PRAISE FOR MICHELLE DIENER

What people are saying about IN DEFENSE OF THE QUEEN:

In Defense of the Queen was an absolute treat to read and I can't wait to get my hands on the next book by Diener and, then of course, the next Susanna and Parker book. I hope I don't have to wait too long. If you like historicals and fast-paced stories, you will not be disappointed in the least. **Rukmini Singh's Blog**

If you love historical fiction that is suspenseful, intriguing and beautifully written, please do yourself a favor and read this book and this series today. **Girl Lost in a Book**

In Defense of the Queen is historical fiction at its best! **Readers Entertainment**

In Defense of The Queen is a very fast-paced and quite an intoxicating ride full of danger and chilling, intense moments. I had to read it one sitting simply because I could not tear myself away from the book until I find out

how it ends. A great read, very much recommended!
Nocturnal Book Reviews

In Defence of the Queen was a amazing addition to the
Susanna Horenbout and John Parker series that I loved
reading. Hard to put this book down . . . **BookFever**

IN DEFENSE OF THE QUEEN

QUEEN

SUSANNA HORENBOUT SERIES

MICHELLE DIENER

Cover Design: 100Covers

2nd Edition by Daisy Crown Press

❀ Created with Vellum

Much thanks and love to Jo.

ALSO BY MICHELLE DIENER

HISTORICAL FICTION NOVELS

Susanna Horenbout series:

In a Treacherous Court

Dangerous Sanctuary (A short story - available for free, exclusively to readers who sign up to Michelle Diener's New Release Notification List)

Keeper of the King's Secrets

In Defense of the Queen

Regency London series:

The Emperor's Conspiracy

Banquet of Lies

A Dangerous Madness

Other historical novels:

Daughter of the Sky

⁓⊰⊹⊱⁓

FANTASY NOVELS BY MICHELLE DIENER

The Rising Wave series:

The Rising Wave (Prequel novella to THE TURNCOAT KING)

The Turncoat King

The Threadbare Queen

Fate's Arrow (Coming February 2023)

Mistress of the Wind

The Dark Forest series:

The Golden Apple

The Silver Pear

~·∙⊰⊱✣⊰⊱∙·~

SCIENCE FICTION NOVELS

Verdant String series:

Interference & Insurgency Box Set

Breakaway

Breakeven

Trailblazer

High Flyer

Wave Rider

Peace Maker

Sky Raiders series:

Intended (Short Story Prequel Available Free to Newsletter Subscribers)

Sky Raiders

Calling the Change

Shadow Warrior

Class 5 series:

Dark Horse

Dark Deeds

Dark Minds

Dark Matters

Dark Ambitions: A Class 5 Novella

Dark Class

Dark Class Epilogue: Free on newsletter signup

To receive notification when a new book is released, and to receive an exclusive copy of Dangerous Sanctuary, a short story featuring Susanna and Parker, sign up at michellediener.com.

CHAPTER 1

> I do not mean that you should be a slave to any
> king, but only that you should assist them and be
> useful to them.
>
> *Utopia by Thomas More (translated by H. Morley)*

The houses on Lombard Street leant against each other
like a crowd of drunks, propping each other up. Parker
moved across the street, away from the shadow they
cast, to catch the afternoon light.

He slowed, pretending to concentrate on avoiding an open
drain, and flicked a glance to the right.

There was someone waiting up ahead, in the darkness of the
alleyway.

A shape moved, small and rounded, and a hand reached out
of the shadows, wrapped strangely in cloth, like a body dressed
for burial.

"Mistress Goodnight?" Parker stopped.

She stepped a little further out of the gloom, and gave him a
smile, showing the browned stumps of her teeth.

"Aye."

"News?" He moved a little closer, feeling for his purse.

"Perhaps." Her eyes followed his hand as it dug deep into the leather pouch at his waist.

"Well?" He stopped when he was still a man's length away from her. He'd learned long ago to keep a good space between them. Her instinct to run was so strong after her years on the streets of London, she sometimes did it even when she knew there was nothing to fear.

"There was talk last night. Along the river."

He made no sound, kept still as she looked around, furtive and beady-eyed as a mouse.

She jerked, as if remembering where she was, and blinked. "Frenchman. Someone said they had seen your Frenchman."

Something cold and dark twisted in Parker's gut, sent a web-fine chill pricking along his skin. "The Frenchman who jumped into the river?"

There was no other, but he wanted to be absolutely sure.

She sniffed, as if insulted by his question, and ignored it. "Story is he's back."

"From where?"

"From the dead, way I hear it. Washed under London Bridge, wasn't he?"

"Where can this ghost be found?" He clinked the coins in his bag together.

Gladys Goodnight looked up, her eyes startling in her wrinkled face. There was a sharpness there, much as a mother would have for a child misbehaving.

"You know I'll tell you all, no matter what you give me. Don't get too high and mighty wi' me, John Parker."

Parker acknowledged her with a nod. Lifted his hand from his purse.

"Don't know where to find him. Just heard he was back to settle a score."

Parker had no need to ask who the score was against. He'd wanted to believe Jean had drowned when he'd leaped into the Thames a few months ago, but there had never been a body, and he had always known Jean would not die quite so conveniently.

"The warning is much appreciated." Parker held out his hand, and hesitantly, Gladys extended hers. Parker dropped the coins into her filthy, rag-covered palm.

"So I see." She looked at the coins, glee lighting her wrinkled face. "My thanks, Parker." She withdrew into the alley again, disappearing into the dark.

"Take care, mistress. You don't want to come to the Frenchman's attention."

Her cackle wafted out of the narrow space, echoing and eerie. "Not likely. He's too busy looking your way, Parker, to worry about the likes o' me."

Parker stood a moment in the failing light, staring into the impenetrable darkness of the alley. If only it were true. But Jean was not after him.

The only reason a professional assassin came back to kill, without payment, was because it was personal.

And that meant he'd come back for Susanna.

"There's someone come for you."

Susanna looked up from the fine drawing of Princess Mary she was working on. Her vision swam as she adjusted it from the minute, intricate work to the housekeeper in the doorway, plump cheeks flushed from the climb up the stairs.

Susanna blinked. "For me?"

Mistress Greene shuffled her feet, agitated and nervous. "Aye. Says he's your brother. Looks like your brother, right enough. Suppose I'd best make up the spare room." The housekeeper turned and disappeared back down the stairs.

Susanna stood slowly and laid down her brush. Lucas was here?

She lifted her shoulders to ease the ache of sitting over her painting for so long and rubbed the back of her neck. Shock kept her feet in place. Shock, and . . . disappointment.

It was hard to admit it, even to herself, but while she was happy to see her brother again, she was equally sorry he'd come, because there could be only one reason for it. He was taking her job from her.

She made her way to the dim landing and started down the stairs.

Lucas stood with his back to her, looking from the hallway into Parker's study. He was just the same, tall and thin, with hair the same red-brown as her own.

He turned when he heard the stairs creak behind him.

"There you are." Lucas smiled, the old grin that was so exactly him.

She smiled, or tried to. She thought she'd have months more, at least, until he came to usurp her. But she couldn't deny it was good to see her brother's face.

"I'm so happy to see you." She took the rest of the stairs down to him, and kissed him on each cheek. "Overcome with surprise, but happy."

He kissed her in return, then held her a little away from him to look at her face. "So. You are about to be married."

"Yes." She held his gaze. "But not for a few months yet. I thought you would come with Father and Mother closer to the time."

He shrugged. "It was a surprise to me, as well, this trip." He looked away without explaining his words. Then he gestured around him at the hallway and the rooms beyond. "I congratulate you. Your betrothed seems a wealthy man."

She didn't know what to say to that. It was rude, and usually, Lucas was charm itself.

Then he pulled her back into his arms, a crushing embrace that seemed a little desperate. "It is good to see you safe and well, Susie."

She submitted to the tight, suffocating hold for a few

moments, then tried to pull back. He loosened his grip and let her go as the front door swung open.

She turned, shoulders relaxing, as Parker stepped inside. His gaze went straight to her, as if he was worried.

"What is it?" she asked, reaching a hand to his, but his attention had moved to Lucas.

"Who are you?"

Lucas swallowed, the sound audible, and he fell back a step. "My lord, I am Lucas Horenbout. Soon to be your brother-in-law." His English came out stilted to her ear. She had been speaking it so long, she could hear how she must have sounded when she first arrived.

Parker did not relax. "If you had let us know you were coming, we could have prepared a welcome." At last he took her hand and drew her closer to him.

"I arrived back from Nuremburg but two weeks ago, and my father put me on the next ship to England."

"But why?" Susanna noticed, for the first time, a pile of bags just inside the door. "What was his reason for such haste?"

Lucas looked away, the movement guilty. "He wanted me to establish myself, find a house and so forth, so he and our mother could join me in time for your wedding."

Susanna opened her mouth. Closed it.

She hadn't spent most of her life listening to Lucas talk his way out of trouble with their father not to know when he was telling the truth. And when he wasn't.

And this time, her brother was lying.

CHAPTER 2

> Now I live as I will, to which I believe, few courtiers can pretend; and there are so many that court the favour of great men, that there will be no great loss if they are not troubled either with me or with others of my temper.
>
> *Utopia by Thomas More (translated by H. Morley)*

Parker could hear the sounds of Horenbout above, in the spare room that sat directly above the study. The artist's striking resemblance to Susanna was in the shade of his hair and the shape of his eyes. But where Susanna was calm and serene, in the little Parker had seen of him, he was sulky and difficult. And irritating.

Susanna stood at the open window, looking out into the garden. A light breeze blew in and scooped out the heat of the day.

He went to her and gently drew her away. If Jean was back, she could not stand outlined in windows until the Frenchman was dead.

She frowned. "What is it? I could see something was wrong when you came home." Her hand came up and cupped his cheek, and he wondered what he would do if she were taken from him.

"Gladys Goodnight heard some whispers on the street. Jean is back."

She looked to the window, and understanding lit her face. "Ah." She took a step deeper into the room. "And you think there is something to them?"

He shrugged. "Jean would not have died so conveniently. And if he were alive, and had the means, he would come back."

"Back for me?" She shook her head. "I don't understand why he would hold a grudge against me more than you, or even the *comte*."

"He sees the *comte* and myself as his equals. You were supposed to be easy." Parker smiled with deep satisfaction. "You were not."

"And my brother?"

Parker frowned. "What about him?"

"It seems strange he would return the same day we hear Jean is back."

Parker hesitated a moment, shook his head. "We knew your brother was coming sooner or later. I can't see how this can be anything but a coincidence."

"Perhaps." She spoke more quietly, tilting her face to the ceiling. "I would agree, if he hadn't lied about why he was here."

"He lied?" Parker stilled, then lifted his face upwards as well, as if he could see through the sturdy wood of the ceiling to the room above. A room which was now quiet.

"I know him too well. He wasn't telling the truth. I thought perhaps he feared I could persuade my father against the plan to give him my position, and rushed here to establish himself before I could do it, but there is something more to it than that. He would be comfortable with that lie, because he believes my job as painter to the king is his due, but he's nervous. My brother is afraid of something."

"Perhaps it's me who makes him nervous?" Parker drew her

close, and let the fragrant air of lavender and rosemary from the garden brush over them.

She gave a small laugh, the delight in it spearing his heart. "You do. But he doesn't know you well enough yet to fear for his life with you." He could feel her smile against his chest.

"You think his fear is linked to his lie?"

"Aye. It makes me curious. Lucas has always done, and been allowed to do, whatever he pleases. Yet he's here against his will. My father would have had to make a significant threat to get him to agree to do something he didn't want to do."

A thought occurred to Parker. "Do you think he will act as your father's proxy while he's here?"

She lifted her head, and laughter still danced in her eyes. "He will notice if I do not sleep in my own room, if that is your meaning."

Parker swore, moved her even deeper into the shadows of the room to kiss her.

He felt a tug against his sleeve and he jerked up his head. In time to see a bolt slam into the door opposite the window with a thud.

❦

PARKER LEAPT STRAIGHT THROUGH THE WINDOW INTO THE garden.

Susanna watched him fly over the sill, then threw herself against the wall. She looked across the room at the bolt, and the cider they had just drunk with Lucas rose in her throat.

If anyone knew to the second how long it would take Jean to crank in a second bolt it was Parker, and she understood he'd gone on the attack before they could be pinned down. But it made it no easier to accept.

She moved until she was pressed against the wall beside the window, then froze at the sound of footsteps in the hall. The door swung open.

Lucas stood in the doorway, and her heart leaped in her chest.

"Down. For pity's sake, get down." She crouched as she spoke, showing him, so he would do it quicker.

"What are you about, Susanna?" He frowned, the look on his face so like Father's when he thought her behavior unbecoming.

He stepped into the room.

"Get down. Someone is shooting bolts at us."

He looked at her, his eyes wide, and at last, he crouched. Scuttled to join her at the wall.

She could see his hands were shaking.

"Where is Parker?"

"Gone after them." She could not help but compare her lover, leaping after the attacker like a wolf on the hunt, with her brother, cowering with her against the wall.

It made her stand up and lean out for a quick look into the garden. Dusk had turned to evening, and it was impossible to see anything.

"Who . . . who would shoot at you?"

The false notes in his question were like poor color mixes on a painting, like an obvious patch-up on a torn inlay of gold leaf. She had thought it was Jean—of course Parker and her both had —but what if it wasn't?

"I don't know." She kept her voice steady. "It comes very close on the heels of your arrival."

He made a sound, a croak from the back of his throat.

Her temper spiked. "If someone you have brought to our door has harmed Parker . . ." She peered out of the window again, listening. But there was nothing to hear. "Why are you really here? And don't say it is to set up house."

He hesitated, and she thought he was weighing up telling her. He looked at the bolt sticking into the door for a long moment, before he drew in a deep breath, his face set. "I couldn't say with your betrothed beside you. He is the king's man, and what I need to give you is not for the king."

"What you need to give me?" She lowered her voice, and saw he was plucking at something inside his jacket.

"Margaret of Austria bade Father give you this to pass to Queen Katherine. It seems the word is the English queen is pleased with you, and so Margaret decided you would be the perfect way to get something to her."

"Get *what* to her?" She waited for him to show her what he had in his jacket, but his hand stayed were it was, as if simply resting over his heart. Like he was swearing fealty.

"A secret letter. The English queen's correspondence is checked these days, according to Margaret's spies, and all suspicious correspondence is passed to the king or his cardinal."

"Margaret wants me to smuggle a letter past the king and Wolsey to the queen. And Father agreed to that?" She was breathless.

"Father works for Margaret." He shrugged, as if this explained everything. "But no. They don't mean for you to smuggle in the letter. There is too much risk with that. They would have you read it, and pass the message on. Whisper it in the queen's ear."

"Father isn't going to be working for Margaret much longer, he's coming to work in London in a few months. And *I* work for the king. If I follow Father's rule, I owe my loyalty to him."

"You're still your father's daughter, Susanna. You obey him above all others." Lucas took out the letter at last, and lifted it up for her to take.

She didn't touch it. She wanted to climb out of the window and see if Parker was all right. Her hand trembled as she set it on the sill, wondering if she should leap into the garden as Parker had. "I'm soon to be the wife of a courtier of the Privy Chamber. A man who is the Keeper of Westminster Palace and the king's private purse. He's also the King's Yeoman of the Robes. And Father would have me commit treason, despite this?"

"Who will ever know?" Lucas's face was in complete shadow

in the now-dark room. "Visit the queen, give her the message, and there is no way to say how she came to know."

"Except the queen herself, Margaret, Father, you, me," she lifted a finger with each name, and then waved her free hand, "and whoever else at Margaret's court is involved." Susanna dropped her voice so low, it was barely a whisper. "And if the person firing bolts through the window is to do with this, someone else knows, too."

Lucas turned the letter over and over in his hands. "I don't know how anyone here could know of this." He looked up at her, what little light there was glinting off his eyes. "I am no good at this skulduggery. But I warn you, whether we're discovered in this or not, if you don't take the message to Katherine, Margaret has told Father she will not pay him for his work this last year. She will ruin him."

"If we are discovered," she spoke slow and clear, so he could not mistake her meaning, "no matter if Father is ruined or not, we are dead."

CHAPTER 3

> For the springs both of good and evil flow from the prince over a whole nation, as from a lasting fountain
>
> *Utopia by Thomas More (translated by H. Morley)*

The bowman was cool. He did not so much as flinch as Parker launched himself across the garden to the back wall where the shadowed figure perched, like a crow.

It must be Jean. He was one of the few Parker had ever encountered who had the steady, nerveless hands of a professional assassin.

"Jean." He shouted the name as the bowman executed a smooth, graceful leap off the wall into the narrow alley below.

Parker jumped at the wall and scrabbled for hand and foot holds, reaching the top with bleeding fingers and scraped knees. He found his balance and looked into the alley.

The shooter was cranking his crossbow at the corner where the alley met St. Michael's Lane.

Parker swore. If it was Jean, Parker would be dead before he took more than a step towards him. Even if it wasn't the Frenchman, he would be a hard target to miss in the narrow back alley.

The bowman waited a beat, saw Parker had thought better of pursuit and lifted a hand in salute. He turned into St. Michael's Lane and disappeared.

Parker stayed where he was, crouched atop the wall, letting the night sounds settle back, letting the blood roaring in his ears abate.

If that was Jean, it was the first salvo in what he knew would be a battle to the death. But the way the man stood, held himself, didn't stir any memories . . .

He couldn't be sure.

If it wasn't Jean, then perhaps Susanna was right.

Her brother had brought more than too much luggage with him from Ghent.

He'd brought trouble.

Susanna ignored the letter, lying where her brother had left it, duty discharged, on the floor by the window.

He'd gone back to his room, salvaging his pride by walking to the door, instead of crawling to it.

She didn't stop him.

Every step he took away from her twisted her feelings of loyalty to her family until they were a knotted, tangled skein in her stomach. She felt the weight of it as he turned into the passageway and left her alone in the room.

She flicked tears from under her eyes, took a deep breath and swung her legs over the sill. She dropped the short distance into the garden and moved forward.

Stopped.

There was a figure up on the wall, as dark and frightening as a gargoyle hanging from a church roof.

She stood very still as she tried to make it out.

"Parker?"

The figure moved, turning towards her, and leaped down. She

could see it was Parker in the lines of his body, in the grace of his movement, and relaxed.

"Was it Jean?" She waited for him to join her, and when he stopped before her, she could not see his face.

"I don't know." He looked over his shoulder, back to the wall. "He was cool enough to be Jean. Accurate enough."

"I hope it was him."

He started, lifted his hand to touch her cheek. "Why do you say that?"

She took his wrist, tried to study his hand in the light coming from the study. It was bloody and moss-stained. "Lucas came in after you went out the window."

She felt his fingers tense against hers, felt the steel in them. "And?"

She drew him towards the window, a finger on her lips, and when they were back in the study, she drew the shutters closed.

Parker stood motionless as she stoked the fire and lit a lantern, watching her every move.

She raised her gaze to his and took a deep breath. "My father has been bullied by Margaret of Austria into getting a secret message to Queen Katherine. He plans for me to pass it to her."

Parker's mouth opened, and then he clamped it shut with a snap. "What is the message?"

She looked at the letter, lying almost at his feet, and he followed her gaze and scooped it up.

"In here?" He reached for his letter knife, and was already breaking the seal as she nodded.

She sat, watching as he unrolled it.

He was silent as he read it and then frowned down at the parchment.

"What is it?"

"You were to pass this to the queen?" He looked up, and she understood why so many stood down to Parker without him having to do more than look their way. She shivered.

"I was to read it, and pass the message on. Not give her the letter itself. Or so Lucas says."

Parker held the letter out to her. She was still reluctant to take it.

She crossed her arms. "What does it say?"

Parker flicked it with his fingers. "You'll have to tell me. It's written in code." His expression, when he raised his head again, was unreadable.

"Code?" The notion was so ridiculous, she finally took the letter, smoothed it out on her lap.

It was in her father's hand, no doubt about that. But the words themselves . . . she gasped.

"This isn't in code." She scanned the page, tightly packed with the unusual markings, and leaned back in her chair, truly shocked.

"You understand it?" Parker stepped closer, crouched down beside her chair.

"It is in the shorthand we use in the *atelier*. It's not only in Flemish, but in a shortened form we've used for years to save paper and time. This letter could not have come from anyone but my father. He has compromised himself."

"And what does it say?" His eyes were on her face, and she raised a hand to rub her temple.

"Margaret sends Katherine a warning. That the Emperor Charles is planning to break his betrothal to her daughter, Princess Mary, and marry Queen Katherine's niece, Isabella of Portugal, instead." She traced the words with a finger. "Why would Margaret want to warn Katherine secretly, though? Why not tell Henry as well?"

"Because treachery by the queen's relatives caused the queen to lose the king's favor before—favor she has never truly won back. And Charles breaking his betrothal vows to Henry's daughter, that is a betrayal."

"The queen would suffer for it, even though she has nothing to do with it?"

"She had nothing to do with her family's treachery last time, either." Parker took the letter back, stared down. "Margaret of Austria has always been an ally of England, and an enemy of France. She knows Henry will be furious if Charles reneges on his betrothal promise to Princess Mary, and he'll possibly break the alliance between them she's tried so hard to build."

"But why would Margaret give the queen advanced warning in secret?" Susanna leaned over the page, and read the message again.

"Knowledge is power. Margaret wants to prepare Katherine. And perhaps buy some time, try to change Charles's mind. Both Mary and Katherine will be far less useful to Henry if Mary is no longer to be the emperor's wife."

"But surely the king loves his daughter?" Susanna spoke without thinking. Then remembered what her own father was asking her to do, asking her to risk. Just to please his employer.

A cold, sick feeling lodged itself in her chest. Her father was most likely acting from desperation. But Henry, she had looked into his eyes before and seen the utter ruthlessness there. He would do whatever he thought in his best interests.

Parker carefully placed a hand on her arm, his touch warm. "The attack tonight could have been to silence you, so you can't deliver the message. Does your brother realize that?"

She nodded. "He said he was sure no one in London could know why he was here, but he was lying again."

"Charles won't want Margaret whispering his plans to Katherine in advance. He would stop this if he could. So most likely someone working for Charles followed your brother here from Margaret's court, or sent word of his arrival to Emperor Charles's spies here in London."

She covered his hand with her own. Looked directly into his eyes. "What do we do?"

He looked towards the fire. "There is no question. We burn this letter and say nothing."

CHAPTER 4

For most princes apply themselves more to affairs of war than to the useful arts of peace; and in these I neither have any knowledge, nor do I much desire it; they are generally more set on acquiring new kingdoms, right or wrong, than on governing well those they possess

Utopia by Thomas More (translated by H. Morley)

"You would not burn it if it weren't in my father's hand. If it weren't brought by my brother." She raised her gaze to his. "You would give it to the king."

"But it *is* from your father, brought by your brother." There was nothing to add to that. The ties to treason in this were too close to her. He would cut them with his sharpest knife.

There was a glitter in her eyes as she bent her head over the letter again. "No matter if we burn it or not, if someone knows of this, I won't be safe until I've had an audience with the queen." She handed it to him.

Parker rolled it up and touched one end of the parchment to the flames without hesitation, made sure it caught well before he threw it into the heart of the blaze.

They both watched it burn.

"Only if that bolt was not from Jean's bow."

The anger he'd been pushing down since learning how her family had compromised and endangered her boiled up again. He tried to keep his voice even. "Henry has spies in Margaret's court, too, or Wolsey does on his behalf. Charles will most definitely have someone watching his aunt. Any of them could be the ones who know of this. Or all of them."

"But if they know or suspect Margaret has given me something to pass on to the queen, would they try to kill me without finding out the details? Without learning the message?" She looked toward the closed shutters and shivered.

"No," he agreed slowly. "Wolsey or Henry wouldn't kill before they found out what Margaret is up to, what message she wants passed to Katherine. They'd have you or your brother in the Tower for a . . . conversation first. Charles, on the other hand, would know whatever it's about, it wouldn't be in his interests. So he may have given orders to kill first, find out what it's about later."

She closed her eyes, her hands gripping her upper arms, as if holding on for dear life. "My father could not have realized . . ."

"Your father has worked at court for many years. He knew what he was doing." He tried to temper the ice in his tone, but she winced. "And because of it, your death would now be convenient to Emperor Charles."

She opened her eyes again, raised her head. "Unless you get me to the queen. Tonight. So whoever knows of this thinks all the damage I can do has been done."

He wanted to run up the stairs and punch Lucas Horenbout until his handsome face was in ruins. Parker turned away from her, opening and closing his fists. He would rather anything than take her out on the streets tonight. But she was right. If she was able to obtain a private audience with the queen, they would at least obtain a temporary reprieve.

No one would know she hadn't said anything to the queen. It would be assumed she had.

He wished now he had been faster across the garden, wished he knew for certain if it was Jean up on the wall or not. It would make this decision so much easier.

"You know it is the best course." Her voice was soft, small, and he turned at last to look at her.

She had risen from her chair and watched him with dark eyes.

"Yes." He said the word on a sigh. His gaze caught the bolt still sticking into the door of the study, and he wondered how fortune could change so quickly.

From kissing his lover by the window to getting ready to race through the darkness to Bridewell Palace, all within the hour.

There was a noise outside the door, as someone came down the passage.

"I hope that's your brother." Parker watched the door, anticipation leaping in him, warming his heart.

"Why?" She looked across to him, and he saw her swallow in shock. "Parker. No."

He did not respond. If it were Horenbout, he was about to lose some teeth.

⁂

PETER JACK TOOK A STEP BACK INTO THE PASSAGEWAY AT THE sight of Parker's face, his hand dropping from the handle like a deadweight.

"Sir?" He half-swallowed his words.

"Come in." Parker sounded resigned.

"He was hoping it was someone else." Susanna could not allow Peter Jack to think that look had been meant for him.

"Who?" Peter Jack stepped into the room, and Susanna pointed upward to the guest room.

"Ah." He grinned. He pushed the door closed and caught sight of the bolt embedded in it. Stood, open-mouthed.

Parker stepped closer and pulled the bolt from the door. Turned it over in his hands.

Susanna reached out and touched the shaft. The wood was smooth and cool. "'Tis well made."

"Yes." Parker held it closer to the light of the fire. "It isn't English made. Italian, or perhaps Swiss."

"What does that mean?" Peter Jack looked between them.

"It means whoever is shooting is from the other side of the Channel, or they can afford the best."

"Like the Emperor Charles." Susanna's heart skipped at the sight of Parker, frowning down at the bolt in his hand. He had been the King's Yeoman of the Crossbows up until only a few months ago and now he looked at the sleek shaft as if it could somehow speak to him.

"The Emperor Charles?" Peter Jack had not moved since he'd stepped into the room. "Why would he be interested in us?"

She could not lie to him. Everyone in this house was in danger, now. "My brother brought a secret message for the queen with him from Margaret of Austria. We think the emperor's agents are trying to stop me passing it on to her."

"Either that, or Jean took the first of many shots at you." Parker's tone made her look up, and despite everything, despite the pit they were sliding into, relentlessly and with no hope of a handhold, she smiled.

"Aye. I do collect enemies, don't I?"

He held her gaze, and his lips curved. "Almost as many as me."

CHAPTER 5

"Among the ministers of princes, there are none that are not so wise as to need no assistance, or at least, that do not think themselves so wise that they imagine they need none; and if they court any, it is only those for whom the prince has much personal favour, whom by their fawning and flatteries they endeavour to fix to their own interests;
Utopia by Thomas More (translated by H. Morley)

The queen would not see them. Parker stared at Gertrude Courtenay, and she shifted uncomfortably under his gaze.

"I'm sorry, Parker, but she's not feeling well and she retired early this evening."

"We had hoped to see her." Susanna's voice was soft, and Gertrude looked between them.

"It is important?"

"Aye." Hope flared, and Parker stepped closer, but Gertrude was already shaking her head.

"Not now. She truly is asleep. But tomorrow. Come early, and I will make sure you gain admittance, if she is well enough."

It was all they could hope for.

The other ladies-in-waiting watched them, the few who were not downstairs taking part in a revel organized by the king.

Parker wondered which of the women in the chamber were spies, and for who. Cardinal Wolsey would have a few in his employ, as would the Duke of Norfolk. The Emperor Charles would have at least one, if he was worthy of his title.

News of this visit would reach all of their ears, or in the case of Charles, his spymaster in England, and because they had not succeeded in seeing the queen, the danger to Susanna had increased. He tried to look as if he was merely disappointed, when he wanted nothing more than to push Gertrude Courtenay aside and force his way into the queen's chamber.

"Until the morrow, then." Susanna dipped into a curtsy and drew him away. He realized belatedly he was dragging his feet.

When they stepped out into the passage, she closed her eyes, her fists clenched at her side. "What now?"

Parker took her arm, and they walked to the stairs. "I think we should speak with the king."

She glanced at him, and a shiver shook her. "Is that wise?"

"I would rather know if he has any inkling of what is happening or not. He must have spies in Margaret's court. The question is, do they know what she's up to? I don't think any agent of the king shot at us tonight, but that doesn't mean they don't know something."

Her steps faltered, and then she nodded. "Aye. It would be better to know."

He squeezed her arm, and let his thumb brush her open palm. "Then into the pit, my love."

ELIZABETH CAREW STOOD JUST WITHIN THE DOORWAY OF THE Privy Chamber.

Susanna let go of Parker's arm as he went to greet a friend and stepped up to her side and followed her gaze.

The king was dancing.

Susanna watched him dip and bow and stamp on the boards to a merry tune.

She looked toward the small band of musicians, but the Flemish flautist she knew was not playing tonight.

The king's partner laughed as he swung her, her color high.

"He has grown tired of me."

Susanna flicked her gaze to Elizabeth, standing with her eyes still on the king.

"I'm sorry." What else could she say to that? Elizabeth had thought the king had grown tired of her before, thought Susanna had been her replacement, but the fierce heat and jealousy on that occasion was missing from the king's mistress now.

She was calm.

At last, she turned her head to Susanna. Her face was utterly beautiful, completely serene. "I am relieved, truth be told."

Again, Susanna did not know what to say. She looked out across the dance floor. "Who is he dancing with?"

Elizabeth shrugged. "The youngest daughter of a minor noble. If he takes her to his bed, it will not be for long. But between him and I, it is over. No doubt my husband will get a new landholding as a parting gift. For lending the king my services."

Susanna stilled. Turned to her again. There had been a thread of steel, and of bitterness, in Elizabeth's voice. "And you? What will you get?"

She smiled, but it was merely a tug of her cheeks, her eyes were cold. "I get a rest. And perhaps, with time, some of the queen's ladies will begin talking to me again."

The dance came to an end, and the king bowed low, with a flourish, to his partner. She giggled and blushed.

Parker came up beside Susanna and touched her arm. "Better you stay here."

She nodded, watched him move through the crowd toward the king.

Elizabeth seemed incapable of moving and Susanna took her arm, steered her to the chairs that were set along the wall.

"Where is your husband, my lady?" She searched the room, but Nicholas Carew was nowhere in sight.

The king clapped his hands enthusiastically, and the musicians started a new, faster, piece. Henry grabbed his partner again, and pulled her onto the floor.

Susanna saw Parker halt, then begin on a new path that would bring him closer to the swirling monarch.

Elizabeth moved, jerky as a puppet, to adjust her skirts. "My husband injured himself in the lists today." Her voice was quite without intonation. "His ribs are painful."

Susanna swallowed, her eyes tracking Parker as he sidestepped the twirling dancers. "Perhaps a stay at your country estate will do you both good?"

Life finally flickered in Elizabeth's eyes. She gazed at Susanna coolly. "Perhaps."

"Did your mother like the pencil sketch I made of you?" Susanna held her gaze and did not flinch, and eventually Elizabeth Carew looked away.

"Aye. She liked it very well, thank you."

"I would still paint you, my lady."

Elizabeth made a face, as if she could no longer imagine a reason for Susanna's interest.

"I am just finished working on a painting of the Princess Mary, so I can start whenever you give me the word."

Elizabeth hesitated. "I do not think my husband would care for what you have in mind." She slanted a look at Susanna. "You still wish to paint me rising from a forest stream?"

Susanna nodded.

Elizabeth watched the dancing in silence a little longer. Drew herself up straighter. "Aye." She stood, her eyes on the king one last time. "You may call on me when you are ready, Mistress Horenbout, and I will sit for you."

She rose from her seat and walked out of the room.

Susanna watched her straight, stiff back, her raised head—pain held together with pride—and memorized the line of her shoulders, the curve of her cheek. Her fingers curled in her palms, and she could already see the scene on canvas.

She started when Parker's hand touched her shoulder.

"The king is slippery as an eel tonight. I cannot pin him down alone. He has started a game of tables. If I'm to talk to him, we will need to watch or play."

Susanna lifted her eyes to his. "You play tables?"

Parker quirked a grin. "I'm a gentleman, aren't I?"

She smiled back. "Ah, you are so much more than that."

CHAPTER 6

> And, indeed, nature has so made us, that we all love
> to be flattered and to please ourselves with our own
> notions
> *Utopia by Thomas More (translated by H. Morley)*

The king was already in play. The Knight Marshal had set up tables along one wall of the chamber, and they had been filled the moment the king abandoned the dance floor.

His opponent was the young girl he'd danced with, and Parker could see she was not familiar with the rules. Even though Henry's eyes were more on the deep shadow between her breasts when she leaned over to throw her dice than on the movement of her pieces, he was already well ahead.

"Parker, Mistress Horenbout." The king slid his gaze over them. "You know Lady Alice?"

Parker bowed. "Alas, no."

Beside him, Susanna curtsied.

"You are fond of tables?" Henry spoke to Susanna.

"No, Your Majesty. I have not had much opportunity to play it."

Parker felt her wariness in the stiffness of her body.

"A game of chance and skill exhilarates. You must learn." The king turned back to his game.

"You need to learn, too, m'dear." Henry beat Lady Alice with a flourish. "Parker, it has been some time. Sit and play."

Parker waited for Lady Alice to rise from the chair, which she did reluctantly, and with a sour glance his way. She did not even acknowledge Susanna as she slipped back into the still-dancing crowd.

The king watched her go, his gaze hot.

As Parker pulled up a chair for Susanna and sat himself, he knew exactly what the king had in mind for later.

"The queen will be sorry she missed this. I know she loves playing tables."

Henry froze, lust melting to fury in his eyes, and Parker wondered why he'd allowed such a foolish comment to escape his mouth. Henry did not like to be chastised.

"What of the queen?"

There was no going back. "I simply heard she was not well, and thought it a shame she had to miss such a merry gathering."

"The queen's courses are causing her great pain." Henry's words were blunt, intentionally coarse. "That is, when she has them. Months go by without a sign of them."

Parker saw Susanna flinch at the king's words. This deliberate discussion of the queen's most private affairs was disrespectful.

He said nothing, setting the pieces back in place to begin the game, truly unsure why he'd provoked the king. He'd seen a hundred girls catch Henry's eye.

"You came here tonight to tell me something?" Henry straightened his pieces meticulously, his fingers shaking a little.

Parker had never seen him so angry, when the anger was directed at him.

"Someone shot a bolt through my window tonight." Parker looked up at the king as he spoke.

Henry's mouth thinned. "You do have a knack for enraging others."

Parker frowned. "Usually on your account, Your Majesty."

Henry picked up the dice and threw the opening play, but there was a softening around his lips, as if he acknowledged the truth of what Parker said.

The dice fell.

Double six.

Henry smiled for the first time since Parker's unfortunate comment. "Do you know who made the attack?"

Parker hesitated a moment. There was no sign Henry knew anything. "Perhaps." He leaned back. "The Frenchman who tried to steal the Mirror of Naples is reported to be back in London."

Henry paused. "Didn't he drown?"

Parker shook his head. "I never thought we would be so lucky."

Henry eyed Parker's move, grunted and threw again. Six and five. "The Mirror is safe?"

Parker nodded. "He's not after the Mirror again. Unless he's mad." He looked at Susanna. She sat with hands folded in her lap, beautiful enough to steal his breath. The expression on her face was tranquil, detached, and Parker realized her mind was working on a painting in her head—she was not with them. "It's my betrothed he's come back for."

Henry stopped the game. Looked at Susanna as well.

"What are you thinking of?"

As if sensing eyes on her, Susanna blinked, coming back from the place in her thoughts.

"Your Majesty?" She had to clear her throat, as if she had been asleep, and she glanced at Parker, puzzled.

"What takes your mind away from us?"

She snapped her head back to Henry, and bowed her head at his direct gaze. "A painting."

"And what is this painting?" Henry spoke without his usual jocularity.

"It is of Elizabeth Carew, Your Majesty." Susanna twined her fingers together. "Forgive my inattendance."

The name of his former mistress made Henry's nostrils flare. He stared at Susanna, as if to discern some hidden barb in her words, and Parker held his breath.

"As my painter, in my employ, you will not paint Lady Carew. Unless I give you too little work to occupy your time?"

Susanna lifted her gaze to the king in astonishment, and Parker resisted the urge to put a hand on her arm. "No, I'm very busy. My idea for the Lady Carew was something quite apart. Not a portrait, but a fanciful scene."

Henry picked up the dice, and threw them over hard. They skittered over the deep sides of the board and onto the floor, spinning and rolling between the dancers.

"Fetch them." He looked straight at Parker, his voice stone grinding on stone.

Parker rose reluctantly.

He was an intimate of the king. He had risen from nothing, and made himself invaluable by his service and loyalty.

He suddenly regretted his success.

He touched Susanna's shoulder as he stepped around her, his finger trailing the smooth, bare skin of her neck. As he was swallowed into the swirling mass of dancers, he had a sense he was leaving her exposed at the very moment he should be standing watch.

SUSANNA TURNED HER HEAD TO WATCH PARKER GO, DISTURBED by his face, by his reluctance. She had missed something while she'd been busy composing the painting of Elizabeth Carew. Something important.

"What is Elizabeth Carew to you?" Henry did not look at her. He kept his concentration on the pieces before him.

Susanna bit her lip. "Lady Carew is very beautiful, and since I first saw her, she put me in mind of a water sprite, or some magical creature. I have wanted to paint her that way since I met her."

"A water sprite?" He sounded bemused. Less angry. "Aye, she is cool enough, to the casual eye."

There was a smugness about the statement, intimating he knew her to be anything but cool, away from the casual eye.

Susanna forced her hands to relax, stretching her fingers along her thighs. Elizabeth Carew had been the king's mistress willingly. She would do well to remember that.

"I could have made a good match for Parker with a daughter of one of my courtiers. His match with you has meant a loss to me. A . . . squandering of a powerful connection."

She lifted her head, and made the mistake of staring straight into his eyes. Even though she looked away, she caught the way his lips curled back in annoyance.

She said nothing. The king had given his permission for their betrothal. He knew why he'd given it. This conversation was a game. A way to show her how much she depended on him.

"I need Parker. I will admit it. But I do not need you, mistress. And you would do well to remember that." He moved, viper-quick, grabbing her fingers in his hand. The touch was shocking and intimate, his grip crushing.

Without thinking, she pulled them back, curling them into her palms so he could not take them again.

He hissed, and when she lifted her head, she could see bright spots of color on his cheeks.

Her heart was pounding, a slow, massive thump, making it impossible to speak.

"You will not paint Lady Carew. You can focus your energies instead on a painting of my son, Fitzroy."

She dipped her head in acquiescence.

What could she lose by doing so?

She was about to lose her place as his painter. Her brother

was waiting in his room at home, ready to take this all from her as soon as he could.

And for the first time, she thought it perhaps not a bad thing. To be out of the royal eye.

Parker returned with the dice in hand, and she smiled at him as he sat beside her, let her bruised fingers rub the side of his thigh to show all was well.

But it was not. Her heart had calmed, but the panic and fear of the king's menace were still with her, making her hands shake.

And for the first time, she considered giving the queen the message from her old patron, Margaret of Austria.

Considered treason.

CHAPTER 7

> Now if in such a court, made up of persons who envy all others and only admire themselves, a person should but propose anything that he had either read in history or observed in his travels, the rest would think that the reputation of their wisdom would sink, and that their interests would be much depressed if they could not run it down.
>
> *Utopia by Thomas More (translated by H. Morley)*

He watched her. He should have been watching the road, watching for another surprise attack, but she was too quiet. Drawn in on herself tight as a hedgehog.

"What did he say to you?"

She lifted her head, and he caught a slight tightening of her mouth. "That I am not to paint Elizabeth Carew."

"He likes to forget them, when he's done with them. Give it a year, and you could paint her then. He won't object."

She nodded. But it was stiff.

"What else?"

She hesitated. "He thought my wanting to paint her was meddling in his affairs. He made a threat . . ."

Parker waited. He felt each second stretch long and thin.

"He said he needed you, but not me. That our betrothal had robbed him of a marriage of convenience between you and one of his courtier's daughters. He said he could change his mind still."

He breathed deep. At last paid attention to the road. "He may change his mind. I will not."

"That is what makes me afraid." Her voice was small, and she leaned into him. "He does not care what you think."

Parker slipped his arm around her shoulders, and the small, slender feel of her wound his resolve even tighter.

Henry used him to keep his enemies in check.

If he were forced into it, Parker would turn every cold, dark corner of his heart, everything that made him a weapon, back on his master.

MISTRESS GREENE WAS WAITING FOR THEM WHEN THEY pulled into the courtyard, outlined against the back door.

Susanna went from drowsy warmth, cuddled against Parker, to awake and drenched in icy fear. She pulled up, stiff and quivering on the seat of the cart and sensed Parker draw his knife.

"The boys?" Before Parker stopped the cart she leapt to the ground and ran forward.

"The boys are well."

Susanna stumbled and caught the wooden rail beside the stairs.

"'Tis your brother."

Susanna clutched the rail so hard she felt the edges dig deep into her palm. "He's been hurt?"

Mistress Greene shook her head. "Not sure. Not sure what

happened. Peter Jack thinks he ran off when he saw Harry hop over the back fence. Thinks Master Horenbout took fright."

"He's not here?"

The housekeeper shook her head. "Harry was out on a job for the master, it seems," she nodded at Parker, "and came over the back wall. Peter Jack thought he heard a cry from upstairs, and a few moments later the front door slammed. Some of your brother's things are gone."

Parker swore softly as he stepped up beside her. "Where are Harry and Peter Jack now?"

"Gone looking for him."

Susanna caught Parker's grimace. Her brother had not made the best impression since his arrival. "We should take the cart, find them."

"No." Parker turned to face the street. "I don't want you out more than you need to be. And I'm not leaving you here unguarded."

She exchanged a glance with Mistress Greene, and the housekeeper shrugged. "The boys'll be back soon enough, one way or another. Want me to wake Eric to stable the horse?" When Parker shook his head, she stepped back into the kitchen, leaving the door open for them.

Susanna looked up at the night sky. "He doesn't know London."

"He's a grown man. Much older than you." Parker led the horse to the stable, and she followed him in as he unhitched the small cart.

Susanna took a deep breath. "I'm worried about him."

"He brought this trouble. He made this mess himself and pulled us in with him." Parker's words were cold.

She leaned against the rough planks of the stable wall. Closed her eyes and let the sounds of him brushing the horse soothe her.

She felt movement and the heat of his body. The sweet smell

of hay and leather enveloped her. She opened her eyes to find him right before her.

He moved closer, until their bodies touched, and cupped her face between his hands.

"We've been in worse straits."

She tried to smile. "We have."

He leaned in to her, his kiss gentle, giving. And then, suddenly, it wasn't. His need, his hunger, ignited her own, until they were both desperate, taking everything they could.

Parker held her high on the wall, lifting her, pushing her skirts up and she arched against him, her legs around his waist as they took from each other's mouths. The feel of his hands gripping her bare thighs made her weak, aching. He wrenched his mouth from hers and began a trail down her neck, where her pulse leapt and sung.

"Sir."

The stable door slammed open, and the horse gave a sharp whinny. Over Parker's shoulder she saw Harry stumble in.

Parker set her down, held her a moment, trembling, as her skirts tumbled back into place. His eyes were closed, his teeth gritted.

He turned to face Harry.

Harry's eyes widened at the sight of them. "'Tis the mistress's brother." His voice wavered.

"You found him?" Susanna stepped around Parker, her legs still unsteady. She grabbed Parker's arm.

Harry nodded. "Down near Old Swan." He looked back over his shoulder, as if he expected Lucas to come through the door at any moment. "We think he's dead."

CHAPTER 8

> There is a great number of noblemen among you that are themselves as idle as drones, that subsist on other men's labour, on the labour of their tenants, whom, to raise their revenues, they pare to the quick.
>
> *Utopia by Thomas More (translated by H. Morley)*

The horse was disgruntled, pulling the cart for the second time that night when it should have been warm in the stable. It tossed its head and wouldn't be hurried, and Parker felt a strong kinship with it.

Susanna sat beside him, wrapped in her cloak, her body bowstring tense. She strained forward, as if that would somehow make them go faster.

Harry tapped his shoulder from behind, pointing right, and he saw Peter Jack crouched on the ground near the dock at Old Swan.

Susanna leaped from the cart before he'd even pulled on the reins, and stumbled her first few steps.

Parker left the cart to Harry, swinging down and reaching Lucas and Peter Jack at the same time she did.

"He's alive. I felt him breathe." Peter Jack lifted a hand and hovered it in front of Lucas's mouth.

Lucas was very still. Parker could see why they'd thought him dead, at first. "Did you see what happened?"

Peter Jack nodded. "I saw two men. One swung something at him from behind and he dropped like a stone."

"Thieves?" Susanna began to touch her brother's head, her long, delicate fingers probing for the injury.

"Don't know. We shouted and ran forward, and they took off. We were too far away to see who it was."

Parker looked along the bank. He caught the quick movement of someone ducking down. "Perhaps we might yet find out." He kept his voice low, stood smoothly and flicked out his knife.

Harry started, his eyes widening, and drew his own knife from his boot. Parker pointed to where the ground sloped down towards the river.

Beside Susanna, Peter Jack stirred, rising up, and Parker hesitated. Shook his head. "Stay here with my lady." He waited until Peter Jack had his knife out before he turned away.

A hand caught his arm, and he looked down at Susanna. She said nothing, her eyes glinting in the light of the lantern they had brought with them, and he wondered how he had lived before she came into his life. Truly could not understand or imagine it.

He lifted a hand to his mouth and open and closed his fingers and thumb together, to show her she needed to keep talking.

She gave a nod.

"We need to get him home and send for the healer." She spoke clearly. "We'll need to move him carefully."

He saw her glance across at Peter Jack—still unsure, by his frown, if he should be pleased to be appointed her guard or be sorry to be left out of the action—and she waved her hand to get him to reply.

Their conversation filled the night as Parker moved to the river.

The bank sloped down at a gentle pitch until it was in line with the wooden dock, then dropped off sharply to the river. The tide was out, and most of the bank was exposed.

Parker dropped to a crouch.

Harry slid past him and Parker let him go, following as quietly as he could. The most likely place to find their watcher was under the dock itself, and Harry knew the best approach. He'd bedded down under Old Swan's wooden boards until only a few months ago.

Slowly, slowly, they crawled closer, until Harry was flat on his stomach, right beside the opening.

He looked back and Parker lifted a hand, signaling him to wait. He gave a nod, rising carefully into a crouch.

In a sudden rush of movement, silent but for the quick in and out of his breath, their prey burst from the narrow gap and took Harry down with an elbow to the face.

Harry cried out in a voice sharp with pain, and Parker leaped, slamming into the man, his arm coming round for a punch to the ear at the same time.

The man gave a keening, grunting exclamation, which cut off as they hit the ground hard, the wind sucked right out of the bastard.

Parker jabbed in another blow, to the ear again, and then they were rolling, flipping weightless for a moment, and Parker braced as they fell into the cold waters of the Thames.

Because the tide was out, Parker was able to find his footing, and haul the man up. He'd swallowed water, and he came up whooping and choking, limp.

Peter Jack stood on the bank, hand out, and with a massive effort, Parker threw the man up onto the grass and took Peter Jack's hand, grateful for the help.

When he was standing again, he rubbed the water out of his hair and eyes, shivering. The day had been warm, but now a cool breeze blew down the river.

It was too dark to see who it was at his feet.

"Parker." There was a sharp edge of panic in Susanna's voice.

"I'm safe." He turned, looking up the bank. Susanna was silhouetted, nothing more than a black shape behind the lantern she held. She picked her way carefully down.

She reached out a hand and touched his arm, as if to be sure he truly was well. "We must hurry. Harry is badly hurt, now, too . . ." She went very still as the lantern light illuminated the man's face.

"You know him." It wasn't a question.

She shook her head. "It can't be."

"Who is it?" He found it hard to speak, his clothes clinging to him, wet and icy cold.

"Jan Heyman. He's a . . . friend." She turned to look at him, her eyes wide, her face white. "He plays flute for the king."

SUSANNA WAS CROUCHED NEXT TO LUCAS WHEN MAGGIE walked into the kitchen. The healer didn't knock, and Susanna saw her eyes widen at the sight of Parker, sitting close to the fire, a blanket draped around him.

He'd taken off his wet clothes, put on new, but even in his dry clothes, he still shivered. He lifted the cup of mulled wine Mistress Greene had made him to his lips, and his teeth clattered against the side of the mug.

"Not you this time, eh?" Susanna saw Maggie take in Lucas laid out by the fire beside Jan and Harry. Jan was still in his wet clothes and he was hunched over himself, shivering as hard as Parker. Parker had tied his hands and feet, and particularly his hands jerked awkwardly with each shuddering breath he took.

Harry sat close to Parker, his head back against the wall, eyes closed.

Maggie went to Harry first, not Lucas, and although Susanna felt a small twinge of guilt, she was glad.

When had Harry replaced her brother in her heart, or if not replaced him, edged him aside?

"That cheek might be broken or cracked." She beckoned behind her, and for the first time, Susanna noticed her little apprentice. Clemence always reminded her of a will-o'-the-wisp, with her delicate bones and her fine hair, white gold against the alabaster of her skin. The only point of color on the girl's face was her eyes, and they were a dark brown, shocking on her palette of white on white.

Despite the circumstance, despite her brother lying senseless at her feet, Susanna's fingers clenched with the desire to pick up a charcoal pencil. Hungered to make that first mark on parchment. To sketch her.

Clemence knelt beside Harry now, her pale beauty a contrast to his dark hair and sun-darkened skin. She soaked a rag in whatever potion was in the bowl Maggie held out and lifted it to his face. He winced as she touched it to his cheek, gentle and light as a butterfly dipping into nectar.

She'd thought at first the girl was no more than eight or nine, but in the months she'd come to know Maggie and her assistant, she'd realized Clemence was at least thirteen, maybe older.

By the way he held himself, stiff and unsure, Harry knew it, too.

Susanna stared at them, and a picture grew in her head, like the roar of a crowd, coming closer. She forced herself to stay kneeling on the floor, but could not help looking toward the passageway and the study, where her bag with her paper and pens were kept.

"Which one next?"

She shook her head clear, and looked into Maggie's direct gaze.

"My brother, here." She shuffled back a little to give Maggie room.

Maggie said nothing, but her gaze slid to Jan, pale, with blue lips and shuddering body. Then she turned her focus on Lucas, and, like Susanna had done earlier at the dock, felt his head, her fingers moving with soft grace.

"There is no crack, or if there is, it's too fine to feel." She looked up. "He should wake. With a headache, and in need of some days in bed, but he should wake."

The edge of uncertainty in her voice forced Susanna to pull herself closer, a supplicant at the altar of hope. "But he may not?"

"Head blows." Maggie shrugged. "Nothing is certain with head blows."

Lucas lay still and pale, but there was a flash of movement to her left and Susanna found Jan watching her, his head bobbing as he shivered, his hair wet and sticking to his scalp. His brown eyes were hot with emotion.

She'd enjoyed Jan's presence in Henry's court, had smiled each time Jan spotted her, and lifted his flute to warble a little hello whenever she had entered a room where he was playing. "Lucas was your friend. I don't understand."

He didn't answer, but his gaze slid to Parker and back to her. And he lifted his bound hands towards her. As if she would simply lean forward and untie him. As if her loyalty was somehow with him.

She stared at him, wondering if he had lost his wits.

A movement beside her made her turn, and she saw Maggie leaning back on her haunches, watching the exchange. "Parker and Peter Jack can carry your brother to a bed. You'll need to watch him, try to wake him in the morning. If he opens his eyes, you call me and don't let him go back to sleep."

Susanna nodded.

"Now him." Maggie gestured to Jan.

"He was the one who hit Lucas and Harry." She saw Jan's eyes widen at that, and his mouth opened. "Parker tumbled him into the river."

"He hit my ear." Jan spat the words as if he still had Thames water in his mouth. "If I'm deafened, I can't play any more. I'm finished." He breathed deeply. "And I didn't hit Lucas. Are you mad? He sent word for me to meet him. I was just in time to see him attacked and then those . . ." he pointed to Peter Jack and Harry with a shaking finger, "ruffians arrived. I was afraid for my life."

There was silence in the room.

Susanna tried to see Peter Jack and Harry as a stranger would. They were only just entering manhood. Still thin from their years living on the street, but at an age where they were growing taller every day.

There was an edge to them, especially Harry. But for all their tough looks, they were at least a head shorter than Jan, and thin and wiry to his more solid bulk.

She looked back at Jan and raised an eyebrow. He turned away, shivering.

"When you saw Susanna, why did you remain hidden?" Parker spoke from the hearth, his words cold and measured.

"I didn't see it was her. By then it was too dark." Jan turned back to her, but his look was not beseeching, it was furious.

"You hurt Harry." She looked him straight in the eye. "We assumed the worst."

"And you could be lying." Parker stood. Took two steps and loomed over the musician.

"Look in my pouch." Jan ignored Parker, his eyes holding hers. "You'll see the note Lucas sent me earlier today."

"I don't know when Lucas could have sent you anything." Susanna lifted the pouch, as wet as the rest of him, and wondered if any note could have survived the tumble into the Thames. Perhaps Jan was counting on just such a likelihood. "He only arrived this morning. How did he know where to find you?"

Jan raised his eyes, and she saw he was trying to communicate something to her. She frowned back and his earnest expression turned confused. Irritated.

He slid his gaze again to Parker and seemed to come to a

conclusion. "We've been writing to each other, now and then. Keeping in touch. He knew where to reach me."

She lifted the flap on his pouch, and pulled it wide, exposing the contents to the light of the fire. There were coins, and a piece of parchment, ruined completely by the water. She lifted it out, but it tore as she tried to unroll it, and what ink had been on it had run to a dark green nothingness.

She knelt closer to him, smelt the stink of mud and wet wool. He was still shivering, little shakes of his body. He shot her another look, loaded with meaning. It baffled her.

Frustration flashed through her, and she slammed her fist on the floor.

"Jan. Enough of this."

Parker turned his head sharply to her. Jan looked up, mouth open.

"What is it you think I know?"

CHAPTER 9

> It seems to me a very unjust thing to take away a
> man's life for a little money, for nothing in the
> world can be of equal value with a man's life:
> *Utopia by Thomas More (translated by H. Morley)*

The musician was arse-deep in trouble, and he was just
starting to realize it.

Parker watched his face as it dawned on him the
ally he thought he had did not exist. That Susanna was not his
savior. Was not in on whatever secret he thought she knew.

Parker had a feeling whatever it was, it was serious. Dangerous. Or he would have been tempted to smile at Heyman's
expression as he realized his mistake.

Smile, and then take the bastard by the throat and squeeze
whatever he knew out of him.

The musician hunched further in on himself, and then spat,
the spittle landing just short of Susanna's shoes.

"*Verrader.*" His whisper sounded over-loud in the hush that
fell over the room.

Susanna went white, her eyes wide. She rose up and stumbled
back a step.

Peter Jack stood, and Harry ducked around Clemence, pushing up on his knees.

Parker moved down into a crouch, smooth and so fast he saw Heyman's eyes widen in surprise. His hands shook with suppressed violence.

"I'm not sure what you just called my betrothed, but from her face, it was nothing good." He lifted his knife, and let it catch the gleam of firelight. Heyman's breath hitched.

The musician had possessed a cocky assurance since they had caught him, but at last reality was settling in.

"Answer Susanna's question." He kept his voice low. "What is it you think she knows?"

"Not here." Jan's hiss was ruined by the chattering of his teeth.

"Here. And now."

The musician looked around the room, and for the first time noticed Peter Jack and Harry were just as focused on him as Parker was himself. Harry's cheek had swollen up and darkened, already turning purple, and Heyman swallowed, the sound audible.

At last—at last—the bastard understood his position.

"I thought she was . . ." He flicked a glance up at Susanna and then miserably down at his soaked boots. "I thought she was one of us."

"One of who?" Susanna folded her arms across her chest, and Parker saw her eyes were hard. Hard as they were when someone mentioned the Boleyns or Wolsey. Whatever he'd called her, Heyman had crossed a line with her and she would not forgive him.

The question seemed to spark something in Heyman. He gave a little nod, as if decided on his course. He leaned forward and waited until Parker tipped his head closer.

"We are—"

Parker had only an instant's warning, a moment, as he saw a

look harden in Heyman's eyes. Too late to move, too late to do anything but take the blow.

Pain exploded as Heyman head-butted him. He fell back, swinging his arm as he did, felt his fist connect with the musician's jaw. The pain in his fist was equal to that in his head.

He rolled, rocked himself up to sitting, cradling his hand. Susanna's arms came around him, and he lifted his fingertips to rub his forehead. *S'blood, it was agony.*

The musician was sprawled unconscious on the floor beside Lucas. Harry stood over him, hard faced.

Parker closed his eyes, the pain in his head hitting like waves on a shore—slap, slap, slap.

"What did he call you?" It was hard to talk, he wanted to do nothing but lie down. Make the pain go away.

He felt Susanna's hands on him again, pressing a soothing, cool cloth against his forehead.

"He called me a traitor."

⁂

SIMON, THE KING'S CARTER, SLIPPED INTO THE ROOM WITH NO announcement.

Susanna lifted her head at the creak of the door, and blinked at him, confused. "What are you doing here?"

Simon nodded to where Parker sat, head back against his chair, and she saw his eyes had opened at her words.

"Who else sends for me at midnight with no explanation?" Simon moved closer to the fire, and rubbed his arms, his eyes flicking to the door, as if assessing his chances of a quick escape.

She frowned. "You sent one of the boys to fetch Simon?" She didn't want Harry or Peter Jack—or God forbid, Eric—out on the streets. She had the sense of being in a maze, or a web, with every turn unknown and deadly. She could not protect them from a danger she didn't understand.

"I got Harry to send one of his boys. No one knows them.

Or, if they do, we are deeper in this mire than we thought." Parker spoke as if each word was painful to get out. There was a lump on his forehead, and Maggie had plastered it and wrapped it, leaving him looking like a casualty of war.

"What trouble this time?" Simon faced them both, and Susanna was not imagining the tension in his body, the way he seemed to lean towards the door. He wanted to be anywhere but here.

They had called on him in the past for help, but Parker always gave back as generously as he took. Simon's current position at court was Parker's doing and Simon knew it. He had never stinted in his assistance before.

"Spies." Parker spoke with no hesitation, and Susanna wondered if he noticed Simon flinch at the word. His eyes were closed again and he took a deep sip of the chamomile tea spiced with cloves Maggie had given him.

Simon glanced at her, and she stared back until he looked away. Towards the door, again. "There are spies everywhere." He kept his voice low.

"Aye." Parker shifted in his chair. "Did you know the king's flute player is most likely a spy for Margaret of Austria?"

"He's previously from her court, so it doesn't surprise me. But what can he know that is of any consequence?"

Susanna stood. "One might say the same of you, Simon Carter. Or of me. We both know for someone who has their ears open, there is much to gather at court."

Simon's fists clenched. "One might say it of you, mistress. But I have no allegiance to another court."

"I spoke of our positions, not our past allegiances." She said the words slowly, reeling at his tone, at the way he looked at her, suspicious and angry. "As the king's carter, you know details of his movements, of the location of his possessions, that others do not. As his illuminator, papers pass through my hands that some may wish to know of. The king calls for music often. What might he have spoken of in

47

the hearing of his players that others would find of interest?"

Simon did not answer, turning from her to look into the fire.

"What is it, my friend?"

He flinched, even though her words were soft. He turned back to her. He opened his mouth to answer, and then his gaze jerked to Parker, held there.

Parker had opened his eyes again, his fingers rubbing at his temple.

Simon's shoulders slumped. "Nothing . . . nothing."

"Have you heard something at court? Something against me?" She almost did not have to ask. There was no other explanation for his behavior.

Parker lifted his head so sharply, he winced. Clutched his temple again. "My head would split in two." A shudder ran through him and he took a deep breath, turned his head carefully towards her. "Why do you ask that?"

"He looks at me as if things are much changed between us." She kept her eyes on the carter, and at last he looked her in the eye.

"Aye." His shoulders slumped. "There are some rumors. Whispered late this evening."

"What do these rumors say?" Parker sat up, his jaw clenched.

Simon's eyes held pity as he spoke. "That Mistress Horenbout has betrayed the Crown. That she is a traitor."

CHAPTER 10

Therefore it seemed much more eligible that the king should improve his ancient kingdom all he could, and make it flourish as much as possible; that he should love his people, and be beloved of them; that he should live among them, govern them gently and let other kingdoms alone, since that which had fallen to his share was big enough, if not too big, for him:

Utopia by Thomas More (translated by H. Morley)

"Who's behind the talk?" Parker rose to his feet, his fists clenched.

Simon winced. "Wolsey."

There was silence. Little spikes of panic and fear leapt in Susanna's chest, and when she spoke, her words were thick and bitter on her tongue. "When did you hear this?"

Simon picked up the poker and stirred the coals, then threw on another log. It caught with a little pop and sizzle as the sap burned up and illuminated the high cheekbones and beautiful curves of his face. "Just a little while ago. I overheard Wolsey telling His Majesty."

"Did the king believe the snake?" Parker sank back down onto the chair, his face too pale, too drawn with pain.

Damn Jan. Damn Lucas as well, for that matter.

"You must have angered him tonight, because he was not in the best of moods where you are concerned." Simon glanced at Parker. Hesitated. "If he had simply been going to bed, Wolsey would have had more luck, but Wolsey delayed the king's departure. I was to take him . . . somewhere, and he was eager to get there. He did not take well to Wolsey telling tales so late."

A look passed between Parker and Simon, and Susanna realized the matter of the king's late night trip was something known to both of them. She thought of the flushed, curved girl he'd danced with earlier in the evening, and came to her own conclusions.

"So, Wolsey's spy in the queen's chamber lost no time running to him with news we wished an audience with the Katherine." Parker took another deep gulp of pain-killing tea. His hand was rock steady. "And it means his spies in Margaret of Austria's court have warned him that something is going on. He may just be guessing at the connection between Margaret's secret dealings and your urgent visit to the queen, but given your father's position, it's a sound guess."

"But we didn't speak with her. And the spy would know that. So why call me traitor before I even had a chance to say anything?" Susanna sat back in her seat, her legs weak beneath her.

Simon turned sharply, his eyes narrowed. "There is something to tell?"

"No." Parker spoke with force. "We were given information, but we had no intention of passing it to the queen." He tapped his lips with his forefinger. "But that is a good question. Why call traitor when it can be proved you didn't speak with her?"

"Perhaps his excitement at having something against me meant he didn't think the matter through." Susanna wondered if that were possible. If Wolsey's hatred of her and Parker would be enough to cause that sharp, cold mind to trip.

"What did the king say?" Parker set his cup down.

"That he would turn his attention to the matter on the morrow." Simon took a step to the door.

"You think they will come for me? That you will suffer for your friendship with us?" Susanna spoke slowly. There was a ringing in her ears, and a terrible, heavy feeling in her stomach. She looked at her feet, and wondered how so much could have changed in a single day.

"If you are not a traitor, then why did you ask to see her?" The words burst from his mouth.

"Someone tried to kill us today." Susanna pointed to the door, to the scar where the bolt had been pulled from its wood. "We hoped they would no longer have a reason to silence us, if they knew we had seen the queen."

"*If* the shooter was not Jean." Parker was watching Simon, his mouth a thin line.

She closed her eyes. "Aye. If the shooter was not Jean."

"You can go." Parker rose up again, and his color was better, his voice stronger. "There is no need to taint yourself with our company, Carter."

Susanna lifted her head. It felt like a lead weight.

Because it was so hard, she forced her chin even higher, at a defiant angle.

"Parker . . ." Simon looked between them. His hand was already on the door. "I'm sorry." He slipped out.

She stared at the door as it swung closed, and wondered how many more would close against her in the days to come.

"What now?" She did not know, for the first time in a long time, what to do next.

"Now we get some rest." Parker held his hand out. "On the morrow, we go to the king."

She nodded. Allowed him to pull her to her feet. "Before he comes to us."

PARKER STEPPED OUT OF THE KING'S CHAMBERS, TO THE HALL where Susanna waited. "The king is not here."

"Where is he?" She frowned.

"Wherever Simon took him last night, I'll wager."

"Ah." Understanding lit her face, and she stared at the door.

Parker lifted his hands and felt her shoulders, taut as the strings of a bow beneath his fingers.

"Do we go to him?"

Parker shook his head. "He is . . . private about these things."

He saw her lips open, as if to say something, and then close.

"Parker and the lovely Mistress Horenbout." Will Somers stepped out of the gloom of the passage behind them, his voice deep and resonant. It was as if he'd been there all along.

Parker would have sworn not, but with the King's Fool, he never truly knew.

"Good morning, sir." Susanna dipped in curtsy, and Parker saw Somers' eyes flicker.

"A good morn to you, too." He took a step closer, his eyes going to the bruise on Parker's forehead. "I see you are still fighting battles, Parker. I know you never take a turn in the lists, yet you sustain many hurts." He rubbed his hands together. "What is afoot?"

Parker did not answer, as Somers knew he would not, and the Fool chuckled.

"You never know, I might keep it to myself." Somers cocked his head as he spoke, and wriggled his hand from side to side.

"I don't trade in maybes." Parker held his arm to Susanna. Time was slipping. A sense of urgency pressed on him, forcing him forward. They needed to confront Wolsey's accusation head on, or he could see nothing ahead but trouble.

Susanna stepped closer to him, to take his arm.

"A word of wisdom, fair lady, for one who always greets me as well as she greets the king himself." Somers hand came out, and gripped Susanna's wrist.

Parker's eyes narrowed, but the Fool ignored him, his gaze locked with Susanna's.

"Go to the queen. Go openly. Make her come out into the main chamber where all can see you, and talk to her of painting. Talk on and on about painting." He let go of her and stepped back into the gloom behind him. "Go now."

CHAPTER 11

> That a king, even though he would, can do nothing unjustly; that all property is in him, not excepting the very persons of his subjects; and that no man has any other property but that which the king, out of his goodness, thinks fit to leave him.
>
> *Utopia by Thomas More (translated by H. Morley)*

"I thought you were to come early?" Gertrude Courtenay spoke sharply, her body blocking the entrance to the queen's inner chamber.

Susanna had never heard her so agitated.

She held herself stiff, and the look she sent Susanna was a little too wild. Her gaze skittered about the room behind them.

"We had a few distractions." Parker did not motion to his bruised head, but Gertrude's eyes flew there, and she had the grace to blush.

"So I see." Her voice softened. "Come, the queen will see you."

Susanna shook her head. "We would not disturb the queen in her private chamber. Perhaps if she feels well enough to join us here?"

Gertrude's mouth fell open, and Susanna struggled to keep herself from wincing. The request was a scandalous one. To presume to set the place for a meeting with the queen was beyond the pale.

She willed Gertrude to read her face, to read the urgency and importance of agreement.

It would not just be she who came under a cloud if Wolsey pushed his suit. The queen was in danger, as well.

"What is it?" Susanna heard the queen's voice from within, and Gertrude spun back, half-closing the door on them.

She glanced at Parker as the sound of murmured conversation filtered through, but he was studying the ladies in the room, sizing each of them up, as if he could somehow identify Wolsey's spy by the look of them.

Some were disconcerted by his open examination, some ignored it. None failed to notice it.

"The queen feels well enough to join you." Gertrude swung the door open, and moved aside as Katherine stepped into the room.

Susanna curtsied low and Parker stepped up beside her and bowed.

"Let us sit and take some refreshment." Katherine made for the hearth, were a small fire warmed the room, and the ladies sitting there stood and moved away.

The queen sank down into the largest chair, and Susanna thought she looked pale and tired. She waved Susanna to a seat, and Parker took up a position beside it, his eyes never resting.

"You wished an audience with me?" Katherine's eyes held fear and worry.

"Yes, Your Majesty." Susanna clenched her fists in her lap, gripped by a wave of frustration. Would that she could speak freely.

It was not to be.

She reached for her satchel, which Parker had placed beside her chair, and lifted out a small oak panel, no bigger than the length of her hand, wrapped in linen. She stood, took a step towards the queen, then knelt before her, holding out the painting as if offering a sacred gift.

The queen caught her breath. She took the wrapped bundle with both hands, and laid it on her lap.

She lifted the linen wrapping with care, and sat still, looking down at the painting of her daughter for a long moment.

"You have caught her." Her words came out in a whisper. "You have taken her very essence and caught her. I shall have it near me always." When Katherine raised her head, tears tracked down her sallow cheeks. She looked old, suddenly—tired and sad.

A faint murmur rose up and spun like a breeze-blown leaf around the room.

A few of the Queen's more intimate friends pushed forward a little, necks craning.

The queen held the picture up, as if it were a baby to be admired, and her ladies cooed.

Behind her, Susanna sensed Parker stiffen and as she turned to him, he strode to the door, his hand to his sword.

He opened the door, and outside, the two guards standing watch were also more alert. Knuckles gripped tighter on their halberds.

She stood. All around her, the room went quiet, and finally they heard what had disturbed Parker and the guards. The sound of marching feet, ringing on the stone floor.

As suddenly as it was quiet, the level of noise in the room rose as the women exclaimed to themselves and pushed forward a little way to the door.

Susanna looked back at the queen. She sat still, her eyes on the door, a deep dread on her face.

Did Katherine think they came for her? Were relations between herself and the king so bad?

Shock doused her, icy and harsh, making the hair stand up on her arms and the back of her neck. She looked about the room, but all eyes were on the door, and then, taking a deep breath, she bent to pick up her satchel. Stepped right beside the queen.

"They come for me."

The queen's head snapped up at her whisper.

"Someone wishes to stop me giving you a message from Margaret—"

"State your business with the queen." Parker's voice rang out from the door, loud and unwavering, and the advancing footsteps faltered.

Susanna looked toward him, and saw his sword was drawn. All thoughts of Margaret, of everything else vanished. He would get himself killed for her. For her brother and her father's stupidity.

She began to move toward him and was tugged back, the grip on her arm surprisingly strong.

"What is the message?" The queen's eyes were desperate, her voice very soft.

Susanna wanted to shrug the hand off, but it came to her in a flash, she would need all the help she could get, in the days to come.

She looked again at Parker. He wanted them to say nothing, but could she let this opportunity go to waste? He stood, immobile, a strong barrier against the forces aligned against her, but he could not win alone. He would be smashed down.

"What is it?" Katherine's voice was no longer pleading. Her harsh whisper was demanding, regal.

Susanna caught her lower lip with her teeth. It was now or never. She took a breath. "The Emperor Charles is going to marry Isabella of Portugal, not your daughter."

Her whisper accomplished what she'd wanted. The queen's hand went slack with shock and Katherine fell back in her chair, dazed.

Susanna moved. Walking towards Parker and the guards.

"We mean no harm to the queen." The man who spoke just

out of her view was subdued, as if realizing the impression he and his fellow guards had made.

"You will forgive our feeling a little uncertain of that, given your weapons and the way you approach." Parker spoke with a dry, amused tone. Allowing some room for face-saving.

"Aye. You are right to chastise us. We took our orders a little too enthusiastically."

"And what are your orders?"

"We are to take for questioning a Mistress Horenbout, who was seen entering the queen's chambers."

"You know who Mistress Horenbout is, Kilburne?"

There was silence. "No. I do not."

"She is my betrothed. The painter to the king, and no higher than your shoulder." Parker looked back at her, finally, his face unreadable. "I did not know you feared women so much, that you needed to storm the queen's chambers with swords drawn to get one."

"Show yourself, those who approach." Katherine's voice came out strong, dripping authority. She had risen from her chair.

Susanna suddenly remembered Parker telling her the queen had roused the English armies while Henry was in France, once. Inspiring them with a speech at Buckingham before they marched against an invading Scotland.

They had won.

Gone was the tearful, sad woman in her middle years. In her place stood a regent.

"Your Majesty." A man stepped forward and sank down on one knee. "My most humble apologies. I am under orders—"

"From who?" Katherine's voice cut him sharper than his own sword.

"From the cardinal."

"And the Cardinal Wolsey thinks it politic to send a guard to drag one of my ladies from my chambers?"

Kilburne, finally realizing the situation he'd leaped into, without a second thought, kept his eyes on the intricate rug at his feet. "We should not have come so loud and so many, Your Majesty. I have erred."

"Tell me, why does the cardinal seek the king's painter?" Katherine spoke more calmly, Kilburne's apology tempering her anger.

"I am to say, on grounds of treason, Your Majesty." Kilburn spoke hesitantly, as if he realized all he thought he knew was false.

"I know of no treason she has committed. But I do know she has rendered great service to the Crown."

Kilburne finally lifted his head, and Susanna saw the agony of indecision on his face. He was truly caught here, and had no way out.

"Where are you to take me?" She spoke directly to him, and he started.

"Mistress Horenbout?" His face fell a little more.

"Aye. I am Susanna Horenbout. Where are you to take me?"

"The Tower."

There was dead silence at his words, and Kilburne dropped his head again.

"If you are to take her to the Tower, you will take her to the rooms I gave to the Duc de Longueville some years ago when he was housed as a hostage of war. They are comfortable and well-furnished."

Kilburne rose to his feet, fast as a cat. "Your Majesty, it shall be done." There was a tremor of relief in his voice.

Katherine gazed at him, steadily, and he shrunk into himself. When she spoke her voice trembled a little. "This is wrong. It should not be, and it will be made right. But until then, not a hair on Mistress Horenbout's head, not a single part of her, will be touched or hurt. Convey my order to the Constable of the Tower. He is to contact me before any change to her situation is made."

Kilburne sent her a look from the corner of his eye, and Susanna wondered if Wolsey had told him to be rough. The cardinal would enjoy thinking of her being man-handled and disgraced. "My word of honor, Your Majesty. She will be treated well."

"I will hold you to account for it." Katherine spoke softly and to hear her, all had gone quiet.

Parker appeared beside Kilburne. When Susanna saw his face, her heart twisted in her chest. His eyes had gone blank, the chill look of a predator before the kill, calculating every eventuality before it leapt. "I will hold you to account, too, Kilburne."

She made a sound, a choked cry, and suddenly she was drawn deep into his arms, and held fast.

He kissed the top of her head, and then turned to Kilburne. Whispered words only she and Kilburne could hear. "And unlike the queen, I know where you live."

CHAPTER 12

> If a king should fall under such contempt or envy
> that he could not keep his subjects in their duty but
> by oppression and ill usage, and by rendering them
> poor and miserable, it were certainly better for him
> to quit his kingdom than to retain it by such
> methods as make him, while he keeps the name of
> authority, lose the majesty due to it.
>
> *Utopia by Thomas More (translated by H. Morley)*

They would not let him through the entrance. As
Susanna stepped into the Lieutenant's Lodgings,
Kilburne held out a hand to stop him, and Parker
reined in an urge to smash his fist into Kilburne's face.

There was a scuffle within, Parker could hear it—Susanna
trying to turn back to say goodbye, and being denied.

He bunched his hands into fists, and heard a roaring in his
ears.

Kilburne braced himself, widening his stance. And it was his
quiet acceptance of the blow that stilled Parker's hand.

"You think you deserve it, don't you?" His voice was rough,
even to his own ears.

Kilburne gave a single, curt nod. "I was a fool, gathering a full company, clattering down the halls to the queen's chamber. S'blood. What did I think I was about?"

"What *did* you think you were about?" Wolsey must have made some promises to light such a fire under Kilburne's backside.

"Wolsey claimed the king would be grateful—"

Parker gave a snorting half-laugh at that, and Kilburne winced. "The king told Wolsey to do nothing until he'd thought on the matter, and as far as I'm aware, he's still thinking."

Kilburne lifted a shaking hand to his face, rubbed it. "What is this about, Parker?"

"Too deep a game, Kilburne. Better you don't know."

"Aye. I think I would prefer to be dumb in this tangle." He stepped over the threshold. "I will go up. Make sure your lady is comfortably settled."

"Where were you to take her? How were you to treat her?"

Kilburne hesitated, and his hand tightened on the door ring.

"That bad?" Parker kept his voice calm. Wondered what would have happened had they not been in the queen's chamber. Had Katherine not intervened.

He thought suddenly of Will Somers, urging them to go to the queen. He would talk to the Fool before this was over, find out how he knew Wolsey's plans. And thank him for his help.

"I'm sorry, Parker. I did not know who she was."

Parker lifted his head, up to the windows above him. "You know now."

Kilburne paused, door half-closed. "I know now. And I have direct orders from the queen. It will help me keep her safe if the cardinal commands me otherwise, either directly or through the Constable of the Tower."

Parker dragged his gaze back. "If Wolsey makes any move against my lady, makes any change at all to the queen's arrangements, send for me."

Kilburne shook his head. "I cannot promise that. It may be impossible to get a message to you in time."

"Then I would have one of my pages in the Tower with Mistress Horenbout. And have him accorded free passage."

Kilburne hesitated, the shadow of the door concealing his expression.

Parker waited. He forced his breathing slow and even. He was not used to being the supplicant. But Kilburne was taking too long, and he could not accept it.

He gathered himself, a snarl already twisting his lips, hands lifted to grab Kilburne by the throat, and when Kilburne finally spoke, his words tumbled over themselves.

"She can have one servant, and he will be free to come and go." Kilburne stepped a little further back, ready to slam the door. "I'll make an arrangement at the gate for him."

Parker gave a nod, his limbs shaking with the force of violence held back. Unable to speak.

Kilburne swung the door shut in his face.

It was probably the first of many.

THEY HAD REFUSED TO LET HER TURN AND SAY HER GOODBYES. Hands, not so gentle now their leader was otherwise engaged, gripped her in a relentless march deep into the house and up the stairs.

She twisted her head, craning back to catch one last glimpse of Parker, and heard him shout as Kilburne denied him entrance.

She wanted to cry out to him, but clamped her mouth shut, grinding her back teeth together. He was capable of plowing through Kilburne to reach her, if he thought her in danger, and she would not have him in more trouble than he was already.

The guards pressed against her so tightly on the carved wooden stairway panic rose up to choke her, as if she were drowning, caught helpless in a maelstrom.

She knew it could be worse.

She could be in the White Tower, going down the stairs to the dungeon, instead of up to rooms in the Lieutenant's Lodgings, tucked neatly up against the Bell Tower. Rooms which had formerly housed a French duke.

She sensed the men around her had expected more rough play—they were reined in and chafing against the restraints Kilburne and the queen had placed on them.

As they reached the top of the stairs and began down a passageway, a hand from behind splayed against the small of her back, slipped around her waist, bold and disrespectful.

Fear clawed at her. She was hemmed in, crowded. Overwhelmed.

She scrabbled for purchase on the smooth wooden floor as another hand snaked out to palm her breast, squeeze it.

They were growing bolder, the further they got from Kilburne.

She took a breath, her fists clenched before her, and stopped moving. She leaned back, her legs locked at the knees, bracing herself for the slam of bodies from behind. She angled herself to make a smaller obstacle as men tripped over her and each other.

She'd caught them by surprise. She had been nothing but cooperative since they had encountered her.

The man behind her swore as he tripped and twisted away to save himself, knocking into another guard. They both fell to the floor, at her feet.

Other men jostled each other to stay upright, grunting and swearing.

"You bitch." One of the men on the floor gave her a slit-eyed glare.

"You were manhandling me. Someone was running his hands over me." She did not flinch from the words and they remained, hanging in the air, clear and accusing. "It is not well done of you." Even she could hear how accented her English was, all of a sudden. Fear and panic had brought her mother tongue back into her head, trying to override her new English speech.

She had not known what to expect, but she saw at least some looked uncomfortable at her accusation. They looked away, or at each other, and she said no more.

The men on the floor scrambled to their feet, and she thought the one who'd called her a bitch was one of those who had been free with his hands earlier.

"What is your name?" She looked directly at him, and for the first time, fear or nerves flickered in his eyes.

He did not want to tell her. He shuffled.

Perhaps he was remembering, suddenly, to whom she was betrothed. Or who had defended her when they had come for her.

"What is this, Merden?" Kilburne's voice made her start. She had not heard him coming up the stairs, and by the panicked looked on his men's faces, they hadn't either.

"Merden." Susanna said the name softly, and the guard turned away, a flush on his cheeks.

"What happened?" Kilburne hardened his tone.

There was silence.

"Your men were jostling me, forcing me along. Some were groping me." She turned to him. "I refused to walk any further."

Kilburne blinked. "Lewis?"

A guard stepped forward, tall and well muscled. She remembered he'd been near the front, leading them, and the men around him would not look at him, now.

"You are second-in-command."

"Aye." Lewis cleared his throat. "Aye."

"And are you deaf?" Kilburne's words were soft.

Lewis shifted, uncomfortable. "No, sir."

"Are any of you deaf?" He waited them out as they shook their heads.

"Then you would have heard the Queen of England giving a

direct instruction on the treatment of this prisoner. You would have heard me give my word of honor to obey it."

A few faces paled. Heads nodded.

"Then, by God, follow it, or you will be held accountable." His shout made them flinch. Susanna could not help flinching, herself.

"And the other? What of his instructions?" Merden spoke with a soft hiss, like a trapped grass snake.

Kilburne stared Merden down. "I cannot have a man under my command who will not follow my orders, Merden. If you would rather ask the cardinal for a job in his household, by all means . . ." He swept his arm towards the stairs, and Merden shifted his eyes from his captain to the way out. Hesitated. Stepped back in line with the other men.

Kilburne gestured for her to continue down the passage, and his men shuffled aside to let them pass.

As she came abreast with Merden, she flicked him a glance and stumbled at the look in his eyes.

"Careful, the going is uneven." Kilburne held out his arm.

Susanna took it, glanced back at Merden, her heart leaping in her throat. "So it would seem."

CHAPTER 13

And this is all the success that I can have in a court, for I must always differ from the rest, and then I shall signify nothing; or, if I agree with them, I shall then only help forward their madness.

Utopia by Thomas More (translated by H. Morley)

With every step he took away from her, Parker's failure weighed heavier on his shoulders. She was so vulnerable, at the mercy of too many who meant her harm.

He needed Peter Jack in those rooms with her. Knife in his boot and eyes open.

He was running by the time he reached Crooked Lane, his chest heaving as he pulled himself up the back stairs. A clawed fear-demon held fast to his lungs, squeezing them, piercing them mercilessly.

Harry, Peter Jack, Eric and Mistress Greene were on their feet as he stepped into the kitchen. White, fearful faces turning to him in expectation.

"She is in the Tower."

Mistress Greene let out a single, whooping sob, then choked back the ones that would follow it. "What is the charge?"

"Wolsey accuses her of treason."

At Harry's shout of protest, he held up his hand.

"He has no proof. Absolutely none. He has moved against her too quickly, and that is at least one thing in our favor. That and she has the support of the queen."

"How will that help her?" Peter Jack's voice cracked.

"It already has. The queen bade the Tower wardens take her to the royal apartments in the Lieutenant's Lodgings, to the rooms she once gave to the Duc de Longueville. Susanna is in comfort, not in the dungeons, as Wolsey would have her."

Mistress Greene sank down on the bench by the fire. "Thank the good Lord."

"What do we do?" Harry moved closer to the door, as if to leave immediately, and Parker felt a lift in the crushing weight that dragged at him.

"I persuaded the captain to allow her a servant. I need Peter Jack there to keep watch on her, and to warn me if Wolsey makes any move. The warden has guaranteed free passage."

"And Harry?" Peter Jack scowled.

Parker cocked his head, looked properly at Peter Jack. "Harry and his lads are going to help me spy on Wolsey. To see who comes to him with information, and to watch where he goes." He kept his voice calm, fighting the urge to roar. He did not have time for anything but immediate obedience.

"They were once my lads, too."

"'Til you gave it all up for this." Harry spoke quietly, hand flicking the air to encompass the kitchen, the house. The security of it all.

"You're in here, too, aren't you?" Peter Jack crossed his arms over his chest. "You look to have gotten the best of both." He turned to Parker, his eyes narrowed. "You always leave me behind, and take him into the thick of the action—"

"Stop it." Eric shoved Peter Jack hard enough to make him

stumble. His slight body, only shoulder-height to his brother, vibrated with rage. "You think you're left out of the action? What about me? You don't think protecting my lady is a worthy job? I'll do it." He spun, facing Parker. "I'll do it!"

Parker flicked his gaze from face to face. How had this blown up now, when every second counted? "Peter Jack, you once told Susanna you'd fight for her—"

"Yes, I'll fight for her. I want to kill her swine of a brother for doing this to us, I want to help stop Wolsey. Not sit in the Tower with her, sucking my teeth."

"I'll watch her." Harry stepped closer to Eric, touched a quivering shoulder. "Maybe we can do it together? You're good in a fight, Eric, but the Tower wardens are big, and if something happens . . . you could get help while I stand guard."

Peter Jack opened his mouth, but Parker had had enough. "Harry, your lads will report to me, or Peter Jack?"

Harry gave a nod. "I'll speak to them." He turned without waiting and left, leaving the door open behind him.

Peter Jack watched him go, a hunted look in his eyes.

"Sir, I—"

Parker held up a hand, and in the silence that followed, he heard a sound.

The creak of floorboards by the entrance.

He launched himself at the passageway, but the front door had already slammed shut. When he flung it open and ran out into Crooked Lane, there was no one there.

He spun on his heel, almost colliding with Peter Jack, and raced back into the house, up the stairs and burst into the spare room.

Lucas Horenbout sat with his head in his hands on the bed. On the floor lay the rope that had tied Jan Heyman, but the musician had gone.

"What did you do?" Parker slapped Lucas's hands away, and his head jerked up.

His face was pale, tinged with green, and his hand shook as he lifted it to wipe away a line of sweat on his brow.

"What did you tie Jan up for? He woke me, begging to be released." His voice was weak, wavering.

Parker took a step back. Breathed deeply. The air in the room was stale, and he could smell the sharp odor of sweat.

"Where is Susanna?" Lucas gently lifted his hand to press the skin around the lump at the back of his head.

"Exactly where you made sure she would go." Parker walked to the window and flung it open to purge the sour air of the room. "The Tower."

⁂

THE WALLS OF SUSANNA'S PRISON WERE WHITEWASHED, AND set with dark beams. Her windows were large, paned with glass, and looked out over Tower Green, to the menace of the White Tower.

There was little furniture in the expansive, comfortable rooms, though, and she could only think that they had been taken for use elsewhere. A table and chair sat under one of the windows and two short benches were angled near the fireplace. That was the sum of it.

Kilburne eyed the room critically and muttered something about finding more furnishings.

She did not care if he did, or not. She wandered though a doorway, and found the bedchamber. There was a bed in it. An enormous one, and she could only think it had not been taken because of the difficulty in moving it down the steep stairs.

The back wall of the bedroom was of grey stone, part of the Bell Tower which the Lieutenant's Lodgings leaned up against. She could feel the tower looming over her, cold and harsh.

"The bell will ring each night to call the curfew. I will interpret the queen's orders concerning you to include the freedom of the grounds. You can take your ease on the green, but when the bell rings, you must return to your rooms." Kilburne stood, uncomfortable, in the doorway of the bedchamber. "I am sure Parker will send your servant soon."

"Servant?" She lifted her head.

"I gave leave for a servant. He will have free passage from the Tower, but if he is outside the Tower after curfew, he won't be allowed back in until the next morning. And he cannot leave the grounds between curfew and morning, either."

"My thanks."

He looked away. Her gratitude seemed to prick his conscience.

"I left my satchel in the queen's chambers. Can I have it returned?" She walked toward him, and he edged out of the doorway, back into the main chamber, relieved to be out of the bedroom.

"What is in it?" His voice took on a sharper edge, suspicious.

"My pigments and brushes. My parchment and charcoal. I have a number of commissions to complete for the king, and I will need them if I am to fulfill my obligations."

"What were you doing this morning with the queen?" Kilburne went to stand by a window, looking out over the green.

"I was there to present her with a portrait of the Princess Mary."

"A portrait? I saw none." He turned, his eyes narrowed.

"The queen held it in her hands when she spoke to you." Susanna kept her tone mild. "It is on an oak panel, about this big." She showed him with her hands. "A small portrait the queen can take with her when she travels with the king. Something she can look at whenever she wants."

She saw he recalled the queen was holding something in her hands, and nodded slowly. "What has Wolsey against you?"

She shrugged. "A few months ago I prevented him from achieving a goal. And he has never forgiven me for it."

Kilburne stared at her a long time, as if trying to understand how a woman with no powerful connections could stand in the cardinal's way. "There is more to this than I wish to know."

"There is more to this than *I* wish to know." She crossed her arms in front of her, and stared back at him. "And yet, here we both stand."

Kilburne shook himself, as if trying to wake from a dream, or shake water from his eyes. "My men will not harm you again." He moved to the door.

"They want to."

Her words stopped him dead. "My apologies for what happened. I don't think it will happen again."

"You'll forgive me if I'm not reassured that you are not absolutely certain."

He rubbed his face with his hands. "You are in more trouble than I first thought."

Susanna smiled as he stepped out her rooms, and knew Kilburne's hesitation before swinging shut the door was because of the bleakness he saw in her face.

She waited for the click as the door closed and tightened her arms in front of her. She was in trouble, that was certain, and being a prisoner in the Tower was the least of it.

CHAPTER 14

> He would rather govern rich men than be rich
> himself; since for one man to abound in wealth and
> pleasure when all about him are mourning and
> groaning, is to be a gaoler and not a king.
>
> *Utopia by Thomas More (translated by H. Morley)*

H orenbout stared at Parker, mouth open. "The Tower."
He stuttered out the words.

"She was arrested this morning."

Lucas jumped to his feet, gasping, and leaped for the basin in
the corner of the room.

Parker watched him dispassionately as he vomited and
heaved, until at last he stood, spent and shaking, his breathing
harsh.

"I never meant . . ." He wiped his mouth with the back of his
hand. "I never thought . . ."

Parker straightened. He had never wanted to kill someone so
badly. Every muscle, every tendon, screamed for action,
screamed for him to flick his arm, palm his knife and throw it.

Straight into Horenbout's throat.

"Don't look at me like that." Lucas's eyes were wide, and Parker smelled the stink of fear in his sweat.

"My life was calm, happy, before you came along, Horenbout. Now my betrothed is in the Tower and my life has gone to hell." He couldn't help it, he did palm his knife into his hand.

"She is my sister. You think I wanted this?"

Parker flicked the knife upward, so it arced through the air. He caught it by the hilt. "You knew it was a possibility. But you endangered her anyway. Without asking her permission, without any precautions. The speed with which your plan has been uncovered tells me this was either done by amateurs, or someone wanted you and Susanna in trouble."

"I didn't engineer this. I'm just the messenger," Lucas shouted, then gripped his head, rocking on his heels. "*Mijn God.*" He looked about to faint.

Parker felt no sympathy. "Why did you run yesterday? Who hit you over the head?"

Lucas groaned, and stumbled to the bed, flopped down on it and lay, eyes closed. "I was upstairs in my room. I saw someone come over the wall. He looked like a ruffian, a thug." Lucas massaged his temples. "I grabbed a few things, and ran out the front door."

"Straight to your meeting with Heyman."

Horenbout's eyes flew open at that. "He told you of our meeting?"

"He thought it would prove he didn't knock you senseless."

"Jan didn't hit me over the head."

"Who did then?" Parker stepped right up to the bed, to read his brother-in-law's eyes.

"I never saw them, they came from behind—"

"Then it could have been Heyman. He was certainly the only one we found on the scene. And he knew where you would be, and when."

"I don't believe it," Lucas whispered. "We . . ." He fell silent, cast a quick glance at Parker from the corner of his eye, and then winced at the pain it cost him. "I *won't* believe it."

Parker took a step back from the bed. Lucas and Heyman both went quiet with fear when he probed their association. Heyman had risked serious harm when he'd refused to answer.

Someone very powerful lay behind this.

Someone they thought could reach right into Henry's court, if they so wished.

"The Emperor Charles." He didn't know he had spoken aloud until Horenbout groaned, and turned away, his head in his hands.

"Leave me alone." He buried his face into his pillow.

"Oh, I will. My lady is locked in the Tower, and I need to find a way to free her without jeopardizing our entire future at court."

Horenbout lifted himself up. "And if you can't?" He looked like a madman, ready for a place in Saint Mary of Bethlehem, his hair standing straight up and his eyes wide and desperate.

"If I can't, I'll have to find a way to free her and escape England."

"You think me to blame for this, but I've sacrificed as well. Tried to protect us all—"

"If there is anything you know that can help me, tell me now." Parker cut him off, sick of the sight of him. He moved towards the door.

Horenbout looked ready to speak, then sank back onto his pillow. Turned his face away.

Parker hesitated at the threshold. "If you know something useful and are holding it back and Susanna is hurt, no place you hide will be safe from me."

He took the stairs at a run, and behind him, he heard Lucas begin to sob.

THE LAST TIME PARKER HAD BEEN THIS NERVOUS BEFORE meeting the king, he'd been young, without connections, with nothing but a dangerous letter and his wits as currency.

Things were all too different now. He had so much more to lose, but he walked past the courtiers and other Privy Chamber gentlemen, towards the guards of the King's Closet, without hesitation or falter.

One of the guards stepped into the room, and Parker heard his name murmured. But when the man stepped back out, he shook his head.

"His Majesty is busy, he can see no one."

Parker wanted to push them aside and walk in, anyway. But after his unthinking comment the night before, he was not as sure of his welcome as he usually would be.

"This is urgent."

The guard hesitated, but he had delivered urgent messages from Parker before, and eventually the man stepped back in. He heard the king's voice, sharp and annoyed, and the guard had a deep flush on his cheeks when he appeared at the door.

"Aye. Proceed." He stepped aside for Parker to enter.

"Your Majesty." Parker bowed in the doorway, and waited for Henry to invite him in.

The king looked up from his papers and gave a nod, and Parker stepped inside. The door closed behind him.

Francis Bryan stood beside the king, freshly returned from some diplomatic mission abroad. Parker had missed seeing him these last few months.

Henry didn't send Bryan out, and Parker knew he was being punished for last night's blunders. Being denied a private audience.

Bryan looked between them, uncomfortable. There were dark rings under his eyes, and his hands shook, the tip of a quill fluttering between his fingers.

"My betrothed was arrested from the queen's chambers this

morning and taken to the Tower." Parker did not let the anger that flared up just saying the words show on his face.

Henry let his quill fall. "Wolsey?"

From the corner of his eye, he saw Bryan's head jerk at the news.

Parker nodded.

"I didn't authorize it." Henry spoke slowly, a frown creasing his forehead.

"I know." Parker flexed his hands. "Will you authorize her release?"

Henry leaned back in his chair, and pressed the tips of his fingers together. "I cannot ignore Wolsey's accusations. If Mistress Horenbout is innocent of the charges my Lord Chancellor has made against her, she will be released soon enough."

"You know why he's done this." Parker kept the fury from his voice with an effort of will. "She was acting for you when she made Wolsey her enemy. Risked her life in your service." Parker took a step toward the king, and Henry shifted in his chair. Scraped it back and walked to the window, looking out at the river.

Parker took a deep breath, relaxed his shoulders. It would help no one if he were to anger the king.

He let his gaze move to Bryan, and saw he was staring at him, mouth slightly open. "What is the charge?" He spoke softly, just out of the king's hearing.

"Treason." Parker looked directly into Bryan's eyes as he spoke. He'd saved Bryan from a charge of treason not too long ago, and if anyone understood the fear and powerlessness that came with such an accusation, it should be him.

Bryan looked away and would not meet Parker's eyes again.

"So that's the way of it?" Parker murmured.

A flush crept up Bryan's face, but he still would not look at Parker.

He would keep the king's favor, no matter who he must shake off to do so. No matter what he owed those he abandoned.

Parker wondered how Bryan would treat his sister, now Elizabeth Carew was no longer the king's mistress.

"Where is she kept in the Tower?" Henry turned from the window.

"Her Majesty bade the captain take her to the Lieutenant's Lodgings."

"The queen was present?" Henry's attention sharpened, and for the first time he looked worried.

"She was."

"When you said your lady was taken from the queen's chambers, I did not realize . . ." Henry's eyes narrowed. "What was your lady doing there?"

"She was presenting the queen with a small portrait of your daughter, Your Majesty."

Henry cocked his head to one side. "I must see it. I didn't know the queen had commissioned such a work. And it reminds me. Last night I asked Mistress Horenbout to paint my son, Fitzroy." Henry slid back behind his desk and picked up his quill. "I will instruct the guards to give her leave to visit Fitzroy when she needs to." He wrote quickly, sanded the page and rolled it. Sealed it with his crest. "And she can busy herself illuminating these writs and communications." He indicated a box of scrolls.

"I will make sure she receives them." Parker wanted to lift the box and smash it to the floor.

He picked it up carefully and tucked it under his arm. "Wolsey will try to move her to the dungeon. And when he's done there, she will be lucky to ever lift a brush again." Could his voice really stay so level, so cool, and say words like that? When they stuck, hard as an almond swallowed whole, in his throat.

Henry picked up his quill again, and began signing the papers Bryan had brought him. "Wolsey will answer to me, if that happens."

"That may be." Parker could hear the bleakness in his own voice. "But if it comes to that, it will be too late."

CHAPTER 15

> Do not you think that if I were about any king, proposing good laws to him, and endeavouring to root out all the cursed seeds of evil that I found in him, I should either be turned out of his court, or, at least, be laughed at for my pains?
>
> *Utopia by Thomas More (translated by H. Morley)*

The men who came for her didn't knock, but thanks to their number and their haste on the stairs, Susanna heard them coming and was ready.

She watched the small, tight group of men enter her rooms, and retreated, shaking, into the stairwell.

She'd been in the Bell Tower, to look at the bell. Otherwise she'd have been trapped in her chambers.

Wolsey would be behind this. Come to drag her from comfort to the place he'd had in mind for her from the start.

The White Tower dungeons.

Her heart beat faster just thinking the name.

She could not go back up the Bell Tower. If they came looking for her there, there would be no escape. She lifted her skirts and ran silently to her chamber door. Pressed herself against the wall.

The men within were moving furniture, cursing and swearing, and with her heart pounding in her ears, she ran past the open doorway, towards the stairs.

As her foot touched the first tread, someone burst from her rooms, shouting, and the angry sound of it, the fear of what he was there for, made her leap the stairs three or four at a time.

She reached the bottom, but before she could take a step towards the front entrance, she heard the handle turn on the big double door. More were coming in the front.

She spun, taking in the dark paneled walls and a twisting passageway as she searched for some escape.

From above, the stairs creaked with the weight of running feet and the front door was thrown open so hard it slammed against the wall. She found herself five paces down the passage before she realized it.

She jerked to a stop as voices called up the stairs, straining to hear what was said. Icy perspiration pricked her brow like a crown of thorns and her breathing was harsh and too fast.

There was a shouted exchange, and Susanna forced her feet to move. She skidded to a stop again as a door in front of her was flung open.

She stared straight into Kilburne's wide eyes.

Relief dipped her knees until she forced them straight. Without hesitation she ran to him, past him, and spun, to face back the way she'd come, with Kilburne standing between her and whoever was thundering down the passage. He looked over his shoulder at her, his mouth open, but then snapped his attention back to the incoming danger.

Kilburne had made promises on her behalf, and she thought he was a man of honor. Her life hung on whether this was so.

"Who goes there?" Kilburne's voice was so calm, Susanna found her gaze sharpening on him.

"Lewis, sir." Kilburne's second-in-command stepped around

the corner, panting. "Seems the cardinal sent some men to fetch Mistress Horebout to the dungeon. We were just disputing their right to be above, searching for her."

Lewis caught sight of her, peeping out from behind Kilburne, and his eyes opened wide.

Whatever he'd shouted up the stairs to Wolsey's men, Susanna noted he had not gone up the stairs to stop them. Had not made a move to find Kilburne, either.

Kilburne stood silent, waiting for Lewis to finish, and did not speak for a long moment afterwards.

Lewis flushed.

"I will require a word with you when this matter is settled." Kilburne spoke very quietly, but Lewis staggered back, as if under siege.

"Aye, sir."

"You got her?" A man stepped into view, addressing Lewis.

Susanna saw the second-in-command go white at what the simple question gave away.

From the way Kilburne stiffened, the implication had not been lost on him, either.

At last, Wolsey's man noticed Kilburne, and then, finally, her.

"And you would be?" Kilburne's tone was still even, but she could see his left hand clenching and unclenching.

"Harris, Captain. In service to the Cardinal Wolsey." Harris reluctantly raised his hat. His men began to mill behind him, and he turned and spoke sharply.

Susanna heard them returning to the front entrance, muttering amongst themselves.

"And what is your business, Harris, that you should storm the Lieutenant's Lodgings and run along its passageways, without first taking my leave?"

Harris' cheeks flushed a deep red, and a little tick started up, just under his eye. "You took into custody a Mistress Horenbout this morning, on my lord's orders, and she is wanted in the White Tower for questioning."

"Who wants her? Where is the writ?" Kilburne held out his hand.

Harris shifted. "I'm only following my orders. I know nothing about a writ."

"I understand. And I can only follow orders, myself. Especially those from His Majesty, the king." Kilburne held up a scroll, with the king's unmistakeable seal.

"What has that to do with the prisoner?" Harris flicked his gaze from Kilburne, to Lewis, to Susanna.

"This is a writ, containing my orders, straight from His Majesty, in His Majesty's own hand, on what to do with the prisoner." Kilburne opened it up. Glanced down at it. "And there is no mention of questioning in the Tower."

"I don't know anything about this . . ." Harris wiped a hand over his forehead, leaving a faint brown line of dust.

"Clearly not, or you would not have been acting directly against the king's wishes, sir." For the first time, Kilburne allowed his anger to show. "Count yourself lucky I prevented you from taking her, or you could well have ended in the dungeons for questioning, yourself." Kilburne was surely exaggerating, but Harris went white at his words.

"Mistress Horenbout will not go to the White Tower unless I have the correct papers and a writ from the king, rescinding his orders. And I and my men will be the ones who will escort her there, should that be the case."

Harris lifted his hat again, and stepped back, with one last, almost longing look at her. Then he turned and walked down the passage towards the door.

Susanna put a trembling hand against the wall and leaned against it. Her throat was too tight to speak.

Kilburne and Lewis exchanged a look.

"You all right?"

She flinched at the sound of a voice behind her. Spun to face the speaker.

Eric stood before her, just inside the room Kilburne had

come from, and behind him she saw Harry. Eric was smiling, but Harry's face was grim.

His fists were white-knuckled, and she knew, with a startling clarity, he had had to force himself not to step forward while Kilburne confronted Harris.

"It is good to see you." She could only whisper. She wanted to sink to her knees at the sight of them, but she was too shaky to get up again, and she would do nothing in front of Lewis to show any weakness.

"I told Parker you could have one servant but with the extra duties required of you by the king, I see that two are necessary. And they have come not a moment too soon, it seems," said Kilburne. "Your rooms will be in need of straightening."

⁂

"HEYMAN ESCAPED?" SUSANNA CLAMPED HER HAND OVER HER mouth, but the shout had already left her throat.

Harry winced. "Your brother untied him."

Susanna gaped. "Why did he do that? Heyman *knows* something . . ."

They all contemplated that for a moment.

"Did your brother not start this?" Harry flung out an arm. "Isn't he the reason you're here?"

Susanna noticed the bruise on his face was settling into a deep greenish-yellow. Her brother was the indirect cause of that, too.

"I can't believe Lucas wishes me this much ill." She wrapped her arms around herself, trying to fight back the dread that hung on her like the weights on the drawbridge just over the wall from where she stood. "He has been jealous of me. He's jealous of the position I hold with the king. But deliberately having me arrested, and possibly tortured? I can't believe it."

"Cannot or will not?" Eric kicked his legs as he sat on the bench beside the still cold fireplace.

Susanna closed her eyes. Thought. "Cannot." She realized she spoke with certainty, and the weights eased a little. "Lucas would not try to harm me like this deliberately."

"So, perhaps he never meant you to end up in the Tower, but he had a hand in it." Harry's mouth was still as grim as it had been downstairs in Kilburne's rooms. "And letting Heyman go, that says he knows more than he's letting on."

He was right. Susanna rubbed her head. "If Lucas untied Heyman, he must be awake and at least better than he was."

"One more person to watch." Eric spoke in a clear imitation of Parker, wry, with an edge of bite.

Despite herself, Susanna smiled. She noticed a small wooden box resting on the chest Harry and one of Kilburne's men had brought up, and bent to pick it up.

She slid open the lid, and saw the writs. "The king has sent more illuminations for me to work on while I'm here?"

Harry nodded, his face unreadable. Then he dug in her satchel, which he'd brought her from the queen's chambers, and held out the king's writ Kilburne had waved at Harris earlier. "You are also to paint his son."

The writ had saved her from the dungeon, and she took it from Harry carefully. "Why did Kilburne give it to you?"

Harry grinned. "He didn't. When we collected your things from his rooms, I saw it on his desk and thought it better in our hands than in anyone else's."

Susanna regarded him a long moment, and started to laugh.

She fought against it, but as some point, the laughter gave way to sobs.

CHAPTER 16

If ill opinions cannot be quite rooted out, and you cannot cure some received vice according to your wishes, you must not, therefore, abandon the commonwealth, for the same reasons as you should not forsake the ship in a storm because you cannot command the winds.

Utopia by Thomas More (translated by H. Morley)

The man Parker was sure was a French spy walked down Fleet Street, unconcerned and relaxed.

Parker watched as he stopped and bought apples at a stall, and was close enough behind him to hear him crunch into one of them. His hand came up and wiped away the juice that spilled out onto his chin with his sleeve.

He'd sauntered out of Wolsey's London residence less than half an hour after entering. The boys in Harry's gang who were watching Wolsey's house had managed to call Parker in time to follow him.

No one knew better than Parker there was no French embassy in London at present—he'd had some part in the

French ambassador's hasty departure from England some months ago.

But the French would have left their spies in place to report on the movements and mood of the English king.

And Wolsey would be sure to keep an eye on those spies, and encourage a rapport with them. The cardinal traded on and used information better than anyone, after all, and between the Emperor Charles and King Frances I, Parker knew Wolsey much preferred the French king.

The spy slowed on the street, and Parker slowed with him, stepping into the shadow of a deep balcony over the front of a baker's shop.

The man was not lost, he'd sensed something.

He started walking again, as if he had his bearings once more, but in a swift motion bent as if to adjust a buckle on his shoe and looked behind him.

The look on his face said more than words he was shocked at what he saw. Very slowly, his hand went slack and his half-eaten apple fell into the dust.

Parker's gaze flicked from his target to down the street, because the Frenchman's eyes had not gone to him, they had gone a little further back than where Parker stood, to the right.

And Parker froze as well.

His chest was in a vice of shock, squeezed hard. He forced himself to draw breath, to look again to make sure.

Stock still, watching the French spy and making no attempt to hide, was Jean.

The French assassin.

The man who was back to settle a score.

He'd been following Parker while Parker had been following the French spy.

It burned in his throat, like the stink of the leather curers' foul mix, that he had not realized it.

But Jean showed no sign he saw Parker standing just a street's width away. His entire focus was on the man who'd been to visit Wolsey.

And while Parker would have thought the two would be natural allies, there was a fear, a panic, in the Frenchman's face as he stood waiting for Jean to make a move, that gave lie to that assumption.

Then, without warning, the Frenchman turned and ran. Blindly, as if he were blinkered and under attack from all sides. He weaved and jerked, to make himself a hard target to hit.

Parker looked back at Jean, and was not surprised to see the assassin had his crossbow raised.

The people around them in the street began to notice the drama unfolding, and there were shrieks and yells when they caught sight of Jean's weapon.

Parker swore. He wanted to speak to the spy, but there was no way he would run after the man and present his back to Jean as a gift of sacrifice.

He had no doubt the assassin would shoot him without a second thought.

But Jean had lowered his bow and clipped it back on his belt as the crowd grew more hysterical. He started after the Frenchman, and Parker stepped into his wake.

He had only gone a few feet when Jean looked over his shoulder and caught his gaze.

There was a smile on the assassin's face.

SIMON COULD NOT KEEP STILL. HE PACED THE ROOM, STOPPING every now and then to throw a log on the fire Eric and Harry had started in the hearth.

It was distracting.

"You'll go through all my wood if you keep that up."

Susanna tried to ease the irritation out of her tone.

Simon jerked at the sound of her voice and bumped his head on the mantelpiece above the fireplace as he straightened.

He swore and rubbed his head, ill-tempered. "That writ is urgent."

Susanna leaned back in her chair. "Then the king should not have had me dragged to the Tower. I would have been done with it by now if I were at home." She smiled sweetly. "Especially if there had been a list amongst the papers he sent me to say which one I should have started with."

She picked up her brush as if she had all the time in the world. "He could always send it off without illumination."

"You know he won't. He loves to send writs and letters that have been worked. You've spoiled him for plain letters, now."

Susanna shrugged. Contemplated the mussel shell holding yellow ochre. She needed to mix more.

"I'm sorry."

His words were so soft, spoken so close to her ear, she dropped her brush and had to grab it before it rolled onto the writ and ruined her work.

She turned in her chair and saw he was kneeling beside her, had ripped off the mask of impatience he'd worn, so hard and inflexible, to reveal nothing short of anguish.

The hard knot of tarred rope that had been looped around her chest since he'd turned away from her last night loosened and fell away. She breathed easy for the first time since Simon had entered the room, all glittering eyes and stiff limbs.

She'd sent Harry and Eric out to find dinner—their hostility to Simon had made her feel worse. They'd once been friends, and her brother's ill-wind had blown through even that.

"You know I forgive you." As always, when emotion gripped her especially hard, her English faltered, and her words were thick with Flemish intonations.

He bent his head. "I found someone. Someone I want to marry."

"Ah." She suddenly understood. "She works in the king's

household?"

He shook his head. "You know you are the exception. There are hardly any women working for the king." He remained on his knees, but his head lifted, at last. "She lives near my mother."

"What will happen to Parker if Wolsey succeeds in this, Simon? What will happen to you?"

"Parker will suffer. There is no possibility of anyone believing he knew nothing if you are found guilty." At last he got to his feet. "For me?" He shrugged. "They know I am a confidant of Parker's, but I am low enough down the ladder, I may be beneath notice."

"You did not want to leave it to chance."

He looked back at her, and his eyes were still anguished. "I did not." He turned away. Fed yet another log into the flames. "I was thinking of myself. Of a life I might not have if the court's eyes swung my way."

Susanna stood, and looked out over Tower Green to the White Tower.

"Even though I know Wolsey isn't there, I feel that he is. Lurking in that dungeon like a spider, waiting to drag me down." She shivered. "He cannot succeed in this. I can't let him. Not for me, although I don't want to find out what he has planned for me in there, but for everyone. You, Parker, the boys."

"You know you have my eyes and ears at court. If I hear anything that might help you, I'll find a way to let you know."

Susanna placed her hands on the windowsill and pressed her face against the glass. "I thank you for it. I will need all the help I can get."

"We don't just need your eyes and ears." Harry's voice came from the doorway, and Susanna turned to see him eyeing Simon with a little more warmth than he had before, his arms bunching under the weight of the tray he carried. "You're the king's carter. Your cart can go anywhere?"

Simon nodded slowly.

"If we have no choice but to flee, will you get us out?"

CHAPTER 17

> For one is never to offer propositions or advice that we are certain will not be entertained. Discourses so much out of the road could not avail anything, nor have any effect on men whose minds were prepossessed with different sentiments.
> *Utopia by Thomas More (translated by H. Morley)*

Parker almost stumbled as Jean looked back. The look that passed between them was as intense as a flash of lightning in a dark sky.

Jean had an air of calm purpose about him, and Parker reached within himself to find his own centered calm. He'd been running on panic, on fear—reacting to events. He needed to take back control.

The spy running before them, a chicken chased by foxes, could not be ripped apart until Parker learned what he knew.

Jean turned his attention back to his prey. He gathered speed as the crowds thinned away from the main way, eating into the distance between himself and the spy.

The Frenchman was running at an angle, leading them a twisting path north west. He didn't go through the arch of

Temple Bar but darted right, up Shire Lane towards Lincolns Inn Fields. Heading for open ground.

Parker saw Jean unclip his crossbow as he ran, and he surged after them both. If Jean caught the Frenchman in an open field, he was dead.

Shire Lane ended in a high wall with a gate, and the Frenchman at last saw his folly.

He looked back, and cried out when he noticed Parker behind Jean. He fumbled for the latch and disappeared through the opening.

Jean was walking slower now, and Parker thought he was favoring his left side, breathing heavily. There was no panic about his movements, though.

He would be only too pleased at the prospect of open ground.

Jean swung the solid wooden gate shut behind him as he went through, a petty mischief that had the smack of a taunt about it, and Parker palmed his knife before he went through the gate after him. What he and Jean would do about each other, he didn't know.

They were two predators circling the same prey and they would have to deal with each other before they could claim their prize.

The last time they'd met face to face, they had fought to kill. There had been a cold menace in Jean's eyes then, a suppressed fury—not this unhurried, smiling strangeness.

It disturbed Parker. He did not know what was going through the assassin's mind.

On the other side of the gate was a small lane, a muddy track with a mound of grass growing down the middle. There was no sign of either man, but up ahead, between the last two houses before the fields, Parker saw another open gate.

He ran, ignoring the puddles and ruts of the ill-kept path.

There was a cry just up ahead, and Parker burst through the gate into a newly ploughed field.

The soil underfoot was thick and clotted, some sort of slick clay, and he slid, only just staying on his feet.

The French spy had not been so lucky. He was lying on his back, churning the earth around him, struggling to gain his feet.

Jean approached, bow raised, one steady step at a time. He stopped a little way away and aimed, and the Frenchman thrashed about like a pike on a line.

"No." Parker's shout echoed strangely in the open space. He would have only one chance with Jean, and he did not waste it.

He ran, his knife ready to throw.

Jean turned, lifting his bow as he spun. As he took aim and squeezed the trigger, Parker threw himself forward. He hit the slick earth and slid, bringing his legs around and under him, one hand out to steady himself, his other arm back, knife at the ready.

The bolt shot over his head.

It made him feel better that Jean was trying to kill him. It made more sense.

He slammed into Jean, grabbing his legs. The momentum threw the assassin over backwards, but he kept hold of his bow, and Parker had to knock it from his hands.

At last—at last!—he had his knife to Jean's throat.

Parker scrambled round and hauled Jean up, keeping the blade tight against his skin.

He looked over at the French spy. The man was watching the two of them with his mouth hanging open.

"What was your business with Wolsey?"

The man closed his mouth with a snap, and frowned. "Who are you?"

Parker felt Jean tense under him. The assassin had nothing to lose. He expected Parker to mete out death and he would try to get free.

He should slit Jean's throat right now, end his problem, but he could not. He had taken lives before, but always in self-defence. Never calmly, with the intent to kill.

He tightened his grip on Jean. "Answer the question, or I will let Jean go. He can finish the job of killing you."

Jean stilled at his words. Parker wondered what he made of them.

The Frenchman pulled himself to his knees. Looked between the two men.

"At a loss for words, Renard? That is unlike you." Jean spoke with a laconic drawl, his accent thick and tart as a mouthful of French plums.

"Answer me. Now." Parker ground the words out, hating that he could only carry out his threat as a last resort. He hoped Renard did not know that. Did not know the dynamic between Jean and himself went far deeper than Parker preventing the assassin from executing a kill. "What did Wolsey want?"

Renard said nothing, he sat still, grabbing handfuls of mud and squeezing it between his fingers.

Jean relaxed back into Parker's hold, as if he were at his ease. "Answer, Renard." He smiled. "Every second you talk, is a second you live, hmm?"

Renard dropped the mud, a measure of hope lighting his face. "Today, I was there . . ." He hesitated, cleared his throat. "I made him a promise that the proof we have on someone he has imprisoned will soon be in his hands."

"And *will* it soon be in his hands?" Parker tuned out the birds calling to each other in the trees, the soft swish of leaves, the distant shouts and calls of Temple Bar and Fleet Street. Renard had his full concentration.

Renard shook his head. "We have nothing. We are simply buying time."

"And who is 'we'?"

Renard frowned at the question, and Jean laughed. "In Renard's case, it is the Emperor Charles whose orders he follows, even though officially he is pledged to France, *n'est pas?*"

"Wolsey knows you're working for the emperor?" Parker felt a grudging respect for the Emperor Charles, swooping in when the French ambassador left London and bribing the remaining French spies to his side. It was a masterstroke.

Renard shook his head. "He thinks I carry word from France."

"And why wouldn't he? After all, you used to work for the *comte*, and Wolsey thinks you still do." Jean spoke with an edge. If he'd been holding his bow, he would have cocked the hammer.

So Jean was here to dispose of a French double agent. Could that be the sole reason for his return? Not a personal vendetta to kill Susanna?

Parker had not wanted to say Susanna's name. He didn't know how Jean would react. But he had no choice now and felt a glimmer of hope that Susanna had never been the assassin's target. "The person you pretend to have proof of treason for, is it Mistress Horenbout?"

Jean went very still.

Renard turned his full attention to Parker, his eyes pleading. "Kill Jean, slit his throat, and I will tell you everything you want to know. Everything."

"You will tell me everything right now, or Jean and I will fight over who has the pleasure of killing you."

Renard flinched. "It is Susanna Horenbout. We had to stop her passing a message her brother gave her to the English queen. The emperor needs more time before the English king learns of his new plans."

"How did you know about Horenbout's message?"

"All I know is Lucas Horenbout has some connection to the emperor. He sent a note to the emperor's man in Ghent, telling him about the letter he'd been ordered to courier to his sister, just before he got on the ship to England." Renard's voice was matter-of-fact, and Parker had to close his eyes and breathe deeply. "He was supposed to arrive in London and come straight to us. We would have told him not to hand the message over, to keep it quiet, but he didn't. We missed him at the appointed place, and he went to his sister's before we could stop him."

"That bolt through the window, that was you?"

Renard went white, as if he suddenly understood who he was talking to. "Not me, I'm no good with a bow. Jules did it. But yes, we tried to kill both the Horenbouts first. It was nothing personal, you understand, we simply had to keep the message from getting out."

"And when you couldn't kill her, you stopped her another way, by telling Wolsey you could prove she was a traitor. And tried to kill her brother again."

Renard lifted his gaze to Parker's face, and his eyes went wide. He nodded, a jerky movement. He would not look at Jean and Parker wondered what he saw in the assassin's face that was even more frightening than in his own.

"How long had you planned to string Wolsey along with your non-existent proof?"

Renard lifted his shoulders and kept them up, in a hunched pose. "Indefinitely. Until it's too late. He thinks French agents intercepted Lucas Horenbout, and stole the message from him. I told him I'm waiting for them to contact me to hand it over."

"And if Wolsey gets impatient, and decides to torture it out of her, rather than wait for your 'proof'?"

Jean made a sound, like a growl, and Parker thought for a moment he should plunge the knife into his throat. Since Renard had admitted to trying to kill Susanna, to having her locked away, the assassin had been still and focused as a snake about to strike.

There was no other conclusion than he really was here to kill her and wanted no one else to cheat him of his prize. Renard must be a mere triviality, a small clean-up of the French king's affairs he was doing on the side.

Renard was shaking his head. "We told Wolsey not to torture her. We told him to wait for the proof. For her to go under questioning—it's the last thing we want. If her brother has given her the message and she talks, then the English king will learn that which the Emperor Charles wishes to keep secret for now."

"How unfortunate for you, and for Mistress Horenbout, the

cardinal does what he pleases, and certainly does not take advice from the French spies he confers with." He had to clamp his teeth together to stop the howl that threatened to rip from his throat.

"Imperial spies." Jean made the correction softly.

"It doesn't matter whose side he takes, who Wolsey thinks he speaks for. The cardinal has tried to torture my lady from the moment he laid hands on her." A half-open jaw of fear held him by the neck, sharp teeth pricking him, at the thought of what Wolsey might be trying, even now.

"And has he succeeded?" Jean spoke in a voice that came from far away. Some icy plain where there was no shelter, nothing but relentless cold.

"To my knowledge, not yet."

Renard lifted his hands, caked with mud, like some strange earth offering. "What will you do with me?"

"Who directs you?"

Parker sensed Jean was eager to learn this, too. The assassin was a statue beneath his hands. Hard, cold, and still.

"Louis de Praet, the former Imperial ambassador to England." Renard looked away. "He is no longer in the country. Wolsey had him arrested for treason in February and sent home soon after. I haven't had time to receive orders from him—my letters on Lucas Horenbout missing a meeting with us and our decision to kill him and his sister to keep them quiet won't even have reached de Praet yet. I had to act as I thought best."

"And the new Imperial ambassador?"

Renard sneered. "Jehan de le Sauch? He's a merchant. He is Imperial ambassador by default, because there was no one else to take the job when de Praet was expelled."

"And tell me, how many of you are there? Did Jan Heyman help you and your friend Jules attack Lucas Horenbout?"

"I don't know who Jan Heyman is. Jules and I knocked Horenbout out. Would have killed him but for some boys who raised a fuss." Renard looked away, and something in the shifty way his eyes darted to the side spoke of a lie, or only a partial truth. But time was running out. He could feel Jean bracing beneath his hands, feel his muscles bunching for a sudden move.

He must either kill Jean or let him go, and he cursed himself for his indecision. Why was it so hard to pull the knife across and end it?

Renard moved, diving away towards the gate they'd come through.

Parker watched, helpless, as he slipped and slid away. He must either let Jean go, and suffer the consequences, or see Renard go free.

A stick came from nowhere, whipped up by Jean from the mud. Even as it struck him on the side of the head, Parker cursed himself for his inattention. Renard had taken too much of his focus.

He fell, slicing the knife with a vicious movement.

Jean jerked back and the knife bit into flesh, but only deep enough to score a red, oozing welt across the assassin's throat.

The Frenchman rolled towards his bow.

Parker scrambled to his knees and stood, but Jean was on his feet already, running to the trees, out of range of Parker's knife.

When he reached the first trunk, he turned and lifted the bow coolly to his shoulder and Parker braced for the bolt.

It sang out, with the familiar whistle, and Renard gave a scream as he went down, face first, the bolt sticking out of his neck. He flopped in the mud like a fish in a drying pond, and went still.

"You are lucky, Englishman, that was my last bolt. And I had a contract for his life." Jean stepped between the trees and lifted a hand to his head in salute. Then he vanished.

Parker watched the shadows of the wood for long minutes, then turned to Renard's body. The spy had taken his untold secrets with him and Parker would have to uncover them the hard way.

A chill rose up from the red earth, clammy, like the arms of death. He shivered.

Jean still seemed relentlessly determined to kill Susanna.

For the first time, Parker felt a sense of relief she was safe behind the impregnable walls of the Tower. Even so, he should have killed the bastard while he had the chance.

He wouldn't make that mistake again.

CHAPTER 18

> But such discourses as mine, which only call past
> evils to mind and give warning of what may follow,
> leave nothing in them that is so absurd that they
> may not be used at any time, for they can only be
> unpleasant to those who are resolved to run head-
> long the contrary way;
> *Utopia by Thomas More (translated by H. Morley)*

They travelled on the river, sailing upstream under the
bridge and past Bridewell, past all the places Susanna
had come to know and grow familiar with these last
months.

Durham House stood proud and regal on the right bank, with
high, crenulated walls and a tower on the downstream side.

The barge angled toward it, and Susanna noticed steep stairs
cut into the bank which led from the river through an arched
entrance. As they bumped to a stop, one of Kilburne's men
leaped off to tie them to the small pier.

Susanna gathered her things, but Harry insisted on taking
them from her, and she accepted Kilburne's offered hand as she
stepped off the gently swaying boat.

The sun winked off the window at the top of the tower to her right, and Susanna lifted her gaze to it.

She thought she saw someone standing there, looking down at them.

"The little prince only has an hour to spare between his midday meal and his lessons." Kilburne led her up the stairs, which were well-kept, scraped clean of moss and slime, and through an archway into a small hall.

A servant was waiting for them, and led the way up two flights of stairs to a large room on the top floor overlooking the Thames.

A small boy, with light hair and blue, blue eyes, stared at them from the centre of the room. He was sitting alone at a table, with the remains of a meal before him, and two servants waited on either side to take his plates.

"Your Highness." Susanna was not sure of the proper address for the king's bastard son. She dipped in curtsy.

She wondered if a six year old would feel insulted by an improper address.

He inclined his head, and pushed away his plate. "Are you the reason I cannot go out and play with my bow?" He eyed her with dislike.

"The king wishes me to paint you, Your Highness, so he has a picture of you always to hand. But I do not see why I cannot sit quietly by and draw my sketches while you practice."

"You mean I can play with my bow?" He frowned.

"Today I need to sketch you, rough drawings that I can use later when I paint you. I can do that while I watch you practice your bow, just as well as if you were sitting still for me."

"That is good." The child stood and seemed at last to notice Harry, Kilburne and the three guards he'd brought with him. "Why do you have so many guards about you?"

Susanna turned to Kilburne and raised an eyebrow. "To keep me safe."

Henry Fitzroy laughed. "Well, you will be perfectly safe here.

I have guards everywhere." He clapped his hands. "Bring me my bow, let us not waste time before my lessons."

A man came through the far door of the room, a frown on his face. He stopped short when he saw her and her entourage. "Mistress Horenbout?"

She nodded.

"Good day to you, I'm Richard Croke, the prince's tutor. Did you not want him to sit for you?"

"He would rather play with his bow in his free time, sir, and I can sketch him just as well doing that. I have no doubt his expression will be happier than if I make him sit still for an hour."

Croke looked at her sharply. "That is well thought of you, mistress. To be sure, I wondered how you would keep him still for an hour, anyway."

"Will you fetch my bow?" Henry asked him.

"I will." Croke smiled, and Susanna saw there was a genuine affection between them.

When he had the bow, and a quiver of arrows, Croke led them all down the stairs and into a garden that ran beside the river, but was walled off from it, with a stone wall at least 10 feet high. Trees grew along it, and they muted the sounds of the river and the calls of the boatmen, so Susanna could imagine they were not in the city at all, but some far country estate.

There were flower beds and a herb garden, as well as a beautiful stretch of lawn, on which sat a large hay bale with a target made of cloth pinned to it.

The prince ran to where a line of white stones had been laid, and stood behind them. He turned impatiently, hopping from one foot to the other in excitement.

Susanna found a seat on one of the extra bales of hay lying to one side, and got out her charcoal and parchment, and her pressing board. Kilburne stood, almost apologetically, behind her, and Harry stood beside him. Two guards with two very different agendas.

Susanna tried to forget they were there.

Henry Fitzroy's excitement and eagerness leaped out at her, and she moved her charcoal in sweeping lines, caught in the thrill of the first mark on a fresh page, as she always was.

It was like fine wine was to some men, or food to a sophisticated palate. She lived for the moment her charcoal or her brush touched the white of a blank surface. With infinite possibilities and endless ways to create beauty before her, she moved the charcoal just so to capture the joy she saw before her.

"What have you drawn?" Henry stopped before her, and Susanna turned the parchment round so he could see.

It was rough, the work of a few minutes, but it captured his excitement, the way he moved. He clapped his hands, delighted.

"That is me."

"Aye. You may have one of the sketches I do today. You can pick the one you like best when I am done."

"I didn't know women could paint and draw." He looked from the sketch to her.

"Well." Susanna looked across at Croke, but he was busy fussing with the target. "Do women have eyes and hands?"

"Yes." He giggled.

Behind her, she sensed Kilburne's gaze on her.

"And do they have fingers?"

He nodded, laughing.

"Well then, they can paint and sketch. But a lot of women aren't taught how. I was lucky. My father is a famous painter. And he taught me. And then, like all painters, I needed time and the right materials to practice. And my father saw I could be useful for his work, and he gave me the time and all the brushes and charcoals and paints I needed. I didn't have to help my mother with the cooking and cleaning, I could paint all day."

"Just like I have to practice my bow?"

She nodded. "Just like that."

"But women can't shoot bows." Henry frowned. He looked up at Kilburne. "Can they?"

Kilburne seemed at a loss for words.

Susanna gave him a quick look over her shoulder. He gazed back at her, bemused.

"I thought we already agreed women have hands and eyes." She smiled as she turned back to Henry.

But his expression was mulish, and he did not like the turn of her logic. "Maybe you need more than hands and eyes for bow shooting. Something only men have."

Harry snickered and Susanna wagered Kilburne was smiling.

She said nothing, and at that moment, Croke called to Henry that they were ready for him, and he spun around, and ran happily to take his bow.

"You draw better than anyone I have ever seen," Kilburne said, suddenly, from behind. "Man or woman."

She twisted on the bale to face him and he fidgeted in place. "I saw the writ you finished for the king, lying on your desk, and I understand why he wishes you to work them for him. Your skill reflects well upon him. No person receiving such a letter could fail to understand the king of England is the greatest sovereign in the world."

She was touched by his words. They were honest, and heart-felt, and without warning, she felt the sting of tears. She opened her eyes wider, refusing to let them fall, and nodded to him. Turned away.

"My thanks, captain. You make a pretty compliment."

"It's no compliment. It's the bare truth." Harry's voice was rough, as if he'd gone too long without speaking. She shot him a look but he wouldn't meet her eyes.

He'd never spoken of her work, and she had always wondered what he thought of it.

She faced the little prince again and watched as one of the guards helped him fit his arrow, with Croke looking on with a smile, and took another piece of parchment from her satchel.

Perhaps, if she drew his son well enough, the king would find her indispensable.

CHAPTER 19

> For in courts they will not bear with a man's holding his peace or conniving at what others do: a man must barefacedly approve of the worst counsels and consent to the blackest designs, so that he would pass for a spy, or, possibly, for a traitor, that did but coldly approve of such wicked practices;
>
> *Utopia by Thomas More (translated by H. Morley)*

Jehan de la Sauch kept a fine house.

Parker looked around the room he'd been left in to wait on the merchant's pleasure, and noticed the fine tapestries and jewel-colored paintings. They had the feel of Susanna about them. Detailed, intricate. Perfect.

That de la Sauch was from the same place as she was, was as clear as the crystal glass that stood at the centre of the table.

It made Parker wonder how homesick she felt. Whether she missed Ghent.

She never mentioned it. But he had never heard her complain about anything, no matter the circumstances, since he'd known her.

It might please her if he bought a few tapestries for the walls and some paintings by her fellow countrymen.

He wondered why he had never thought of it before.

"John Parker?" De la Sauch stood in the doorway, a lean, handsome man, with hair a strange shade between blond and brown. His grey eyes were quick and intelligent, and there seemed to be no fear, no nerves in him at this surprise visit.

Parker bowed. "I am told you are acting as the Imperial ambassador?"

De la Sauch nodded slowly. "Not just me. I came here with a number of other merchants around the time the former ambassador was expelled. We became ambassadors by default. But it has come about that I have shouldered the majority of the duties."

"How quickly can you get a message to Louis de Praet?"

De la Sauch stepped back, his eyes narrow. "Why would you want to get a message to de Praet? Who are you?"

Parker wished he had worn his chain of office, but it would have only been a hindrance to him while he'd followed Renard. He was aware of the mud on his hose and his doublet. He'd wiped most of it from his boots on the way. "I am the King's Keeper of the Palace of Westminster, and his Yeoman of the King's Robes."

"A gentleman of the Privy Chamber." De la Sauch's eyes widened in surprise. "What business has the king with de Praet? He is disgraced here in England."

"My interest is personal." Parker gave a bitter smile. "One of de Praet's spies has fabricated a story of treason. He has given false information, and I want de Praet to retract it in writing. To the king. Not to Wolsey. I don't care if it foils the emperor's plans."

"What plans?" De la Sauch's face turned wary.

"His plans to break his betrothal to Princess Mary, and marry her cousin Isabella instead." He spoke baldly, and de la Sauch flinched.

"I know nothing of that." He held Parker's gaze a moment, and then sighed heavily. He sank down into a chair, and motioned for Parker to do the same.

"Truth be told, I'm ill-equipped to deal with being ambassador. I'm a merchant, not a diplomat, and the Cardinal Wolsey and I . . . " He hesitated. "Well, I am a plain-speaking man. I have no patience for innuendo and pretty speeches that mean nothing."

Parker felt the first stir of warmth for the man. "You and Wolsey do not see eye to eye?"

De la Sauch looked as if he regretted his honesty, but shook his head.

"Is Jan Heyman an imperial spy?" Parker slipped the question in easily, and de la Sauch paused and then stared at him, open-mouthed.

"Is he? You seem to know more of my business than I do, sir."

"Yes. He is. He is reporting to de Praet, and recently to a former French spy living in London, who has been turned to the imperial cause, I assume because de Praet is paying him well. There is a third man, Jules, although I think his role is more that of henchman than true spy."

De la Sauch closed his eyes and leaned back in his chair. "I am not the man for this job."

"Too bad." Parker's harsh tone had de la Sauch open-eyed and braced in his chair. "You are the one in place and I am telling you that de Praet's man has lied to Wolsey, fed him a story so he would imprison one of your fellow countrywomen in order to stop her talking."

"Her?" De la Sauch was truly alert now. "A woman?"

"My betrothed." Parker stood and paced to the window. "Her name is Susanna Horenbout, and—"

"I know Susanna Horenbout." De la Sauch surged to his feet, as well. "I know her father. He painted a portrait of my family, it is right there." He pointed to a small picture, one of the ones that had reminded Parker of Susanna a little earlier, with a deep, deep blue sky, a beautiful house on a river in the background. In the foreground stood de la Sauch and his wife and three children, their clothes, their expressions, were exquisitely rendered.

Parker stepped up to it. "She has his talent."

"So I've heard." De la Sauch's tone was calmer, warmer. "She is here in London?"

"Her father received a commission from the king for a painter from his *atelier*, and he sent her."

"And since coming to London she has been betrothed to you?" De la Sauch sounded uncertain.

"She has." His words were fierce. Defensive.

"De Praet would not have had anything to do with getting her into trouble. That I can promise you. If his agent has acted to endanger her, it would have been on the agent's own authority, not de Praet's, and I'm convinced de Praet will be quick to reverse what has been done."

"Any letter from him may be too late, but I would have you reach him and tell him every moment counts." Parker swung around. "Though how can you be so certain de Praet will do whatever he can to have Susanna cleared?"

"De Praet was mayor of Ghent for years before he became Imperial ambassador to England. He is a close friend of the Horenbouts."

Parker folded his arms across his chest and stared at de la Sauch, shock reverberating through him.

Now he knew to whom Lucas must have sent the note Renard had spoken of. Not to a minor agent, but the spymaster himself. De Praet.

Renard had implied it, but now he had proof. Lucas Horenbout was an Imperial spy.

Susanna stood in the sun, on the edge of Tower Green, lifting her shoulders and releasing the ache of too many hours bent over her desk.

She had spent her second night in the Tower hunched over the portrait of Henry Fitzroy, until her eyes burned and her hands were too unsteady to continue.

All the while, hanging like a chain around her neck, stifling her with every movement, was the certainty Wolsey had not given up.

He would try again and again, until he had her.

She eyed the White Tower. It sat, squat and implacable, a declaration of strength and might. The sun winked off the glass of the arched windows and she shivered at the thought of who might be behind them, staring down at her. Plotting to drag her within, to the bowels of the beast.

"A word, my lady." A soft call broke through her thoughts. A woman, covered with a cape and wrapped against the cool, brisk wind that was blowing, even though it had just turned June, stood near the entrance to the Lieutenant's Lodgings.

Harry stepped from the shadows by the door, and the woman started when she noticed him.

There was something familiar about her, and Susanna walked towards her with a frown.

She was holding a covered basket uncomfortably, as if she had never had cause to carry one before, and her eyes darted, low and frightened, as if she had no right to be there and was waiting for someone to call the alarm.

"Lady Courtenay." Susanna breathed the words softly as she reached Gertrude, and the queen's confidant snapped her head up at last.

"Do not say my name." Gertrude spoke between gritted teeth. "Is there somewhere private we can talk?"

"Not my chambers. Unless you have good reason to be here if someone comes knocking?"

Gertrude shook her head.

"Let us walk then." She held out her arm, and Gertrude took it.

Harry took up position just behind them and Susanna glanced quickly back at him.

There was a suppressed excitement in his face, in the way he moved, but she did not think Gertrude was coming with a way out. The queen had been helpless against Kilburne and his men. She would be even more helpless in the face of the king and Wolsey.

"You have news from the queen?"

Gertrude nodded. "She thanks you, truly, for the risk you took in telling her what her nephew plans. She has written to him, begging him to keep his word in the betrothal. If he does marry Isabella instead of Mary . . ." Gertrude stopped and set the basket on the ground, opening and closing her hand, her fingers white from the weight of it.

"The king already blames her for no sons. His only compensation would have been his daughter married to the Holy Roman Emperor. He could see his grandchildren the rulers of England and the whole of Europe, and the thought of it soothed the disappointment of a lack of a male heir. But if that is taken away . . ." Gertrude fell silent.

"Then neither his wife nor his daughter are very useful to him, any more." Susanna looked at Gertrude as she spoke, and the lady dipped her head.

"As you say," she whispered. "With the queen's health as it is . . . she will not bear another child."

"And the king is left with only a bastard son and a daughter."

"Yes." Gertrude looked down at the basket as if it held a snake.

"He must feel the wolves breathing down his neck." Susanna angled herself against the breeze, wrapping her cloak tighter against its chill, over-familiar fingers.

"He could have fended them off with Mary married to Charles, but if Charles truly intends to renege . . ." Gertrude lifted a hand to her temple and rubbed. "I fear for the queen. Wolsey already has more spies than we can guess at in her chambers. I cannot trust anyone there, now. Not a single one."

"And if the queen cannot persuade Charles to keep his word and marry the princess?"

Gertrude looked up, and Susanna saw her eyes were ringed with shadows. "Then Wolsey will help the king put Henry Fitzroy forward as regent-in-waiting."

"The nobles won't like that. Some would think they have better claim to the throne than the king's bastard son." Susanna wondered where this would lead. Henry's court seemed always to be balanced on the knife's edge of war. With each other, with France.

She tired of it.

"I care nothing for the king and his problems." Gertrude spoke fiercely, and at last there was a fire in her voice. "I care only for the queen, and what this would mean for her." She looked around her, at the towers and walls that closed them in, and shuddered.

"I hope to God I never end up in this cursed place. It weighs me down, just to be within the walls."

"Thank you for coming to give me word." Susanna touched her shoulder in a soothing gesture.

"I am here under the pretense of fetching some things from the queen's chambers in the White Tower." Gertrude eyed the massive building with trepidation. "I had better be about my business."

"Wait." Susanna's grip on her shoulder tightened. "Does the queen see a way out for me?"

Gertrude pulled back. Shook her head. "She will try. You have my assurance on that. But the winds are changing, and the queen fears . . ."

"Fears what?" Her whispered words were ripped away by the breeze.

"That the king has no more use for her."

CHAPTER 20

'If a man,' says he [Plato], 'were to see a great company run out every day into the rain and take delight in being wet—if he knew that it would be to no purpose for him to go and persuade them to return to their houses in order to avoid the storm, and that all that could be expected by his going to speak to them would be that he himself should be as wet as they, it would be best for him to keep within doors, and, since he had not influence enough to correct other people's folly, to take care to preserve himself.'

Utopia by Thomas More (translated by H. Morley)

Parker found himself staring up at the redbrick walls of Bridewell. He couldn't remember what he'd been thinking of for the last few minutes.

He ran his hands over his head, shrugged his shoulders. After seeing de la Sauch late yesterday, he'd come here, only to find the king was away, no doubt tucked somewhere warm and private with the giggling Lady Alice.

Or perhaps someone else.

He had gone home to sleep, but it had been impossible. The empty side of the bed, where Susanna usually lay, had refused to let him.

He'd longed to smash into Lucas's room, and demand answers, but Maggie, leaving just as he arrived home, had forbidden him from rousing the artist. He'd gone back into a deep sleep and she thought it dangerous to wake him.

Parker wondered if Horenbout had willed himself back into a senseless state, so he did not have to face what he had done.

No matter. He would have to wake sometime. And he would account for his actions.

"You do not look your best, Parker." The cool amusement in Norfolk's voice sliced through his reverie like a poison-tipped dagger, and he straightened.

Norfolk stood just beside him, dressed in ermine and velvet against the unseasonably cool day.

"I believe you are right." Parker smiled.

Disconcerted by his reply, Norfolk narrowed his eyes. "I hear your little Flemish artist is in some trouble." His voice was half-baked bread soaked in bacon fat—oily and sickening.

"I'm surprised you're so delighted, as it is Wolsey who put her there." Parker began walking towards the main doors of the palace.

"Anything that would cause you pain or trouble delights me." Norfolk stepped in with him, although he was considerably shorter than Parker and had to scurry to keep up.

As if sensing the disadvantage of this, Norfolk stopped, and Parker continued on without him.

"Parker."

Norfolk's call stopped him. There was an urgency about it. Parker turned and raised a brow.

Norfolk glanced sidelong, making sure they were far enough away from the crowds going about their business for privacy. "What is this arrest about? What is Wolsey plotting?"

"What do you care, Norfolk? It is indeed causing me trouble and pain. According to you, that is enough."

Norfolk pressed his thin lips together, making them disappear completely. "I will offer you aid to free your lady, if you tell me."

Parker said nothing, and as the seconds stretched out, Norfolk began to fidget. "You do not believe me."

Parker held out his hands, palms up, his shoulders raised a little. What did Norfolk expect?

"I see you are perhaps not as devoted to your betrothed as everyone seems to think, that you would not even consider an offer to save her—no matter who it comes from." Norfolk's lip curled up. "It makes me wonder why you play the lovesick fool."

Parker allowed himself a small, tight smile to hide the fury that boiled and leaped within him. "How can you help save her if you are coming to me to find out why she's imprisoned in the first place? If your offer of help is merely a word in the king's ear, we both know whose word counts for more in that quarter."

Norfolk drew back as if struck. "Very well. I have resources enough to discover this plot for myself. I had hoped not to go to the trouble, but as you do not trust my word as a nobleman, so be it."

Parker could not help it. He let out a laugh. "Your word as a nobleman?"

Norfolk gave him the cold-fish stare of a pike and turned on his heel. Stalked towards the gates out of Bridewell.

Parker watched him go.

It was not that he resented Norfolk's attempt to weasel information when he was at his lowest. He would expect nothing less from the turd. It was the temptation to risk giving him what he wanted in return for whatever crumbs of aid, if any, he would throw towards saving Susanna.

His lips had wanted to form the words, his throat had held them just out of his mouth, while he struggled with himself.

He was so used to walking the tightrope of pleasing his king and keeping the balance at court and beyond.

He turned back to the doors.

Enough.

He had had his fill of the fine, wire-tight tangle, now. He cared only to get Susanna free, even if he had to hack with a sharp knife to do it.

If he started a war or a diplomatic storm in the process, so be it.

⁂

THE KING, DRESSED IN LOOSE CLOTHING, WAS CHOOSING A blunted practice longsword in the inner courtyard.

Around him, Parker saw the usual cronies. Bryan, Carew, Boleyn and others. Thomas Wyatt sat to one side, slightly apart from the crowd.

He lifted his head when he felt Parker's eyes on him, and gave a brief dip of his head.

Will Somers stood near the door, watching the antics of the courtiers as they chose swords and challenged and insulted each other with a quiet concentration.

He turned as Parker stepped into the room, and his long, expressive face broke into a smile. He winked.

Parker raised a hand in response. He wanted to talk to Somers but could not risk missing an opportunity to address the king. He began weaving through the men, toward where Henry stood.

Henry caught sight of him, and something flashed in his eyes. Shame, or perhaps embarrassment.

The back of Parker's neck went hot at the sudden fear something had been done to Susanna. He had yet to hear from Eric or Harry, but that meant nothing.

He closed the distance even faster than before.

"Your Majesty." He bowed and when he looked up, Henry was tossing his longsword lightly in the air, finding the balance.

"You are just in time, Parker. It has been too long since we had a turn at bouting." Henry's eyes were steel-blue, they brooked no argument.

Parker bowed again and turned, undoing the buttons down the front of his doublet as he walked toward the array of longswords. He shrugged the snug-fitting garment off and was surprised to find Will Somers before him, hand out, to take it.

He nodded his thanks, turning his attention to the practice longswords hanging in a row before him.

He found one with a double fuller blade, and lifted it out. The balance was beautiful. He tucked it under his arm and looked for someone to lend him their gloves. Bryan already had his off, and tossed them to Parker. A recompense, perhaps, for his lack of support the day before.

When he had them on, he swung the sword in an arc, and turned.

The men had moved back, leaving an open corridor with the king at one end. Carew looked as if he wished to be in Parker's place, but most were simply intrigued. They knew about Susanna, knew there was more to this than sport.

"What rules?" Parker ignored the courtiers, and spoke directly to the king.

"Low Countries." Henry smiled. Moved deeper into the courtyard, where they would have room to move. "I am King, you are Champion."

Parker nodded his acceptance. Each free play bout had a King and a Champion in Low Countries rules, with the King having the advantage.

Henry had claimed that advantage, as was his right.

They squared up, and lifted the swords, double-handed, before them. Parker bent at the knees, sinking low, as Bryan called the start.

He had not bouted with the king for nearly a year, and in that time, had only ever drawn his sword in earnest. Free play felt alien to him, after so long.

He fell into an easy rhythm, binding and winding against Henry, warming up, as they displaced each other's strikes but stayed back, giving each other room. He had to remind himself the Low Countries rules allowed only two-handed grips, no one-handed technique or half-sword, and he began to find pleasure in the challenge of winning under their restrictions.

He usually fought with none.

The courtyard went silent, as they all recognized a turning point in the play.

Parker started to circle, twisting the sword right, and struck underhanded with the inner flat, for a hit under the arm.

Henry caught it, pushing it aside, and closed in, letting his blade slide down Parker's to the hilt.

They were as close as lovers, breathing hard after their warm-up, eye to eye.

Parker heaved, and leaped back, disengaging the hilts.

Henry stumbled back a step and righted himself, but Parker was already winding left for a neck blow, forcing Henry into an upward counterstrike.

This time it was Parker who closed in, sliding his blade down to Henry's hilt.

"There is a fire in you today." Henry spoke in short gasps, a little winded, but still strong.

Parker was close enough to see every drop of sweat on his forehead.

"I find I have a lot to be angry about."

Henry heaved him off, and they struck together, the flat edges slamming against each other with a high-pitched ring.

Parker felt the vibration in the ache of his wrists, and from the way he winced, Henry felt them, too. His sword slipped a little in his grasp.

Henry's lips drew back in a snarl and he let the momentum of the slip carry the sword in an arc downward, with a chop to Parker's side.

Parker spun in close, and Henry's sword bit air. He thought the king had cause to be glad of choosing the Low Countries rules, prohibiting *corps-à-corps*, or Parker could have struck him with an elbow to the face or sternum.

He danced to the side, and spun again, and now he was behind the king, in the perfect position for a back or side thrust. Or even a neck blow.

He didn't take the back strike. He waited for Henry to turn.

As he did, Parker crouched down, so the king's neck strike passed harmlessly overhead, and he brought the flat of his sword against Henry's side.

Bryan called the strike, but as King, rather than Champion, per the rules, Henry had the advantage of an after-stroke. He took the single step allowed, and countered.

Parker brought his sword up to block, and for the last time came in close, the two swords resting against each other's hilts.

They stared straight at each other for a moment, before Parker dropped his gaze.

"Well played." Henry stepped back, forcing his breathing slow and even through his nose. "You always fight as if your life depended on it, Parker."

"That is because my life often does." Parker did not say it was usually on the king's business. He didn't need to.

"You think we merely play games here?" Henry's eyes flashed, but Parker was already shaking his head.

"I think I need to come here more often. It is good to practice." His response was truthful, and Henry accepted it with a grunt.

"Why did you come today, if not to take a turn with bouting?"

"My lady still sits in the Tower, Your Majesty. I have no time for anything but seeing she is released."

"Wolsey has yet to bring me any proof of her treason, or even tell me what that treason is, and her confinement is slowing down the portrait I would have of Fitzroy." Henry stripped off his gloves, and tapped them against his leg.

"I will give Wolsey until tomorrow evening to bring me proof, and if he has none, I will sign her release myself."

It was more than he'd hoped for.

Parker bowed. "My thanks."

Henry nodded his acknowledgement, and turned away, calling to Bryan to match the next opponents.

Parker looked up and saw Wolsey just within the ranks of spectators. For a beat, their gazes clashed, and Wolsey took a step back in surprise. He recovered, drew himself tall and turned on his heel, robes fluttering about him as he strode from the inner courtyard.

Parker felt a frisson of satisfaction. *Run and beg for proof, cardinal. You won't find it.*

He turned back to hand Bryan his gloves and stopped midway as he saw someone slip from the courtyard after the cardinal.

He frowned. The man trailing Wolsey was Will Somers.

CHAPTER 21

> I must freely own that as long as there is any prop-
> erty, and while money is the standard of all other
> things, I cannot think that a nation can be
> governed either justly or happily: not justly, because
> the best things will fall to the share of the worst
> men; nor happily, because all things will be divided
> among a few
>
> *Utopia by Thomas More (translated by H. Morley)*

"Υou feel it, too?" Susanna's words halted Harry in his tracks at the far end of the room. He turned, but instead of pacing back, he stood still. Grimaced.

"Feel what?" Eric looked up from his letters, and Susanna was pleased to see his progress. He would be reading in no time.

She enjoyed the thrill this small act of subversion gave her. Very few women could read, and certainly very few—man or woman—of Eric's station could do so. That she could teach him, give him this weapon that would serve him a thousand times over for the rest of his life, was a matter of deep satisfaction.

"We've been lucky to have two nights, as it is." Harry did not soften his voice, he spoke baldly.

"I would have thought if they were going to take me, they'd have tried earlier today." She said it, because it was what she wanted to think, but she did not truly believe it herself. They would be back. It was only a matter of time, and time was running out.

"They can't come at night, though." Eric dipped his quill into the ink again. "When curfew is announced, no one can come through those gates."

"They could already be here. Hiding in there." Harry stepped over to the window and looked out at the White Tower. "All they need do is take you to that dungeon, and their problems with you are solved."

"I don't think they will try after curfew." She knew Kilburne and his men enforced the curfew strictly, and she didn't see Wolsey's thugs trying to get to her then. It was easier during the day, when so many outsiders had access to the Tower, going about their business.

"It's not long to curfew now." Eric joined Harry at the window, and all three of them looked out at the darkening sky.

"You don't often get a sky that purple." Harry spoke reverently.

Susanna wanted to answer, but she was too busy staring at the color. It was so amazing, if she painted it, it was sure to be taken as an artistic impression. She would do it, anyway. She was already choosing the pigments she would need to mix to get the right shade.

"Funny how beautiful it is, no matter where you are." Eric pressed his nose to the glass. "You would think from in here, the view would be worse somehow, just because it is here."

The knock at the door, so firm and authoritative, made them all jump.

Harry had the knife from his boot before he'd crossed the room. He stopped at the door and raised his hand, ready to strike down, as he swung it open.

A figure stepped through, in dark monks' robes, with the

cowl pulled deep over his face. A long, bony-fingered hand came up to push it back. "You don't seem pleased to see me." The King's Fool smiled his death-mask smile.

They stared at him in shock.

Susanna was the first to recover. She curtsied and when she lifted her face again, she saw Somers had a strange glint in his eye.

"There are all sorts of rumors flying about the court regarding you, Mistress Horenbout." He made no move to step deeper into the room.

"What do they say?"

"Very little of substance." Somers smiled. "I should know. I've started most of them."

Harry's grip on his knife tightened, and Susanna shook her head.

"My guess is those rumors have been in my favor."

Somers chuckled. "Well, let us say the rumor the king has imprisoned you while you work on a portrait of his son so none can see it until it is finished is holding its place as the favorite. Especially as two courtiers saw you arrive and leave Durham House yesterday accompanied by a guard but not restrained by them in any way. The original rumor from the night you saw the king, that you were a traitor, has been quite forgotten, or dismissed."

Harry let his knifehand drop. "They believe the king would lock someone away to keep a painting private?"

Somers turned to stare at him as if he were simple minded.

Harry shrugged. "It sounds ridiculous."

Somers let out a truly deep belly laugh. "As ridiculous as they are themselves."

"My thanks for the distraction, sir. If I am able to return to court, I would rather it not be with whispers of treason about me."

"Why doesn't Wolsey say why he's got you here?" Eric frowned. "He would like you disgraced in everyone's eyes."

"I'm sure he would like to. I would say his natural prudence is at war with his need to crush Mistress Horenbout, but until he has his proof—"

"You know he has no proof?" Susanna stepped closer to him.

Somers lifted his hands to his ears and pretended to flap them. "I can be invisible, when I wish. And I've taken quite an interest in the cardinal of late. I just happened to be skulking at the right place at the right time. It is just a pity that I cannot repeat the conversation I overhead to the court." He sighed, his face turning hangdog. "Some wonderful material dropped like a coin down the gong."

"Wolsey has no proof, and he cannot be sure he will get it. So he's said nothing, lest he has to release me later, and look a fool." Susanna spoke slowly, turning the words over on her tongue like a gold-leaf covered confection.

"Better to be a Fool than look a fool." Somers spoke deadpan, and then gave a quick, sly smile when Susanna's cheeks heated in embarrassment.

"What did you hear?" Harry watched the Fool in bemusement.

"The king has given Wolsey until tomorrow evening to present proof or release you. Wolsey is having difficulty persuading his source to provide the proof, so his new solution is to extract it from Mistress Horenbout herself. As painfully as possible."

Susanna fisted her hands as he spoke. She had known this was a possibility, but to hear it . . . She breathed deep, the sweetness of Wolsey's inability to label her traitor had gone. "Go on."

Somers sent her a sympathetic look. "I heard him informing one of his thugs to be ready to accompany him tomorrow. He has not been able to get a writ signed by the king, giving you over to him for questioning, but he has decided if he comes with his own writ, in person, Captain Kilburne or, if necessary, the Constable of the Tower himself, will have to acquiesce."

"They may. He is the cardinal, after all." She bent her head. "Although Wolsey is surely risking the king's displeasure."

"What is your play in this?" Harry stepped between Somers and the door. "Why did you risk coming?"

Irritation flashed in Somers' eyes. "I owe no explanation to you." He turned to Susanna. "Will you trust me?"

She had wondered herself why Somers was taking the risks he had. But she didn't doubt his honesty. Ever. She nodded.

He nodded back, and extended his leg in a pretty imitation of courtly manners.

"When tomorrow is he coming?" Eric had waited his turn, and now he clutched at Somers' robe.

"I don't know. I would think it best if one of you were to watch him. Slow him down on his journey here. And meanwhile get Parker to have the king intervene in some way."

"If I'm to go, I have to go now." Eric went to gather his cloak. "Curfew is in a few minutes."

Somers lifted his hood. "I will walk out with you. With luck, they will think you my acolyte. If Wolsey has spies watching, it's better they don't see you leave."

"Eric." Susanna looked between him and Harry. "Tell Parker all is well with me. That I love him."

"You want me to go instead?" Harry was looking at her, and she shook her head.

She did not want anyone in danger, guarding her, but her choices had been taken from her. "Eric, promise me you'll be careful. That you'll go straight to Parker."

He drew his cloak about him and lifted the hood. "I won't do anything to endanger you. I swear."

He joined Somers at the door.

"I have one last thing for you. And if you can, I would have it back when this is over, because it doesn't belong to me." He held out his hand and Susanna extended hers. Something heavy dropped onto her palm. Somers closed her fingers around it.

"As a last resort," he whispered, and then closed the door.

Susanna opened her hand and gasped. She was holding a worked piece of jewelry, masculine and ornate.

Somers had stolen her the king's ring.

KILBURNE HAD INVITED HER TO DINNER, COMING TO THE door so soon after Somers and Eric had left, Susanna had stuttered her way through her acceptance, sure he was there to say they had both been taken to the dungeons.

Harry accompanied her, standing behind her at the table like one of the king's sewers, ready to respond to her slightest wish.

As she sat opposite Kilburne, the king's ring lay heavy in the hem of her sleeve. It was the only place she'd had time to put it.

She could not wear it. But where it was, she could lay hands on it in a moment. And if Wolsey came for her, a moment might be all she would have.

"You seem nervous, my lady." Kilburne leaned back as the last dishes were taken away.

Susanna pushed an unused spoon to one side. "I do not trust the calm, Captain." She sipped his fine wine.

He nodded. "I do not trust it, either." He cupped his goblet with both hands. "I have word I must take you again to the prince. The king is anxious that you complete his portrait as soon as possible."

Susanna lifted her brows. She had done nothing but work on Fitzroy's portrait since she'd returned from Durham House. "Is there an occasion for which he wants it?"

Kilburne looked uncomfortable, as if he had been given too much information. Been drawn deeper into this than he wanted. "Henry Fitzroy will be officially presented to the Order of the Garter on the 7th of June." He tapped the table with his fingers. "The king would like to have it by then."

Susanna did not flinch. She'd been hearing unreasonable

demands from royalty since she could first understand her father's occupation.

"I could have a charcoal by the 7th, but then I would have to stop work on the painting." She rested her chin in her hand.

He seemed disconcerted by her calm. "He wants a painting, not a sketch. Like the one you had done of the princess. He would present it at the meeting for all to see."

She didn't like it. It felt as though he would replace one child with the other. But who was she to voice that opinion?

"Then I had better be back to work." She stood. "Let us hope the cardinal does not interfere with the schedule by dragging me to the White Tower."

Kilburne's chair scraped back, and he made no comment to that.

Harry preceded her to the door and opened it, making sure the passage was clear. Kilburne lifted a brow at his caution, but said nothing.

He could not call him to account for what amounted to an insult on Kilburne's security. He knew as well as they did, they had reason to worry.

He walked with them to the front hall.

"Thank you, and good night." Susanna curtsied and Kilburne bowed before going to the huge double doors leading out and opening one side.

"It was my pleasure, Mistress. I will take you and one of your servants to Durham tomorrow afternoon again."

If Wolsey had his way, that wouldn't happen, but Susanna smiled and watched him step out into the night to check on his men.

She felt again, nervously, for Somers' gift.

How had he taken the king's ring? It swung in her sleeve, and she crossed her arms in front of her to hide that it pulled the fabric a little.

"What was that? That Somers gave you."

Harry waited for her at the foot of the stairs, and she took the arm he held out. "The king's ring."

He stopped, the movement jerking her back. "How do you know?"

"I've seen it once before. The king gave it to Simon a while ago, and he showed it to me."

"Do you think Somers stole it?"

Susanna urged him up the stairs. "What else can I think?"

"Why does he help you?" A frown etched deep in Harry's forehead. "I do not like that we know nothing of his motives. He could be doing this for sport."

"I don't know why he does it. But it is not for sport. He risks a charge of theft if I use this ring unwisely. If I use it at all. Wolsey will have to let me go if I invoke its powers, and he will surely inform the king I had it in my possession." She kept her voice soft—they were still in the open, although they had reached the top of the stairs now, and the door to her room was ahead. "I think it may be as simple as Will Somers likes me."

"Theft from the king means death. He's risked his life, if you're right."

Susanna shrugged. "Perhaps there are not many people he likes?"

They were in the last stretch of passageway, walking in near total darkness. A wall lantern shone from the top of the stairs behind them, but the one between the stairs and her door had gone out, and there was no light beyond to the stairs up to the Bell Tower.

Harry put an arm out in front of her, forcing her to stop, and put a finger to his lips. Then he pointed.

Susanna saw a faint glow just beneath the door to her rooms, a slice of gold in the darkness.

Someone was in there.

Harry drew his knife from his boot, and she sensed him gathering himself, ready to leap.

He slammed open the door with a cry, knife raised, and came to a stumbling halt.

Susanna took a step in after him, hesitant but curious.

Parker's eyes, warm and creased at the corners, glittered at her in the light of the candle he'd placed on the table.

"How . . .?" She put a hand against the door post to steady herself.

He stood and she flung herself across the room to him, each breath a tight, painful joy.

"I had to come." He whispered the words into her hair. "I can't seem to sleep if you aren't with me."

CHAPTER 22

> They think it is an evidence of true wisdom for a man to pursue his own advantage as far as the laws allow it, they account it piety to prefer the public good to one's private concerns, but they think it unjust for a man to seek for pleasure by snatching another man's pleasures from him;
>
> *Utopia by Thomas More (translated by H. Morley)*

"Gertrude Courtenay *and* Will Somers have been here today?" Parker knew his mouth was agape, but he could not help it.

"We have been quite popular." Harry slid another log on the fire, and then came to sit at the table with them.

Susanna held Parker's hand in a vice grip, and Parker drummed the fingers of the other on the table. "I saw Somers follow Wolsey today. They had both vanished by the time I was able to go after them."

"Do you think Somers speaks true? That Wolsey plans to force Kilburne to hand Susanna over for questioning?" Harry lifted a cup of mead to his lips and set it down beside his plate.

Neither he, nor Parker, had eaten, and he had uncovered the tray of dishes he'd gathered earlier for dinner; game pie, bread, cheese and apples.

"I don't know why Somers has involved himself in this. Or why he weaseled his way in here when he could have come to me." Parker tore at a piece of bread with his teeth. Its earthy yeast flavor filled his nose, and he breathed it in deep, savored the chewy texture.

Since Susanna had been taken to the Tower, he had barely eaten, and every mouthful he had taken had been flat and tasteless as gruel.

"Perhaps you aren't easy to find. Whereas I do not go anywhere." Susanna paused. "Except to Durham House."

"That damn portrait." Parker swore softly. "Henry's obsessed with it. There must be something special about Fitzroy's official induction into the Order of the Garter. The king is planning something. Some change of significance."

"He is going to put Fitzroy forward as his heir apparent." Susanna stood abruptly. Angrily. "The queen feels he is going to abandon her. He has certainly abandoned all hope of her producing another child, let alone a boy."

"He needs a son." Parker thought of all the noblemen, carefully working their family lines back to the throne, waiting for their chance. "The nobility will not easily accept a daughter. And, after all, he *has* a son."

"I have nothing against the boy. I like him." Susanna hugged herself close. "The queen has spent years falling pregnant and losing child after child. She has prayed and fasted and begged God for a son. She is old before her time because of all the energy and dedication she has given to trying to producing one. And now that she is used up, even though she has a beautiful daughter, she will be cast aside. Her daughter cast aside with her. His own child." She spoke the last sentence in a whisper.

"He is a hard, cold man." Parker chose his words with care.

"He has cut down his enemies as ruthlessly as a tyrant. But he is also capable of great friendship, he can be generous, and he loves song and dance. To keep his hold on the throne, his royal line's hold, he will do anything. Crush anyone. Cast anyone aside. Even his own daughter."

Susanna sat down again. Leaned into him, and he pulled his arm tight around her. "It is wrong."

"I don't care over-much who will take the throne now. I don't care for the wrong or right of it. I just care that you are released."

She said nothing, and a stillness filled the room, broken only by the breathy sigh and crackle of the fire.

"Have you ever met Louis de Praet?" Parker asked, thinking of his conversation with Jehan de la Sauch.

"I have." She straightened in surprise. "It's been a long time since I've heard that name."

"He was Imperial ambassador in London until February. In fact, you would have almost passed each other on your way from Ghent to London." Parker started to wonder at the timing of that. "Wolsey had him arrested and expelled for treason."

Susanna's eyes were wide. "Where is he now?"

"In France, on Imperial business. But he is still controlling the spies here. The men who were forced to take over his ambassadorial duties are only temporary. They know nothing about running spies."

"And Uncle Louis does?" Susanna frowned.

"Uncle Louis knows a lot of things, it seems." Parker did not hide the sour note in his voice. "It was his spy who went to Wolsey and gave you up to him. The spy doesn't have any proof against you, we burned the only thing that would link you to their cause, but as long as you're in the Tower, the emperor thinks he has time to negotiate his marriage to Isabella. They don't seem to know you've seen the queen, or if they do, because you didn't see her privately, they think no message was exchanged between you."

"And Lucas? What is his role in this?"

Parker shook his head. "He's involved. Up to his neck. But what his part is, I don't know. He won't tell me."

"How is he?" Harry chewed a piece of apple.

"He was awake yesterday. Claimed Heyman couldn't have hit him, but never saw who did. So I don't count Heyman out. But he went back into a very deep sleep last night, and Maggie couldn't wake him. I haven't been back to the house today."

"What about Peter Jack? Is he watching Wolsey?"

"He was." Parker took some butter and slathered it on another piece of bread. "Since I followed de Praet's spy and worked out Wolsey's role in this, I've had him looking for Heyman."

"I wonder what Heyman will do." Susanna leaned back in her chair, and her eyes never left his face, as if she wanted to commit every line of him to memory. "He could go back to the palace, but he has reason to be afraid you will say something to the Knights Provost about him. He may have to find a place in the city to hide."

"I should think he'll go to other Lowlanders." Harry bit into the game pie with a shower of crumbs. "What else can he do?"

"What about the spy who visited Wolsey? Would he take Heyman in?"

"Perhaps he would have, but he's dead." Parker realized with a deep sense of dread that he hadn't told Susanna about Jean. "Jean killed him."

She drew in a sharp breath, leaned forward. "Jean? What was he doing there?"

"He was following de Praet's spy as well, he had a contract to kill him from the French king. The spy wasn't a Lowlander, he was a Frenchman, turned by de Praet through his agents here when the French ambassador was out the way. Wolsey thinks he's getting his information from the French."

"So Jean is here to deal with a traitor." Harry tripped over the last word, and it hung in the air for a moment.

Parker nodded. "I was able to stop Jean and question Renard first, but when he got free, Jean killed him with his last bolt. I'm lucky he chose to complete his contract, rather than use his bolt on me."

"If it was a contracted kill, Jean wouldn't have let Renard go for a personal vendetta."

"I know." Parker touched her hand. "But what worries me is Jean knows exactly where you are now."

"Is he back for me? If it was de Praet's men shooting at us in Crooked Lane, and Jean is returned to take care of a double agent?"

"I think he's only too happy to combine his revenge with carrying out his duties for the French Crown."

"He can't get me in here, though." Susanna smiled. "At last, I'm in the safest place you could think of."

"Gertrude Courtenay and Will Somers had no trouble gaining entry. All I had to do was tell the guard I needed to look at the crossbows in the Armory, even though I haven't been King's Yeoman of the Crossbows for over two months. And they let me in without a second look. Why not Jean?"

They were all quiet a moment, contemplating the truth of it.

She drew a deep breath and held her hands, palm down, before her. "I don't feel as afraid of Jean anymore. I'm more afraid of Wolsey. I don't want to lose the use of my hands."

His throat closed at the thought, and he had to force the words out. "It won't come to that."

"It may." Harry spoke quietly.

"Over my dead body."

HARRY LEFT THEM. TO TAKE BACK THE TRAY, HE SAID, AND TO chat for a while with the other boys who served in the kitchens and gardens of the Tower.

Susanna knew it was to give them some time alone.

Parker had consumed the meal Harry had brought up with the zest and concentration of a man long starved, and as she closed the door behind Harry and turned back to him, she saw he was looking at her the same way he'd eyed the feast on his plate.

Ravenously.

Need flared within her, but it was tempered with caution. She felt too exposed here, too vulnerable.

Kilburne, Lewis, anyone could storm the room and she did not want them to find her doing anything but work. She wanted no ideas in their heads of her naked, or with her clothing in disarray.

They must also not catch Parker. The rules were clear. He had to be out by curfew. Which had long since come and gone.

If he were caught in her chambers, he would be in serious trouble.

"You look afraid." He stood and walked towards her with deliberate steps. She shivered, felt the anticipation brush down her spine like a lover's hand.

"You are as much at their mercy while you are in these rooms as I am."

"Who are you afraid of? Wolsey can't come here until tomorrow." He reached her, pulled her close to him.

She let her cheek rest against the soft velvet of his doublet, and closed her eyes as his fingers curled around her waist. "Some of Kilburne's men . . . wish me ill. They are working for Wolsey and they'll be watching me closely. Especially if he plans on taking me tomorrow."

"Which of Kilburne's men?" He spoke quietly, and she lifted her head to look at him.

"His deputy, Lewis, and another man, Merden." She didn't mention the way they'd manhandled her on her first day. From the darkness she saw in his eyes, she would be forfeiting their lives. She needed nothing more on her conscience.

"I will deal with them." He pulled her closer, rubbed her back. "You are so stiff."

"I cannot be easy here." The Bell Tower loomed over her, the White Tower lurked just outside her window, and all around her were those who would see her broken and crying for mercy.

Lucas had done this. Lucas, and her father.

"What did Lucas hope to achieve?" Her voice cracked on the last word. "Is he really playing spy for Uncle Louis?" She shook her head, and he buried his hands in her hair, forced her head up to look at him.

"Whatever the reason, there is more to this than we think. Lucas told me he had made sacrifices to try to get you out of trouble. I don't know what he means, but when he's awake again, I'll find out."

"And tomorrow? What do you plan to do?"

"I'll get a stay from the king." Parker dipped his head and kissed her cheek, warm and sweet as sunshine.

"Will he be amenable?"

"He wants you to paint. You will not be able to if Wolsey has you in the dungeon. I think it will be easy to persuade him to sign a writ to keep you safe."

"He has already. It will not stop Wolsey if he comes tomorrow with one of his own."

"It will, if I deliver it myself." Parker spoke between soft kisses, but despite the feather-light touch of his lips, his words were hard and cold.

She reached for him, skimmed her fingers along his jaw. "Take care." He closed a part of himself off when he was like this. Forced every soft corner, every gentleness in his soul, into another place. She knew it took its toll.

Another crime to lay at Lucas's door.

"Enough of Wolsey." Parker turned her face so he could kiss her mouth with soft, sweet brushes of his lips, as if he were tasting fine wine. "If Harry is half as bright as I think he is, we have a little time."

Susanna hesitated again.

Parker pulled away a little and lifted his knife. The candle-light caught the gleam of its blade. "This goes through the eye of the first person who interrupts us."

Susanna laughed, leaned in to kiss his neck. "Then I hope Harry is really, really bright."

CHAPTER 23

> None are suffered to put away their wives against their wills, from any great calamity that may have fallen on their persons, for they look on it as the height of cruelty and treachery to abandon either of the married persons when they need most the tender care of their consort,
>
> *Utopia by Thomas More (translated by H. Morley)*

Peter Jack and Eric were standing, stiff and turned away from each other, waiting for him, as Parker stepped through the gates of the Tower. The red sky of dawn had only just been burned away by the morning sun, and the pale stone looked pink in the light.

He smiled as Eric bowed his hello.

"I found Heyman." Peter Jack looked up at the Bell Tower, his face drawn. Parker wondered if he had slept.

"Good." Satisfaction curled through him. "Where?"

"Where Renard was staying. There is another man there, perhaps the Jules Renard spoke of? He took Heyman in."

"They will be sweating by now, wondering what has happened to Renard." He turned for a last look at the Tower. He would need to get home and get his horse. Get to Bridewell and see the king before Wolsey made his move.

"Eric, you need to go back inside. Find some way to watch this entrance from the inner wall, or from the Bell Tower. Make sure you're able to see who is coming."

"And if I see Wolsey coming?"

"Then I have failed." He contemplated that possibility, but his mind refused to accept it, slipping away from the thought like an eel in the reeds. He heaved in a breath. "If you see Wolsey, my lady must hide, or escape. You have to run and warn her. You and Harry must try to get her away."

"How goes it in there?" Peter Jack's voice was low.

Eric refused to answer him, turning away a little more, so he only faced Parker. "May Fortune be with you."

"And with you." Parker clasped his arm, so thin and fragile, in a gesture of respect, and Eric gave a tight nod.

Then Eric ran to the entrance, calling a cheeky hello to the guards, who grumbled and laughed as they let him through.

"He thinks I have let my lady down. Refusing to guard her in the Tower."

Parker shrugged, started to jog along the cobbled road. "You did well, finding Heyman. You are doing your share."

"He's right." Peter Jack sounded as if he would be happy to throw himself in front of the cart that was rumbling towards them, loaded with grain from the barges.

"You get any sleep last night?"

Peter Jack frowned. "No. I was watching Heyman. Wanted to see if anyone else came to the house."

"Did they?"

"One man. One of Harry's boys followed him when he left, but I haven't spoken to him again. I don't know where he went or who he was."

"I'm sorry, but you can't sleep yet. You need to round up as many of Harry's lads as you can and watch Wolsey's house. At least it's spring tide, so he can't take a barge—it won't go past the bridge. He has to take the roads. If he leaves for the Tower, stop him any way you can, and get one of the lads to call me."

Peter Jack nodded, his back a little straighter. "Does my lady think ill of me?"

Parker looked at him in surprise. "No. She doesn't."

It was as if his words had toppled a huge weight from Peter Jack's shoulders. He grinned. "I'll get the lads."

He peeled off up Fish Hill, and Parker turned at a run into Crooked Lane.

One of Harry's boys was waiting for him near the house, and he forced himself even faster.

"Yes?" He was gasping for air as he drew near.

"Simon Carter saw me near Bridewell last night, following a cove for Peter Jack. Gave me a message."

Parker heaved a deep breath, and bent, hands on his knees.

"He said to tell you, just after dinner last night, the king had a fancy to be hunting, and away from London and more private. He packed up with a few friends and left straight away for one of his courtier's homes near Epping Forest."

Parker slowly lifted his head in horror. "Which estate?"

The boy said a name, and Parker tried to remember where exactly it was, and who owned it. Came up with a distance of at least an hour, at full gallop, just to the house. If the king was out hunting in the forest, it would be near impossible to find him.

"Is Simon with the king?"

The boy nodded. "Found me just before he had to go."

Parker went still. "Did you say he found you while you were following a cove for Peter Jack? Was this the man you saw going into Renard's old house?"

"Don't know 'bout anyone called Renard, but yes, we saw someone go in to the house we were watching and then go out 'bout ten minutes after. I followed him."

"He returned to the palace?" Parker heard the blood pounding in his ears. It made the tick, tick, tick of a clock, wound too fast.

"Went to one of the houses next to the palace."

"Whose house?"

"Duke o' Norfolk, 'parently."

Parker wondered when the bad news would stop coming.

HE'D TAKEN TOO LONG. HAD RIDDEN TOO FAR.

He had a hastily scrawled writ from Henry, smudged with the blood of the deer he had just brought down, in his pouch, but as Parker squinted up at the sun, now well past the midday mark, he tasted the bitterness of failure on his tongue.

If Wolsey knew of the king's late night trip to Epping Forest, as he surely would, he would be crowing now, certain there was no chance of Parker stopping him.

He would see his chance, and grab it.

If Parker was too late, if Susanna was harmed, the cardinal was dead.

He was *dead*.

Parker bent low over his horse and urged him on, and the familiar fields leading to Bishopsgate began to flash past.

He passed Hounds Ditch at a gallop, and as he thundered towards Bishopsgate he was thankful he'd worn his chain of office. The portcullis was raised but it was guarded, and when the watchmen saw his speed and the evidence of his rank, they stepped smartly aside.

His mount began to slide on the cobbles as soon as he passed under the arch and turned onto Grass Street and he was forced to slow down. He shouted himself hoarse at the milling crowds blocking his way, and carried on down Fish Hill with his sword drawn.

It had the desired effect of clearing the way.

He caught sight of a woman with a child, a brief glimpse, her face a mask of fear, her arms rising to protect her daughter as if from the Grim Reaper as he flashed past her.

He was so close to the savage within, the beast that he kept carefully fenced, and with every sharp strike of his horse's hooves on the stone cobbles, he felt that wall crumble. Grow weaker.

He was shouting by the time he turned at Lower Thames Street towards the Tower, a long, continuous battle cry. He could hear himself, but he could not stop. His horse reacted under him, tossing, wild-eyed, trying to dislodge the maniac on its back, and Parker fought it under control.

Wolsey would come this way from Bridewell. If he were still on his way to the Tower, Parker would encounter him. Or at least run Peter Jack or one of Harry's boys to ground.

The thought steadied him and he managed to clamp his mouth shut, weaving the horse through the carts and pedestrians on their way to the dock at Belin's Gate with more restraint.

"Sir." A voice cried out from the side of the road.

He pulled so hard on the reins, the horse lifted its forelegs and tried to unseat him, dancing sideways in alarm.

It had been one of Harry's lads, Will, and Parker twisted on the saddle to see if he could find him again.

"Here." Will dodged around a cart, and ran toward him.

"Wolsey?"

"We've been trying every trick to slow him." The boy pointed to a cart overturned and half blocking the way up ahead, another cart abandoned next to it. Parker realized the overturned cart was from his own stable. "His men pushed that aside a few minutes ago. But they couldn't get the cardinal's cart through. They're walking the rest of the way."

Parker swung down from the horse and threw the reins to Will. The crowds coming in and out of Belin's Gate, hauling fish and grain, would make the going faster on foot. Something Wolsey had realized, as well.

He ran, sword still raised, and palmed the knife he kept in his sleeve as well.

He leapt over the front of his cart, and saw a flash of crimson a little way up the street.

The cardinal, in full regalia. All the better to intimidate Kilburne with.

"Wolsey." His shout echoed, bouncing off the water to his right and the houses to his left.

Even over the noise of the small port, he thought the crimson-clad figure heard him. Hesitated.

He pounded forward. "Wolsey." He held the shout this time, drawing it out, and the crowds parted, people turning back to stare at him as he ran, moving out of his way when they saw his sword.

He didn't see the men Wolsey had set on him until it was far too late.

His concentration had been on the cardinal's crimson robes, but Wolsey had brought his henchmen.

He missed them in the crowds, dressed as they were, not in the cardinal's colors, but as merchants and traders going about their business.

The first man slammed into him and they bounced against each other, Wolsey's man losing his footing on cobbles slick with river water and fish scales. He gripped a nearby trader as he went down, trying to stay upright.

Parker dodged past him while he was still struggling with the passerby, but someone grabbed his arm, and pulled him back.

He staggered, and bent into a crouch, turning in a circle to see how many.

He was surrounded.

He didn't hesitate. These men had thrown themselves into Wolsey's service, and every second they delayed him, was a second longer Susanna would be in their master's clutches.

With a roar, he lifted his sword and spun.

The men leaped back, standing on toes, elbowing the crowds as they tried to stay away from the honed blade.

There were mutterings from the traders, and Parker heard his name called.

He'd worked Belin's Gate as a lad, hauling loads here, and he was known.

"Sir." Peter Jack called from just outside the circle.

"What's happening?" Parker lunged at one of the men and he countered, trying to jump back against the growing wall of people hemming them in.

"The cardinal is nearly at Tower Gate."

"Stop him any way you can." A calm came over him, he felt it settle on him, like a cloak of feathers. Light, weightless.

He lifted his sword again and the man in front of him looked him in the face and turned, squealing like a pig, and tried to burrow his way through the crowd pressing in.

Parker spun away, his longsword angled for a neck hit, and connected with another of Wolsey's men. The blood sprayed high, a rain of warm red, and the people closest screamed and turned away to avoid it.

He lunged in the same move as he pulled his sword free, thrusting his knife to take another of his attackers just under the breastbone and up.

The man fell screaming, hands clutching his stomach, trying to hold the blood in.

Parker stood back, blood dripping from both his blades, and the rest of Wolsey's men tried to melt back into the crowds.

Parker saw the traders and dockers bumping them, hitting the backs of their heads, watched them being tripped, as they tried to get away.

"Please let me through." His voice was nearly gone from his shouting from before but a way opened up immediately and he ran, ran harder and faster than he could ever remember running.

The crowds thinned past Belin's Gate, and he could see Peter Jack launching himself at Wolsey, grabbing the cardinal physically by his robes and falling to the ground. A deadweight for Wolsey to drag with him.

Wolsey had kept two men about him and three of Harry's lads buzzed around them like flies around dung, getting in their way, forcing them to slow. Preventing them from helping the cardinal.

They hit out at the boys, and caught one a backhander, tossed the other two aside. They pried Peter Jack off the cardinal and threw him, easy as if he weighed nothing, to the side of the street.

The cardinal turned up Sporiar Lane and disappeared from sight.

A howl swelled up in his throat and Parker bit it back, forced himself even faster.

He saw Peter Jack and the boys stagger to their feet. Peter Jack called an instruction, and the boys ran after the cardinal, scooping up stones and pebbles as they went. Ammunition.

Peter Jack turned then, not up Sporiar Lane, but through the gate of the house on the corner.

He was going to take a shortcut, beat the cardinal to Tower Gate. Warn Eric.

Parker laughed, one short burst of triumph, then clamped his mouth shut and focused on breathing, on pumping his legs and arms as fast as he could.

He followed the path Peter Jack had taken, dodging around the side of a massive mansion and slamming through the wooden gate at the back of the garden onto Beer Lane. He crossed the street and took the next gate, ran through an orchard and out onto Petty Wales, the open lane that led to Tower Gate.

He could see Wolsey turning right out of Tower Street, his stately progress ruined by the need to duck and shield from a rain of pebbles thrown by the lads. Twice he stopped while his men tried to chase the boys off, but as soon as they started toward the Tower again, the boys edged closer, more missiles in hand.

Straight ahead, at the main gate, he could see Peter Jack. He was leaping and waving in front of the Tower like a madman, jumping and pointing back to the cardinal.

Warning Eric at his look-out post.

Parker walked slowly out onto the road, his chest heaving, his legs shaking from exertion, and took a stand directly in the cardinal's path.

He took out the king's writ, and held his sword ready.

Wolsey could see him now, and satisfaction licked up his chest and warmed his heart as he saw the cardinal falter at the sight of him standing in his way.

Peter Jack was still shouting behind him.

"Call for Kilburne." Parker hoped Peter Jack could hear him over the racket he was making. He wanted the captain to witness the delivery of the king's writ.

Wolsey was capable of claiming to have never received it. Capable of anything.

And then, a strange noise came from behind him. His focus was on Wolsey, his whole body quivering with eagerness for the confrontation, but the noise seemed out of place.

Ahead, Wolsey stopped, his mouth open.

And finally Parker heard it properly, amazed he had not understood before. It was the sound of the bell in the Bell Tower, ringing out with urgency.

The bell that was rung outside of curfew time only to signal the Tower was under attack.

The portcullises began to come down, their chains clinking and sliding in a grating rumble. The massive drawbridge creaked and groaned as it was raised.

The Tower was locked up tight.

Parker threw back his head and laughed.

No matter what happened, the cardinal would not be entering any time soon.

CHAPTER 24

Nature inclines us to enter into society; for there is no man so much raised above the rest of mankind as to be the only favourite of Nature, who, on the contrary, seems to have placed on a level all those that belong to the same species.

Utopia by Thomas More (translated by H. Morley)

"The cardinal is coming. The cardinal is coming." Eric was breathless as he burst into the room. "We have to hide."

"How close?" Susanna stood from the table and met him at the door, Harry just behind her.

"On the approach to the Gate. He's just turned onto Petty Wales. Five minutes away."

"Let's go." Susanna stepped out into the passage and then ran along to the end, through the door into the Bell Tower.

"We'll be trapped up there." Harry stood firm, near her door.

"We aren't going to stay there. We're going to ring the bell." She'd thought about it all morning. Ringing the bell when there was no actual threat to the Tower may land her in trouble, but it couldn't compare to the trouble she would be in if Wolsey was able to walk through those gates with his writ.

Eric was already behind her, and Harry followed, still reluctant.

"What will that do?"

"Kilburne told me if the bell is rung out of curfew times, it signals the Tower is under attack. The guards lock the gates and raise the drawbridge."

"The cardinal won't be able to come in." Eric laughed.

"And we give Parker more time to reach us." She was gasping as she spoke, near the top now.

She burst into the open-air belfry and grabbed for the rope, hooked neatly over its holder.

"I might need help." She pulled down, and the bell swung, but not enough to touch the clapper. Eric took hold just below her own hands and pulled with her a second time. The clapper made a small twang against the side. Harry reached above her hands, and the three of them jumped and pulled down with everything they had.

The bell rang out, the clearest, sweetest sound, and they did it again, and again.

"Listen." Eric let go, and pointed toward the gate, and then she heard it too. The sound of the drawbridge coming up, the rattle of chains as the portcullises dropped.

"We did it." Harry shouted a laugh, the sound of it drowned out by the counter-swing of the bell coming down for one last ring.

"Let's find somewhere to hide." Susanna spun to the stairs.

"I'm afraid that won't be possible." Jean's voice came just as the bell fell silent, his words clear and loud in the belfry. He stood a few steps from the stairs, to the left, and he moved his crossbow a little to the side so she could see his face.

Susanna's mouth hung open. She closed it slowly and continued to stare at the assassin. He was dressed in the uniform of the Tower guards.

Then they all heard the sound of someone running up the stairs, and they all turned to the door, as Kilburne burst through.

"What is this?" Kilburne stood at the top of the stairs, breathing heavily, his sword drawn. He frowned at Jean, trying to place him among his men.

"I'm afraid your bell rung a little too late." Jean spoke with laughter in his voice. "The enemy is already within."

Kilburne almost stepped back in shock, catching himself just in time before he fell backward down the steep stairs. "Who are you? You aren't one of my men."

Jean flicked his crossbow right, indicating Kilburne come round to stand with the others, and the captain reluctantly complied.

"You're right, I'm not one of your men, but I'm sure some of them will be along soon, Captain, so . . ." Jean pointed the bow at Eric. "Mistress Horenbout, you will come with me, or I will shoot the little boy."

Susanna did not hesitate. Better than anyone, she knew Jean would do whatever he threatened. She took a step toward him.

"Wait." He held up a hand. "First, I'd like you to drop that knife you have up your sleeve." He took aim at Eric again, and she pulled her sleeve up, and unstrapped the blade Parker had given her. Dropped it to the floor.

Kilburne looked at her with eyes wide with horror.

"Good. I learned my lesson from last time we met, *madame*. Now come here."

She went to stand by his side, and Harry gave a strangled cry of frustration as Jean drew her in front of him, and placed a knife to her throat.

"If I hear a footstep on the stairs before I reach the bottom, I will slit her throat, and you can explain *that* to your master."

Harry fisted his hands and she saw agony in his eyes as Jean pulled her after him, down into the Bell Tower.

She was surprised when he put her in front of him, but did not keep his hold on her throat, letting her move under her own power. She could feel the knife near her neck, the blade touching her lightly when she didn't move fast enough. It made her shiver.

The weight of the king's ring pulled at her left sleeve, and she thought it ironic her last resort was worthless to her now. The ring would mean something to Wolsey, would stop him in his tracks, but it meant nothing to Jean. Except as something to steal.

"How did you get in?"

He snorted. "That was easy enough. It is how I am going to get out now you have raised the alarm that occupies my thoughts."

"Why are you here? Why didn't you simply kill me in the Bell Tower belfry, rather than having the inconvenience of dragging me down the stairs?"

Jean clucked his tongue. "Despite what I threatened your young bodyguard above, I am not here to kill you."

Susanna almost stumbled on the step, and his hand came out to steady her. "What do you want with me, then?"

"Two things, as it happens."

She was silent, waiting for him to go on.

"The current whereabouts of the Mirror of Naples, naturally, and I also have an offer to put to you."

"An offer?" She stopped on the stairs and turned to look up at him.

"Yes. I am not sure what your answer will be, but I will take the chance of rejection. Would you come away with me, to France?"

"Come away with you to France?" She repeated the words, unable to take their meaning.

He sighed, as if she were a very slow child. "As my lover."

PARKER COULD NOT HELP THE SMILE ON HIS FACE AS WOLSEY approached, walking slower now he could see there would be no quick entry into the Tower. Peter Jack had reached his side. He was limping, and he stopped just at Parker's left shoulder. Parker risked a quick look at him before he turned back to Wolsey and he did not hide the pride and respect in his eyes.

Peter Jack held his gaze.

"Your Grace." Parker turned to Wolsey, but did not bow.

The cardinal did not reply.

Parker saw Wolsey's eyes flick to his face. He raised a hand and wiped away the blood from the man he had cut at Belin's Gate. It was already beginning to dry, and it flaked off from his cheek as he rubbed.

They said nothing.

There were two dead men, and their deaths were on his and Wolsey's hands, both. The weight of them was as heavy as if both bodies were draped across Parker's shoulders.

"They died for nothing." Parker looked beyond Wolsey, to his two men, standing just behind him. "The king issued a writ to stay you, Wolsey."

Wolsey made a hissing sound, like a kettle boiling dry. "The king is away."

"The king is away, you are right. Away in Epping Forest. And he was none too pleased to have me track him down there in the middle of his hunt and ask him to stop you damaging his artist beyond repair, searching for proof that doesn't exist." Parker paused. "Might I clarify, none too pleased with *you*."

Wolsey's eyes flared, hatred and frustration burning bright. "You interfere in everything, damn you."

Parker eyed him like he would a rabid dog. "That is my betrothed you planned to torture, Cardinal. Did you think I would stand aside and watch?"

"Your loyalty to the king should come before your loyalty to her." Wolsey spat the words.

"You did not have her arrested out of concern for the king, you hypocrite. You did it to punish her for what happened a few months ago. When Renard came to you with a story, but no proof, you were only too eager to believe it."

Wolsey flinched as he said Renard's name. "How . . ?"

"I know all about Renard." Parker watched Wolsey's face with interest. "I know he's no French spy. He was turned by de Praet. He's been feeding you false information since the *comte* returned to France."

Wolsey turned white-faced. He staggered a little, as if about to faint.

"Renard wanted Susanna imprisoned because he thought she might know something to the king's advantage. Something that would put the emperor in a difficult position." He laughed softly at the irony. "The one person who could help you win the king away from the emperor to support France, and you had her locked up and planned to torture her."

Wolsey finally had control of himself again. His hands shook, and his lips were pursed, but he had drawn himself together, his shoulders stiff.

"Let me see the writ." He held out his hand.

"I want an independent witness. I will not have you tear it up or throw it to the wind." Parker crossed his arms over his chest.

Wolsey choked in outrage, but the sound was drowned out by the clank and rattle of the drawbridge being lowered again and the portcullises raised.

There were shouts behind him, and Parker turned to the side, still keeping Wolsey and his men in sight.

Harry and Eric were running towards him and Kilburne followed behind at a half jog.

He had a terrible sense of wrongness. Their faces, the tears on Eric's face, brought a rushing of fear, a waterfall of panic that drowned out all other noise. "Where is Susanna?"

"I'm sorry. I'm sorry." Harry was gasping, fighting back tears himself, and Parker felt a chill run down him. He had never seen Harry cry. Ever.

"What happened?" Peter Jack spoke for him.

"Jean took her." Eric threw himself into his brother's arms. "He grabbed her and put a knife to her throat and dragged her away."

Parker turned to Harry, sure there must be—

"He has it right." Harry scrubbed at his face. "That bastard appeared, cool as you please, and took her."

"Is this the only gate that's been opened?" Parker grabbed Kilburne's arm.

"Aye."

Parker tucked the writ back in his pouch. "Then they are still in there, somewhere."

CHAPTER 25

> Thus, upon an inquiry into the whole matter, they reckon that all our actions, and even all our virtues, terminate in pleasure, as in our chief end and greatest happiness; and they call every motion or state, either of body or mind, in which Nature teaches us to delight, a pleasure.
>
> *Utopia by Thomas More (translated by H. Morley)*

The shouts and cries of the guard rang out just the other side of the double doors to the Lieutenant's Lodgings.

Jean did not seem panicked. He guided her right with a cool, steady hand on her shoulder, along a short passage. At the end was a low door, and he stretched past her to open it.

Beyond lay another passageway, although this was clearly in a different house, older, more run down. It lay parallel to the river, clinging to the inner-curtain wall.

He opened a door to the left, to a room with a window out onto Tower Green, and crowded behind her, forcing her in.

The sure way he'd done it, the lack of caution as he entered, made her certain he'd been using the room to watch for her. He knew it would be empty.

"Now, down to business." His hands grabbed her shoulders from behind, and pulled her back against him. Before she could hammer an elbow into his stomach, he looped his arms around her at her waist, tightening his grip so her arms were pinned to her sides.

She struggled against him, and he laughed, breathless enough to make her skin crawl, and placed his lips where her neck met her shoulder.

She forced herself still and stiff, when every muscle screamed to wrench and fight free.

He sighed. "You will escape from me the first moment my back is turned if I take you to France by force." He said it as a statement.

"You know I will."

"Such a pity." He let her go as suddenly as he'd grabbed her, and she stumbled forward to the window, hands out to catch herself.

"Not by the window." The way he spoke, every word a threat, forced her to turn back to him, and she saw his crossbow was raised. She moved into the corner of the room, to the left of the window, her hands half-raised.

"What is it about the Mirror of Naples, that you will risk your life for it, again and again?"

Jean lowered the bow slightly. "It has been my only official failure."

"Even if I knew where it was, if you took it, it would mean war between England and France."

Jean shrugged. "They are almost at war anyway."

That was true. Susanna bit her lip. She had nearly given Jean the Mirror of Naples once before, in exchange for Parker's life, and her loyalty to Henry had been shaken these last few days.

Henry had no right to it, anyway. It was part of the French Crown Jewels.

"You know where it is, don't you?" Jean narrowed his eyes, and took careful aim. "Your lover has taken it somewhere special, kept it even safer since I tried to steal it last time. And he does not hide anything from you."

Her blood started to beat in her ears, a heavy, erratic thump, as she looked straight at the bolt. It was overkill this close. The bolt would go straight through her and bury itself in the wall behind her.

She had a moment of clarity. It would be this way until Jean got the Mirror or he was dead. There was no room in his mind for failure.

And he thought she would go with him, when right at this moment he was threatening to kill her . . . She shook her head.

In the past he'd hit her, choked her, held a knife her throat. That he imagined she would put herself under his power voluntarily . . .

An icy feeling of fear ran down from the base of her skull, and with sharp, pricking fingers, raised the hair on her arms, on the back of her neck.

He was mad, or so unable to see his actions for what they were, it was almost the same thing.

"You are right. I do know where it is." She leaned against the wall, willing her shoulders to relax, and her legs to hold her up. "But there is no guarantee you will let me go if I tell you. Why should I trust you?"

He looked thoughtful. "Nothing I say in answer to that will make any difference. I could still kill you anyway. I hold all the cards."

Susanna lifted a brow. "No. I hold at least one."

"All right. A swap, then. Information for information."

"You have some information you think I would be interested in?" She shot him a look of challenge.

He smiled. "Yes. Something that will clear your way with your king. Make you a hero instead of a prisoner. That would be worth something, no?"

It would be worth the Mirror of Naples. If he spoke the truth.

"I see that *would* be of interest." He cocked his head to one side. "My word of honor, I will give you the information and let you go, in exchange for the location of the Mirror." He waited a beat and in the brief silence, they heard the gates opening again, the creak as the drawbridge was lowered. "We are agreed?"

"It would have to be a very, very useful piece of information for a jewel that is worth a king's ransom." She watched his face, but he had no expression, he had spent years burying his emotions, and she would have no way of knowing if he were lying or not.

"This is one of the reasons I wish you to come with me." Jean took two long strides and reached over to touch her cheek with a finger, his face cold and hard. "You are clever, *madame*. You are brave and you are resourceful. And beautiful, also, but that is not the main attraction." He smiled, suddenly, a quick, fox-sly quirk of the lips. "And I will admit, that you are Parker's, and that you defeated me last time, would make it a victory over him, and over you all at once, which would add not a little sweetness to it, as well."

The breath she drew in shuddered through her, and she jerked back from his touch. "You understand, I will not go with you."

A shout came from across the green, by the main gate, and Jean moved back from the window, his whole body alert and ready.

"Time is wasting, and I do truly want that jewel." His crossbow was aimed at the window now, his eyes never leaving the movement of men beyond the panes.

She wanted so much to push him aside and see who was out there—see if Parker had somehow made it back from the king— it took all her willpower to stop herself.

"If it helps to make up your mind, the jewel will disappear completely. It will not be flaunted on Francis's robes as a reminder to your king that he was bested. I intend to go into retirement with it."

"You are not stealing it for King Francis?" She blinked.

"I am not. Despite almost dying to get it last time, my efforts were not appreciated, and I find I am tired of this life." He lifted a hand off the bow and waved it. "The diamond can be cut down into a few smaller stones, the pearl sold separately. I would think it will last me far into old age." While he spoke, his gaze never left the window. He vibrated with an eagerness to shoot.

She felt a little lurch in her chest. Who would have that effect on Jean but Parker? Could it be?

"If that is so, then you will have to astound me with the information you have." Susanna set her mouth in a grim line. "Or I say nothing."

"I could make you tell me." There was an edge of anticipation in his tone, and at last he turned to look at her.

She held his gaze. "Not easily, and not quietly."

He nodded. "You are right. But you have promised me the jewel before, and reneged on it."

"Last time, I could have been accused of treason if I'd given it to you." She crossed her arms. "Give me something of worth, and I will tell you where to find it. It still won't be easy to take, but this time, I won't be implicated in its disappearance."

He nodded again, slowly. "So be it. I have heard something I think your king would be most interested to learn. Something that might earn you a free walk out of this Tower, he will be so grateful."

Susanna waited as he gazed out onto the Green. "I heard a certain nobleman was looking for an assassin for a special job, and naturally, I take an interest in these things. The word is, the target is a little boy. The bastard son of the king."

Susanna froze. "Henry Fitzroy? The child is only six years old."

"And one day he will be twenty-six, and a contender for the throne, no?" Jean spoke without a trace of emotion.

"Do you have proof of this?"

"A letter, passed to me by someone who thought I would be interested, if the money was right. I will give it to you if I'm satisfied you've told me the truth about the Mirror."

"Which nobleman?"

Jean laughed softly. "None would be so stupid as to put their name to parchment in something such as this. Someone power-ful, I would think, someone who might have a chance at the throne himself, if there was no son to take over."

Susanna tipped her head back against the wall as she took in the full implications. Norfolk? Would he be mad enough? "When is this assassination planned?"

Jean slipped a hand into his pouch, and lifted a letter out a little way. "The location of the jewel, first."

"I do not trust you. Tell me when, and I swear I will honor my word."

He hesitated, then shook his head. "No. I do not trust you so easily again."

She worried her lip with her teeth. Tried to think of a compromise. "I will tell you the building it is in, but not the exact location. If you tell me when the assassination will happen, I will give you all the information you need."

He lowered his crossbow a little more, waited for her.

"You are looking at it." She spoke quietly, and at last had an excuse to move to the window. She pointed to the White Tower.

He swore, pressing up against the window. "In that damnable fortress?"

"Nice and safe," she murmured. She searched the green as fast as she could, but there was no sign of Parker. If he had been there, he was gone, now. "When did the mysterious nobleman want the killing done?"

He grimaced, but pulled the letter out completely. "The boy will be presented before the court in a way that shows him to be the king's heir. It must be done before then. Before the seventh day in June, I was told."

Only a few days away. Henry Fitzroy could be assassinated at any time. She took the letter from him and unfolded it. Read the cryptic offer of money for the death of the little prince. "Did someone take the job?"

Jean laughed. "When that kind of money is on the table, you can believe someone took the job."

"But not you?"

"Would I tell you of it, hand over this letter, if I had taken it?"

"Perhaps." She kept her eyes on his face. "You would do it just to make it more of a challenge."

"Ah." He reached for her again, but stopped just short, pulled back. "You do understand me so well. Perhaps it is your artist's eye. But no, in this case, that job would interfere with finding the Mirror. I turned it down."

"If what you tell me is true, I have one more condition before I tell you where the Mirror is." Her chest was tight, her hands clenched, that she was even going to ask him this.

"And what is that?" He slanted her a look, hard, sharp, barely containing his anger.

"I need to get to Henry Fitzroy." She turned her eyes to the White Tower. "You must help me escape."

CHAPTER 26

> There are many things that in themselves have nothing that is truly delightful; on the contrary, they have a good deal of bitterness in them; and yet, from our perverse appetites after forbidden objects, are not only ranked among the pleasures, but are made even the greatest designs, of life.
> *Utopia by Thomas More (translated by H. Morley)*

P arker had never realized before now what a rabbit's warren the Tower complex was. There were too many towers. Too many houses and rooms and cells.

"There is no way you will find her unless you get very lucky." Kilburne was breathless from chasing after him. "And he's dressed like one of my men. He won't stand out."

"Susanna will though."

Kilburne looked at him pityingly, and Parker knew he was thinking Susanna had long since had her throat slit and was lying somewhere on the grounds, dead.

"Why did he take her down the stairs if he intended to kill her?"

Kilburne didn't answer, and Parker knew again what he was thinking. That Jean wanted to rape her first.

He knew it was what Kilburne was thinking, because it was what he was thinking himself. His hands trembled, his heart skipped—each beat of it painful. Every second he did not find her, was a second longer Jean had her at his mercy.

There was no other reason Jean would deal with the inconvenience of a hostage, unless he had plans for her. Plans that were better suited to a private room than the open belfry of the Bell Tower.

Something caught his eye, a guard making for the door of the Lieutenant's Lodgings across the Green. There was something furtive in his movements. "Who is that?"

Kilburne shaded his eyes against the afternoon sun and his demeanor changed as the man slipped through the entrance and closed it behind him. "It's hard to say, but it looks like Merden."

The name made Parker still. "I've heard of him."

Kilburne glanced across. "Mistress Horenbout believes he is following the cardinal's orders, rather than my own."

"So I gather." Parker made for the door.

"We have no proof, Parker, and I cannot allow you to intimidate or injure my men." Kilburne's warning was soft but clear to his back, and Parker tightened the reins on his bloodlust. Hurting Merden would not save Susanna. It would only waste time.

There would be plenty of opportunity for revenge later.

"It is hardly likely Jean will be in the Lodgings." Kilburne's eyes tracked the inner curtain wall.

"Where did he come from?" Parker kept his eyes on the Lodgings' door, but allowed Kilburne to draw him away, towards the inner towers.

"I don't know. He was in the belfry before I got there."

"And where were you, when Susanna rang the bell?" Parker stopped short. Turned to wait for Kilburne.

"I was in my rooms on the Lodgings ground floor."

"And Jean got there before you." Parker looked up at the Bell Tower. "He's fast, but not that fast."

"He was inside the Lodgings all along." Kilburne's mouth gaped.

"And if he'd been hiding there without discovery before, then why not go straight back to his hidey-hole?" Parker turned back and ran for the Lodgings door. He burst into the hallway and took stock, and Kilburne was right behind him.

"Right is to my chambers—if he was there, I heard nothing. Left is just a short corridor leading to the next house, but the door is locked, it isn't in use. Upstairs is to Mistress Horenbout's apartments and there is a door into the Bell Tower along from there."

So most likely it was up. He'd been hiding right next to Susanna in one of the upstairs rooms or in the Bell Tower itself. It was audacious enough for Jean to attempt. Parker looked back to see if Kilburne was following him, and took the stairs two at a time.

"Helping you escape would be most inconvenient." Jean hooked his crossbow onto his belt, and pushed away from the window. "You will have to make your own plans."

"Then I will not tell you the exact location of the Mirror."

He rounded on her, his face tight with anger. "I may never have another chance to get into this cursed place again. I am here now, within its walls—to help you leave and then come back in? No! You ask too much."

They stared at each other, and Susanna realized she was breathing hard, as if she'd been running.

"Well, well. You are a difficult woman to find, Mistress Horenbout."

Susanna spun to the door, registered Merden and saw his eyes go wide.

Jean had his crossbow raised, no trace of fear, or annoyance on his face. He was blank. Expressionless. And she had never been more afraid of him.

Merden and Jean stared at each other for a long moment, and then Merden broke, trying to dive out of the door.

Jean squeezed the trigger, unhurried, and Merden fell. Soundless but for the thump his body made falling to the wooden floor.

She could not see where Jean had hit him, she could only see Merden's boots lying just inside the door. The rest of his body lay out in the passage.

She forced her gaze from the smooth-worn soles of Merden's boots to Jean. He was calmly loading another bolt, cranking his crossbow, ready for another shot.

"He may not be alone. We will have to move." Jean spoke in a tone that matched his expression.

"He . . ." Her voice cracked and she could not help her eyes going to Merden's body again. The harsh, bitter taste of bile rose in her throat and she forced it down. "He may have been coming to look for me on his own. As a favor for the cardinal."

"He's the cardinal's man?" Jean looked at his victim with interest for the first time.

"He tried to get me into the dungeons." She shivered.

"He wanted to touch you." Jean finished with his bow, clipped it again to his belt. "I could see it in his eyes when he spoke. He was so eager, he didn't even notice me at first. Did he manage it?"

"Once. Briefly." She stopped. Unwilling to speak about this with him.

"It is a pity then I could not gut-shoot him and leave him to bleed out." He did not change his inflection. "It'd make too much noise, though."

"This may mean the cardinal is in the Tower, and looking for me. If he gets me . . ." She tried to look one last time out the window, but Jean blocked it completely. She shuddered. "I can't stay. Not just for Fitzroy, but for myself as well. If Parker is not back and Wolsey is here looking for me, there is nothing to stop him taking me to the dungeons."

Jean pursed his lips. "I would hate the cardinal to get his way in anything. I have developed quite a dislike for him." He tapped a hand on the stock of his crossbow. "*Bien*. This man was to take you to the White Tower to the cardinal? Perhaps that is what we will do."

Susanna pushed herself hard against the wall, as if she could burrow into its safety. "You want me to go with you, into the White Tower?"

"It is a solution. We go together, to get the jewel and to leave the Tower. We help each other."

"But then I will be implicated in the jewel's disappearance. It will change nothing for me."

"Where the jewel is kept, will it be noticed missing right away?"

She thought about it. Shook her head.

"Then a guard bringing in a prisoner, taking them away again, this happens nearly every day, I would think. What blame could be laid at your door?"

It may be the only way she could escape. She pushed away from the wall. "Let's go, then."

CHAPTER 27

> For if you consider the use of clothes, why should a
> fine thread be thought better than a coarse one?
> And yet these men, as if they had some real advan-
> tages beyond others, and did not owe them wholly
> to their mistakes, look big, seem to fancy them-
> selves to be more valuable, and imagine that a
> respect is due to them for the sake of a rich
> garment, to which they would not have pretended if
> they had been more meanly clothed, and even
> resent it as an affront if that respect is not paid
> them.
>
> *Utopia by Thomas More (translated by H. Morley)*

Jean was not hiding above and Parker wanted to howl at the time he'd wasted.

They arrived back at the main entrance and Kilburne silently indicated left, to the dark corridor leading to the adjoining house.

Parker nodded and raised his knife, moved quietly down the narrow passage.

The door swung open under his hand.

Kilburne was behind him, and he realized he did not want the captain there. Did not want anyone to witness what he might find, until he had some grip on himself.

But before he could turn and suggest Kilburne try to the right of the hall, to his own rooms, he smelled the sharp, iron scent of blood, and he could not speak.

He moved forward, turned the corner, and saw Merden lying face up. He was missing an eye. A bolt was embedded in the wooden panel wall behind him. It had gone right through the guard, and Parker did not want to look too closely at what was leaking out the back of his head.

"God above." Kilburne reared back mid-stride, and nearly unbalanced. He stared at Merden in horror. "What was he doing here?"

"Looking for Susanna?" Parker edged around the body, and stepped into the room he had been in when he was shot. "Perhaps he was doing a little private searching for the cardinal?"

Kilburne was too shocked to answer. He did not move, staring at Merden's face.

"If they were in here, they left." Parker knew the order in the room, the lack of a sign of a struggle, did not mean anything, but hope sent a tiny green shoot through the dark overgrowth of fear within him.

Kilburne was still looking down at Merden's body. "You say he is a French assassin. What business has he here?"

"He's after Susanna. And he still has her." Parker spoke sharply, trying to jolt Kilburne out of his shock. "Unless he's left her body somewhere hard to find, she is still with him, at his mercy."

Kilburne grabbed his hair with both hands and tugged. "I do not know what to make of this, Parker. What is he about?"

"Nothing good." Parker stepped over Merden's body. Realized Susanna would have had to do the same. He fingered her dagger, which Harry had handed him, and thought what she would try to do. Thought what Jean would want.

And then it came to him. He tried to keep his body loose, relaxed, so Kilburne would not notice a change in him. But he would have to get rid of the captain to make sure of things.

If Susanna had told Jean where to find the Mirror of Naples in exchange for her life, he thought the exchange more than fair. But to everyone else, it would be treason.

IT SEEMED THE WHITE TOWER, WITH ITS SINGLE ENTRANCE UP an outer wooden staircase to the first floor, was a simple matter to get into.

Susanna hoped it would be just as simple to leave. Carrying one of the largest diamonds in the world.

"She's wanted upstairs." Jean spoke without a trace of an accent for a change. When he spoke to her, he seemed to relish accentuating his words, as if reminding her they were both foreigners here. But now, he could have been anyone.

The guard at the table frowned at him, as if trying to place him, but Jean moved past, as if he had announced his intentions as a courtesy, rather than a requirement.

Susanna recognized the watchman from the day she had been taken from the queen's chambers, and the sight of her seemed to be all he required.

"The cardinal is in the chapel vestry," he called after them, and Susanna felt Jean freeze at the same moment she did.

It took him less than a second to recover, though. "Move." He pushed her between the shoulderblades. "Please, do not tell me that is where the Mirror is." His breath was hot in her ear.

She shook her head. "It's in the State Apartments, which are on the floor above."

Jean was silent.

They had reached the top of the stairs and heard the murmur of conversation behind a small door to the left. The chapel ran the whole length of the floor, with wide double doors in the center.

Susanna pointed to the next set of stairs, and Jean kept his grip on her as he moved toward them.

Then, from above, they heard the scrape of a shoe, and someone coughed, raw and wet.

They froze.

Jean relaxed suddenly behind her. And she thought of the way he'd looked when he'd shot Merden.

"I can't go up there. Then I truly will be implicated. And you can't kill the guard without alerting everyone to the fact the Mirror is gone." She spoke so quietly, Jean had to bend even closer to her.

His hand tightened on her arm, squeezing it hard enough she had to force herself not to cry out. Then he let go, and she rubbed where he had bruised her, angling her body away from his.

He walked toward the doors to the chapel and tried the handles. One opened soundlessly.

Jean motioned to her and together they stepped into the silent room. She could hear Wolsey talking to someone in the vestry, the sound muffled but very close.

Jean pointed to one of the pews, set in shadow against the wall. "Stay here. I'll get rid of the guard."

"Don't kill him." Despite her fear of him, she clutched at his arm. She did not want another life taken, especially in this devil's bargain she'd made.

He gave her a strange look and shook her off as a bear would a troublesome dog. "You're right, his death will bring too much attention. It wouldn't make sense to kill him."

She nodded, tight and short, and stepped away, making sure she did not brush against him.

He swung the door shut, closed it without a sound and left her in the gloomy, jewel-lit light of the stained glass, the image of his face still clear in her mind.

Deadly, focused.

Those words could be used to describe Parker as well, but Jean had lost one thing Parker still had in abundance. His humanity.

The cough came again, and it sounded as if it were in the chapel itself. Susanna tensed, and realized at last the chapel's high ceilings extended up into the third floor.

She moved away from the door, and looked up, saw a gallery ran along the top, with a door leading out to the landing above and the State Apartments. The king could attend church merely by walking from his rooms into the gallery, and look down on the service from above.

The sound of the rustle of clothing filtered down to her, and she guessed one of the gallery doors had not been properly shut.

She heard Jean call softly from halfway up the stairs, and then heard his footsteps as he climbed all the way to the top floor.

"Yes?" The guard spoke loudly, and Jean shushed him. Every sound carried down to her, clear as if she were beside them.

"The cardinal is working in the vestry below." Jean's voice was now so low, she had to strain to hear it. "He is irritated by your cough. He says it's disturbing him."

Susanna heard Jean's low laugh, and wondered if the guard had made a rude gesture in the cardinal's direction.

"I know, my friend. I know."

His voice was so warm, so sympathetic, Susanna shivered. He would have killed this man if it hadn't been inconvenient.

"Think of it this way, you have some time off. I'm to replace you. Is it just the king's chambers you watch up here?"

The guard gave a snorting laugh of his own. "Aye, I suppose time off won't go amiss. The king and queen's chambers and a few of his courtiers' rooms. That's all you need to watch."

"Good." He waited while the guard hacked another cough.

On her floor, Susanna heard the door to the cardinal's chambers swing open.

"Will you be quiet with that infernal racket."

Susanna heard the door slam, and wondered if it were one of Wolsey's thugs or his secretary. Whoever it was, they had played directly into Jean's hands.

"That's your signal to be off, my friend."

"S'pose so." The guard moved down the stairs, unhurried, coughing all the while. Far more than he had been doing earlier.

Susanna smiled.

The handle of the door rattled, and shock at how fast, how silently, Jean had returned froze her for a moment. She stepped back in place just in time.

"Where is the Mirror?" Jean's face loomed at her, backlit by the weak light of the landing, and she wondered how she could create that effect in a painting. A devil leering through a door, with the fires of hell in the background.

"The Mirror." He grabbed her by the shoulders, shook her, and she blinked.

This would be the hardest part. "In the king's chamber in a small box." She showed him the size in the small space between their bodies, hoping he would release her and step back. "It's probably inside a chest."

"Which will no doubt be locked."

Susanna lifted her hands. "Did you think it would be easy?"

He pushed her away from him, and she stumbled backward. She put out a hand to steady herself, and it connected with a small table beside the door.

Jean leaped forward and caught it before it clattered to the floor. He placed it down with deliberate movements and then spun for the door. Let himself out without a word.

Susanna stared at the closed door, waiting for her pulse to calm.

At last she sat on a bench, still in shadow, and looked up at the light streaming in through the high stained glass windows, the floral rainbow pattern soothing her.

If he hadn't been afraid she'd cry out, Jean would have hit her because of the table.

She knew it.

His behavior was mercurial. One moment, entranced by her, the next, furious that she would not obey him to the letter. That she would not cower.

She thought of Fitzroy, being stalked by a killer, and wondered if she dare trust Jean to get her out of the Tower. The way his eyes had flared before he left—she hunched her shoulders and stood slowly.

Could it be he was done with her? He could take the Mirror and keep walking. Leave her to the wolves.

Leaving her only a wall away from the Cardinal Wolsey. Even the weight of the king's ring did not soothe her at that thought.

Her hands were shaking and she lifted them up in the half-dark, willed them to still. When they were steady enough for her liking, she focused on listening. Wolsey was quiet now, but she could hear the occasional thump of a drawer, and was certain he was still busy within his vestry.

Above her, in the gallery, she thought she heard the faintest creak of wood. As if someone were adjusting their position.

Jean?

She had given him what he needed, and she would only slow him down now, and could still turn on him.

Perhaps he'd decided he was better off with her dead.

The darkness above seemed to loom over her, now. She imagined shadows in its depths, with crossbows raised.

With a sudden sense of urgency, she made for the door, opened it and walked out to the stairs. She looked up, but there was no sign of Jean on the landing.

She hesitated. Wondered if the guard below would fetch Kilburne if she asked them too, or if they would call up to Wolsey.

And then she remembered. Kilburne was set to take her to Fitzroy's this afternoon. She was supposed to be painting him.

Her hand gripped the banister. She had completely forgotten. There could be no simpler way to have access to the little boy.

She hoped Wolsey had not convinced Kilburne he had a right to question her, or that the king's wish for her to paint Fitzroy counted as more important than Wolsey's questions.

Above her, she heard the creak of boards, and she moved as quietly as she could down the stairs toward the guards.

She would take her chances with Kilburne.

She had had the tiger by the tail and had let it go. It was time to put a safe distance between herself and the assassin.

CHAPTER 28

> And yet it is wonderful to see how this false notion
> of pleasure bewitches many who delight themselves
> with the fancy of their nobility, and are pleased with
> this conceit—that they are descended from ances-
> tors who have been held for some successions rich,
> and who have had great possessions; for this is all
> that makes nobility at present.
>
> *Utopia by Thomas More (translated by H. Morley)*

Kilburne had been easy to get rid of. He was so shocked by Merden's death, it had been a simple matter for Parker to steer him to his chambers to collect himself before he called his men to move Merden's body.

Parker hoped he would be sufficiently occupied for some time. He reached the top of the wooden stairs and opened the door into the White Tower. The gloom of the inside enveloped him, and he stood still a moment to get used to it.

A guard at a table stood, and saluted him. "The cardinal is up on the second floor, working in the vestry."

Parker nodded his thanks. Walked past and up the central staircase. He wondered where Kingston was in all this. But the

Constable of the Tower would not be concerned with so lowly a prisoner as Susanna, not with an efficient captain like Kilburne to rely upon.

He moved softly up the stairs, not sure if Wolsey would have his men standing outside or in the vestry with him.

There was a soft scuffle of feet just ahead, as if someone had heard him, and stopped dead.

He lunged forward, leaping up the steps, and slammed into—

"Parker." Susanna went limp against him, and he could feel her whole body shaking. "I thought . . ."

Parker tightened his hold on her, his mind not quite sure of the evidence in his arms.

"You are all right." He wanted to laugh it out loud, but forced himself to whisper in her ear.

"Jean is above, looking for the Mirror in the State apartments."

If he didn't have to choose between killing Jean and getting Susanna out of the White Tower safely, he would have taken the stairs without a second thought, knife in hand.

"We need to get you to Kilburne. I have the writ from the king. Wolsey can do nothing to you, and tonight, if he still has no proof against you, he has to let you go."

"I need to get to Durham House, not back to Kilburne." She looked wild, her hair half-fallen from its neat twist, her eyes wide. "We have to get to Fitzroy."

He frowned. "The king will understand your delay on the portrait, and it will be one more mark against Wolsey for causing it."

"No, not to paint him." She raised her eyes upward, to the State Apartments. "Jean told me a nobleman has contracted an assassin to kill Fitzroy. I have the letter he was given as proof."

Parker choked. "An assassin?"

"Yes, someone offered the job to Jean but he turned it down. But he swears someone else would have taken it. And it must be done before the seventh day in June."

Parker heard the door open above, and the murmur of voices. Kingston and Wolsey. So that is where the Constable was.

He gripped Susanna's hand and climbed the stairs to the landing, felt her resist a moment, and then place her trust in him.

It would be best to get this confrontation with Wolsey over with, and he could ask for no better witness than the Constable of the Tower.

"Parker." Kingston gaped at him as they stepped into view. Wolsey stood behind him, his eyes hooded. "There seems to be some confusion about a certain prisoner . . ." Kingston tailed off as he noticed Susanna.

"There is no confusion, sir." Parker pulled the hard-won writ from his pouch, and presented it. "The truth of the matter is, the cardinal acted unwisely, and from false information. He made an arrest before ascertaining any facts, and when the king demanded he produce proof or release Mistress Horenbout tonight, he decided to extract a false confession from her with torture, rather than lose face. I appraised the king of this, and he has made his opinion on the matter clear."

Wolsey's cheeks burned with sudden color.

Kingston took the writ and read it slowly. Looked between the two men.

The silence stretched, uncomfortable and heavy, and eventually Kingston cleared his throat and shifted in place. "It seems clear enough the king wishes no harm come to his painter, and unless the questions you have to put to her are in my office, and without force, cardinal, I suggest she be returned to the Lieutenant's Lodgings, which I hear from Kilburne was the queen's choice of accommodation for her." He bowed to Susanna and she curtsied back. "Apologies that my wife and I have not had the chance to visit you yet, mistress."

"It is quite all right, sir." Susanna ignored Wolsey. "As it happens, the cardinal's arrival interrupted a schedule set out by the king, for me to attend to his son, Henry Fitzroy, at Durham

House this afternoon. I am busy painting a portrait of him, and the king is anxious for me to continue work on it."

Kingston looked to Wolsey as if expecting him to deny it, but when he again said nothing, the Constable blushed. "I will need to speak to Kilburne about this. But if that is what the king requires, by all means, you should continue as usual."

"My thanks, sir." Susanna dipped in another curtsy. "I am eager to get back to work."

Parker noticed a quick movement overhead. Jean was in the shadows above, watching them.

"Kilburne is dealing with the death of one of his men, sir." He spoke to Kingston, but he kept Wolsey in his line of sight. "A guard named Merden. He was discovered in an unused house next to the Lieutenant's Lodgings."

Kingston gasped, and Wolsey snapped to immediate attention.

"That would have been your doing, Parker." Wolsey could barely speak, rage distorted his mouth so badly.

"Captain Kilburne and I noted the man entering the Lodgings and followed him inside. We were together when we discovered the body." Parker held Wolsey's gaze while he spoke.

"I will confirm that with Captain Kilburne, but it does seem clear you are not responsible." Kingston gave Wolsey a strange look. "I notice you've requested Merden's services most often, of all the men here, Your Grace. I am sure it is merely grief that causes you to lash out so."

"The cardinal is surely bemoaning the waste of so valuable a man." Parker spoke without inflection, and Wolsey spun around and walked back into the vestry. Slammed the door shut.

Kingston's eyes went wide.

"With your permission, I will accompany Mistress Horenbout to Durham House in Captain Kilburne's stead, sir." Parker spoke with respect. He intended to go with Susanna, whether Kingston gave his permission or not, but this mess was not of the Constable's making. His powers ended at the walls of the

Tower, and nothing could prevent Parker from accompanying Kilburne, if Kingston insisted his captain make the trip.

"That would be delicate, sir. As I am to understand she is your betrothed." Kingston looked agonized.

"Yes, she is. And if I fail to return her, my place at court is gone and her life is forfeit. You could have no better guard for her than I."

Kingston was silent and in the heavy pause, Parker heard the faintest shift of cloth from above. Jean biding his time, waiting for his moment to escape without notice.

"What you say is true, but if you fear her life is forfeit anyway, that there is a chance of her guilt, then you could just as easily escape with her. And I would be held accountable." Kingston lifted his head and looked Parker in the eyes.

"True. If you want Kilburne to take her, then that is your prerogative." Parker dipped his head.

"I would feel better about it. I am sorry, Parker."

"I will take her to Kilburne immediately." Parker held out his arm to her, but as she took it, Kingston coughed.

"I would feel more at ease if one of my guards accompanied you—"

"I will take them, if you will, my lord." Jean swooped down the stairs, and stood in the half-shadows.

Kingston started, and recovered when he saw the uniform. "Aye. That would be most useful."

Parker held himself still. Having a guard who was not a guard escort them would be most useful, indeed.

Even if it that guard was a murdering bastard.

CHAPTER 29

The Utopians have no better opinion of those who are much taken with gems and precious stones, and who account it a degree of happiness next to a divine one if they can purchase one that is very extraordinary, especially if it be of that sort of stones that is then in greatest request, for the same sort is not at all times universally of the same value, nor will men buy it unless it be dismounted and taken out of the gold.

Utopia by Thomas More (translated by H. Morley)

"For once our interests are aligned, courtier." Jean leaned forward from behind them as they descended the stairs, his voice soft. Smug. "Well, perhaps not for the first time."

She felt the whisper of air as his fingertips danced just short of touching her. Parker's hand came up, grasping Jean's fingers and pulling him down, so he almost toppled between them.

"Beware our mutual interest is not overwhelmed by my need to see you dead, Frenchman."

Susanna stepped away, giving Parker room, and she saw his

dagger was in his hand, had probably been in his hand from the moment Jean appeared. It was pressed against Jean's neck.

Jean lifted his one free hand in surrender. "I have no wish for anything but a quick exit, courtier. Something I think you wish for just as much. Why don't we help each other?"

"Once we are out of here, there will be no further mutual interest." Parker waited a beat. "Do you understand?"

"Only too well. Whichever one of us sees the other first, is the one who has the pleasure of the kill."

"Just so." Parker released him, and Jean stepped back, a gleam in his eye.

He looked too pleased with himself not to have found the Mirror. Susanna hoped it meant she would never see him again.

As if he sensed the direction of her thoughts, he turned to her and gave a cramped half-bow in the narrow confines of the staircase. "My apologies for what happened in the chapel, *madame*. I am usually not so short-tempered, but when it comes to you . . ." He shrugged.

"Were you going to kill me or leave me to be discovered?" She watched him as he straightened his doublet, twisted in the scuffle with Parker.

"Leave you to raise the alarm against me, knowing you had nothing more to lose? I will be honest. I was going to kill you."

The hairs on the back of her neck rose, just as they had earlier. She had had the tiger by the tail, but she had only thought she'd let it go. If she'd stayed in the chapel, she'd have died with a bolt through her eye.

Parker's eyes were on Jean's face and when the assassin straightened, he stared straight back.

"Ready?" Parker's hand was clenched around his sword hilt, and, impossibly, she saw it tighten more when Jean gave an unhurried nod.

They continued down the stairs, past the guard on the first floor and through the door to the outside stairs.

"What now?" Jean whispered.

Susanna flinched at the nearness of his lips to her ear.

"We keep walking. Straight out the front gate." Parker started them on a course past the Lieutenant's Lodgings.

"Parker." Kilburne hailed them from the entrance, and Jean went stiff at her back.

"He has seen me before."

"Then you had best disappear." Parker lifted a hand in greeting and stopped.

Susanna looked towards Kilburne herself. He was walking fast, his eyes fixed on them, and her gut clenched at the thought of explaining Jean's presence. There would be only one explanation when the Mirror was found missing.

And Parker was with her now. There would be no escape for him, either. He would be as implicated as she.

"You are unharmed?" Kilburne's gaze focused beyond them, his eyes narrowed.

Susanna turned, and saw Jean's back as he climbed the stairs to the White Tower. She hadn't even heard him go. She felt a twist of fierce satisfaction that he was forced to go back into the heart of the Tower, tempt the fates for a little while longer.

Parker did not turn. He drew her close, blocking Kilburne's view of Jean. "The assassin took her into the White Tower."

Kilburne frowned. "Why did he do that? What did he want?"

Susanna kept her eyes on the White Tower a moment longer, and then faced Kilburne. She was prepared to lie, to dissemble and invent to keep Parker and herself safe, and she would partly use the truth to do it. Weave a pattern so tight between what was and was not, even the cardinal himself would falter at trying to separate it.

"He wanted revenge. But he found trying to exact it here too difficult. He intended . . ." She drew a deep breath, and had no need to fake the shiver that ran through her. Kilburne shifted uncomfortably. "He didn't have the time or the privacy he needed to kill me the way he wanted to. And when Merden sought him out, interrupted him—"

Kilburne swore softly at the mention of his dead guard. "Merden knew him?"

"It seemed to me that he did." She felt no shred of remorse about implicating the dead guard. The look on his face when he'd found her earlier was imprinted on her memory. "If I were to guess, Merden helped him get inside, and gave him the uniform of your guards. Perhaps he was in the assassin's pay?" Susanna lifted her hands. "But they argued. I didn't hear why, but the assassin killed Merden, and took me as a prisoner to the Tower, to find the cardinal. It was as if they had a deal, and Merden and the cardinal had reneged on it."

She glanced up at Kilburne, but he flinched away from her gaze. She was outlining treason and deceit at the highest level and as she'd hoped, he wanted no part in it. "He left me in the chapel, and then never returned. I'm not sure if he met with the cardinal or not. I eventually found the courage to leave. Parker found me on the stairs coming down." She laced her fingers together, head down. "I would guess he is long gone."

Kilburne exchanged an agonized look with Parker. "Tell her not to speak of the cardinal and the assassin as if they have some tie, I beg you, Parker. Or Merden." He turned to her. "My lady, it will serve to do nothing but make more trouble for you."

"I will say nothing. It was simply an impression I had, that there was some connection there. When he had me prisoner, he said a few other things that gave the strong impression . . ."

"No more." Kilburne lifted a hand, his eyes scanning the Green to make sure there was no one nearby to hear.

"Very well." She dropped her gaze, her aim achieved. Wolsey had once been in league with Jean, but they had long since fallen out with each other. He would find any association with the assassin hard to explain. If it was discovered the Mirror had gone missing while she had been with Jean in the White Tower, it would be impossible not to mention the cardinal had been there too. And he had once promised the jewel to the Frenchman in return for favors from France.

No. If Wolsey had anything to say about it, all evidence of Jean being in the Tower would be suppressed. And if Jean was to be left out it, so would she and Parker.

Parker stretched out a hand and took her fingers in his. Lifted them to his mouth. As his lips brushed them, there was barely concealed laughter in his eyes.

Then he glanced back at the White Tower, and his face hardened. "We spoke with Kingston and Wolsey while we were in there. I suggested to Kingston I take Mistress Horenbout to Durham House in your stead, given Merden's death—"

"Durham House." Kilburne's face lost all its color. "I'd forgotten." He squinted up to the sky. "My lady was to be there after the midday repast."

"If I am still to go, I'll need my satchel." Susanna took a step towards the Lodgings.

"What did Kingston say, about your going in my stead?" Kilburne's words stopped her, and she looked back at Parker.

"He told me he would be happier if you accompanied her." Parker did not hesitate to answer truthfully.

Kilburne grimaced, his eyes on the White Tower again. "Aye. No doubt he is right. If anything happened . . ."

"I'm coming anyway. I will not let my lady leave my sight until she is released this evening on the king's orders. She will ride with me."

Kilburne gave a nod. "I wish we could use a barge, but the tide is still too low. I'll organize a horse and meet you in the Lodgings shortly." He turned away from them, to the stables.

Parker watched him go, then held his arm again, to walk her to the Lodgings. "He is a good man."

"Yes." She flicked a glance at him. "I am guilty of manipulating him. Saying what I did . . ."

Parker shook his head, and the grin he sent her made her catch her breath and stumble. "That was a masterstroke. Remind me never to cross you, my lady. If you were to put your mind to it, you could have the court tied in knots."

A shout sounded from near the main gate, and Susanna's gut clenched, her fingers tightened on Parker's arm. But it was not the guards, or any new threat, it was Harry and Eric.

And as they raced across to her, as she held her arms out to them—part of her family too, who also needed protection—the last trace of her guilt evaporated into the blue, blue sky.

CHAPTER 30

> Nor can they comprehend the pleasure of seeing dogs run after a hare, more than of seeing one dog run after another; for if the seeing them run is that which gives the pleasure, you have the same entertainment to the eye on both these occasions, since that is the same in both cases. But if the pleasure lies in seeing the hare killed and torn by the dogs, this ought rather to stir pity, that a weak, harmless, and fearful hare should be devoured by strong, fierce, and cruel dogs.
>
> *Utopia by Thomas More (translated by H. Morley)*

Parker did not want Susanna to go back to the Tower again.

As its imposing walls disappeared behind the roofs of the houses in Hart Lane, satisfaction gripped him, and he tightened his hold on Susanna, sitting before him on his horse.

They turned onto Lower Thames, moving as fast as the crowds would allow, weaving their way through the throngs coming and going from the madness of Belin's Gate docks.

As they passed the docks, he looked into the mass of traders and merchants, to the place where he'd had to fight for his life, and wondered what had become of the bodies.

Knowing Belin's Gate, they had been picked clean of every useful item and either left in the gutter or tossed into the river.

He knew none here would speak against him. If he did not want the tedium and paperwork of the magistrates, he could avoid it. The men had been Wolsey's, and as such, Wolsey would want the matter dropped.

But two men had died, and he found himself unable to leave that thought alone.

No death was meaningless. He had never taken a life lightly, and since he'd met Susanna, killing weighed even heavier on him.

"What is it?" Susanna turned her head, her eyes solemn.

He cut a final glance at Belin's Gate. "Wolsey's men tried to stop me getting to the Tower with my writ."

"You had to fight them." She spoke quietly, and stroked her fingers over his own where they gripped the reins. "Did you kill any?"

He nodded, a quick dip of his head. "Two of them. The rest fled."

She leaned back into him, ran a light, comforting hand down his forearm.

They both had to do things they did not like in this affair. She as much as him.

She said nothing more, just continued to stroke him, and a heaviness he had not realized he'd been carrying lifted off him.

They were falling behind Kilburne, and he urged his horse faster, skirting carts and wagons struggling with the pitted, slick street.

At this rate, Harry and Peter Jack, and Harry's lads, would be at Durham House before they were.

Parker had given them word the moment they had left the Tower. He wanted eyes on the house. If Jean was to be believed, Fitzroy was in immediate danger.

Susanna was their only way in to get the boy, or Parker would have made sure she was somewhere safe.

"Will we tell Kilburne what is happening?" Susanna twisted her head back to speak to him, her cheek brushing against his throat.

He had missed her so much these last few days, but this close contact, the warmth and life in her, made his hands shake on the reins.

"He'll want to know how we know. We can hardly say we learned it from the assassin who killed his man."

"You could say your sources heard it on the street." She pressed back against him, as intent on physical contact as he.

"The danger in telling him is he will try to interfere. We are going to spirit the king's son from his protected home. And I don't want to take you back to the Tower. Both those things will not inspire trust in us."

"Could we not guard Fitzroy at Durham?"

Parker shook his head. "For all we know, the assassin has insinuated himself inside. Or has a helper within. And we have no control, and no authority, in Durham House. It is best to get Fitzroy out."

"We'll only be in trouble until we get Fitzroy to his father." She leant forward to balance herself as they moved over uneven ground.

"Yes." Parker conceded the point, but his tone was dry. "If his father has decided to return from his hunt."

THEY WERE LATE, AND SUSANNA LET KILBURNE STUMBLE OVER the apologies. Croke did not try to hide his annoyance.

"He cannot miss his lessons, and his hour with the bow is almost up."

"I think you will find the king would prefer his portrait

finished, lessons or no." Parker crossed his arms over his chest, and Susanna noticed Croke take a step back.

"Who are you . . . just a moment, aren't you the Keeper of the Palace of Westminster?"

"John Parker, at your service, Master Croke."

"What are you doing here?" Croke blinked at him, looking between the three of them with surprise.

"I am Mistress Horenbout's betrothed." He said no more than that, and Croke blinked again, as if not sure what that signified.

"Sir, the sooner I have my hour of work, the sooner you will have your pupil back at his lessons." Susanna smiled at Croke, and he rubbed his forehead.

"Certainly." He breathed out a pained sigh. "Certainly." He gestured to the stairs. "He is in the garden practicing."

Parker tensed beside her, and Susanna knew he was thinking how exposed Fitzroy would be in the garden. She gave a curtsy to Croke. "Let us go down to him."

To her dismay, Croke followed them down the stairs and out into the garden, perhaps determined to give them no more than an hour.

As they stepped out onto the lawn, Susanna was aware of Parker scanning the trees along the walls. The chances of an assassin choosing the very moment they arrived to make his move seemed unlikely. And yet, there were only a few days to go before the seventh, and what better chance for a quick kill and a quicker get away than from the river-side wall.

Croke passed them all, and made his way to Fitzroy, but Parker slowed to a stop, turned full circle, noting every part of the garden.

There were too many places to hide here. The assassin would not even need the help of an insider if he was good enough with a crossbow or bow. She could see too many deep shadows, and the thought of someone crouched amongst the branches, bow raised, made her fight a shiver. The skin on her neck pricked uncomfortably, and her whole body went tense, as if anticipating a bolt.

"What is it?" Kilburne had glanced at Parker, and stopped as well, his eyes narrow. "What is wrong?"

"Nothing, yet." Parker turned to him, and she could see him come to a decision. "Kilburne, I've had word someone means the little prince ill. The king plans to officially usher him into the Order of the Garter in a few days, and I hear there are plans to give him a number of titles and holdings a few days after that. The king will be all but declaring Fitzroy his heir."

Kilburne said nothing, but like Parker, he began looking for anything out of place in the garden.

Parker faced towards Fitzroy. "The way I hear it, a sum was offered for the boy's death, and most certainly someone would have decided the money is worth the risk."

"You don't know who?" Kilburne was looking at him, that gleam of steel she'd seen in him before coming through.

"If I did, I would not be standing here, putting Susanna in danger of a crossbow bolt, along with Fitzroy."

Parker began walking toward the little boy, who was aiming at the target once more. She followed, and Kilburne was forced to trot after them.

"What do you plan to do?"

"I don't think it safe to leave him here. Too much chance someone has paid a servant for access. This plan was hatched at least a few days ago, plenty of time for someone to have set the scene."

"We cannot simply take the child away without permission." Kilburne stopped again, his eyes wide.

"Perhaps you can't, but I will." Parker reached Croke, tapped his shoulder. "I have no time to be subtle. Your charge is in danger from an assassin, immediate danger. I need to take him away to safety."

She had expected Croke to be confused, but instead he cocked his head to the side, and she could see why he was considered an excellent tutor for the king's son. Intelligence gleamed from his eyes.

"So that is really why you're here. I've heard before you are sometimes the sharp end of the king's sword." He looked Parker up and down. "Danger from whom?"

"I have word of an assassination planned by someone high in the nobility. Someone who does not want to see the king raise his bastard son to the throne."

At his bluntness, Croke reeled back, but he recovered almost immediately. "I had wondered," he said softly, "how the king's plans would be taken by some."

"It is safe to say, not well."

Susanna reached out and touched Croke's sleeve. "I think we should get his lordship inside, at the least." She looked at the trees again. "It feels too open here."

"What is it?" Fitzroy had noticed them, and come over, his eyes on Parker, curious, and she could see, a little awestruck.

"We need to go within." Croke slipped a hand on his charge's shoulder, and began drawing him towards the house, but Fitzroy balked.

"No. I want a few more turns. I nearly hit the bull's eye, last time. I want to get it before I go in today."

Croke shook his head, and Fitzroy wrenched himself from out of his grasp.

At that moment, Susanna heard the high whistle of a bolt. It flew between Croke and the prince, and buried itself in the ground just beyond where they stood.

They both turned and looked at it dumbly.

Susanna lunged forward, grabbing up Fitzroy and spinning around, looking for a place to take cover. Perhaps their sudden arrival had forced the assassin's hand. Whoever lurked deep in the shadows must have realized the secret was out and there would be few or no other chances for a kill.

"To the house." Parker shouted, his sword raised.

The two guards who had been helping Fitzroy with his practice had their own swords raised, and so did Kilburne.

But against a crossbow, they were all helpless.

She ran, holding Fitzroy against her, so her body covered him completely from view.

He clung to her, his bow and arrow still in his grasp, his breathing fast and too shallow.

She looked over her shoulder and saw Parker moving backward toward her, still facing the way the bolt had come, but trying to act as a shield.

As she turned, she caught a glimpse of Kilburne doing the same. Stepping sideways to block them from the line of fire, his arms wide.

The whistle of a second bolt ripped the air from between the leaves of a huge oak in the corner of the garden and Kilburne cried out, his shout a scream of agony.

The shallow stairs up to the house were ahead. She wanted to turn, to run to Kilburne's aid. But she was holding Fitzroy close, his heart beating quick as a hare against her, and she forced her focus straight ahead, closed her ears to Kilburne and kept running.

CHAPTER 31

> They look on the desire of the bloodshed, even of beasts, as a mark of a mind that is already corrupted with cruelty, or that at least, by too frequent returns of so brutal a pleasure, must degenerate into it.
> *Utopia by Thomas More (translated by H. Morley)*

P arker angled himself between the shooter and Susanna for agonizing seconds, until she was through the door. As the wooden barrier slammed shut he ran to Kilburne, and saw the bolt had gone through his side.

He needed to get Maggie to see to this. Kilburne's chances of surviving a doctor were low.

"Take cover." Kilburne's eyes were overbright, and his face was far too pale.

"He was after Fitzroy, and Fitzroy is safely inside. Come my friend . . ." Parker bent to lift him. As he did, a third bolt flew over his head, and slashed through the large bush behind him in a rattle of branches.

Parker lifted his head, his eyes on the trees. The guards had started to creep toward the assassin with the first bolt, but since

Kilburne had been hit, they had dropped to the ground behind the hay bale that Fitzroy used as a target.

"Looks like he wants you as much as he wants Fitzroy." Kilburne coughed up the words.

Parker stood without answering, calling to the guards. "Get the captain inside. Carefully and gently."

Then he ran as fast as he could toward the oak tree where he thought the shooter perched.

Kilburne was right. The second bolt could just as easily have been meant for Parker, with Kilburne's timing unlucky. He had stepped into Parker's path just seconds before he was hit. And the third bolt had definitely been meant for him.

He was running out of time, every second he took to get to the tree was another second the assassin had to reload, and sweat dampened his hairline as he lengthened his stride.

Chasing a crossbowman down was either a bold move, or a foolish one. Depending on how fast you could run.

Parker heard someone swear, just ahead in the branches, and a bolt dropped to the ground.

He'd unnerved the man, running straight for him. He had expected people to duck and take cover, and now he was rattled.

Parker reached the tree and leaped for a branch, grabbing hold and using it to scrabble up the trunk.

The shooter gave a strangled cry, and by the time Parker'd reached the thick, sturdy branch the man had been using, he had scrambled along it to where it overhung the wall.

As the shooter dropped down, he looked back, and Parker caught a glimpse of his face, strong, sharp, panicked.

Parker got to his feet and ran, balancing along the branch in a half-crouch, and swung down after him.

But the shooter had thrown himself into a boat, was already moving downstream, his oars slapping the water in his haste to get away.

There was no handy boat for Parker to give chase, and he

bent, hands on knees, gasping for breath, watching the boat get further and further away.

Slowly, he became aware of someone standing just to the right of him, in the deep shadow of the wall. He turned his head, his knife already in his hand, and then relaxed again.

"When did you get here?"

Peter Jack stepped into the dappled light coming through the trees. "Just as he was rowing away."

Parker grunted in acknowledgement.

"Do you want to know who he is?" There was an edge of glee to Peter Jack's words.

Parker spun to face him, his head cocked to one side. He waited.

Peter Jack grinned. "That was Jules. The other French double agent working for de Praet. The one who has been hiding the flute player from Ghent."

Parker looked toward the water again, to where Jules and his boat were disappearing around the bend in the river. "Of course." He slipped his knife back into place. "The bastard who shot the bolt through my window."

THERE WAS A CRY FROM OUTSIDE, ON THE STRAND, AND Susanna held Fitzroy even tighter to her.

He flinched at the sound, clinging to her in the narrow hallway at the front of the house where they crouched out of sight. For a moment he allowed himself the comfort of a normal child, and then straightened, pulling himself free, still clutching his bow and arrow as if he had no need of protection.

Croke had been pacing the floor, but he went still when they heard the cry.

The guards moved toward the front door, swords ready, and Susanna noticed even Kilburne, weak though he was, lifted a little from where they'd lain him on the floor, and fumbled for his weapon.

"What is it?" Parker stepped through from a room at the back, and the guards turned, white-faced, until they realized who it was.

Susanna blinked away tears at the sight of him. Her last glimpse had been of him running straight for the shooter. She lifted a trembling hand to him, and he took it.

"How did you get past the locked door?" Croke stepped closer, and looked past him, as if expecting an attack at any moment.

"I got in through an open window. This place is not secure, although the assassin has gone for the moment."

"Someone cried out, in the street." Kilburne struggled to sit even higher, then gave up the fight and slumped back.

One of the guards looked out of a parted curtain, trying to see the road, but Parker motioned him back.

"My page and some boys who work for me are out there, watching the street for us." He opened the door a little way, and stepped out, closing it behind him.

He came back in almost immediately, with Harry on his heels.

"Someone got Will. He's been knocked down. He's breathing, but we can't wake him." Harry's gaze flicked around the room, noting Croke, his eyes going wide at the sight of Kilburne's blood-soaked doublet.

"When?" Parker tried to control his surprise, and an icy hand stroked its fingers down Susanna's spine.

"Right now."

"Then there's more than one of them. Peter Jack and I watched the shooter row off down the Thames. There's no way he's had time to double back and knock out Will."

"What do we do?" Croke looked at Parker.

"How many servants work here?"

"About twenty in all." Croke spoke automatically, then went still. "You think one of them . . ."

"I think it would be foolish to take the chance they are all trustworthy, and give a traitor an opportunity to get to Fitzroy. We need to get him out of this house."

It was only because she knew him so well that she saw the tension in him as he spoke of taking the prince out into the city.

"But guarding him in the open will be almost impossible." Kilburne's voice was getting weaker.

"Better to keep moving, to places they don't know. They've most likely been studying Durham House for days. It will be safer on the outside."

"I know where we can take him." Kilburne shifted uncomfortably from his place on the floor. They all turned their attention to him. "The Tower."

"Why not Bridewell?" Croke asked, "or Greenwich?"

Parker shook his head. "Whoever is behind this is at Bridewell, most likely, and with the king not in residence, Greenwich will not have the security we need to protect the prince."

The Tower. It was the last place she wanted to return to. Jean had still been there when they'd left, although she was sure the assassin had long since made his escape. It was hardly an excuse she could use with Kilburne, anyway.

Wolsey might still be there, and some of Kilburne's guards were in his control. It was not much, but she voiced it. "Wolsey is at the Tower."

Kilburne coughed. Breathed deep. "Wolsey is the prince's godfather. Whatever your feelings are of him personally, he would never harm Fitzroy."

Susanna nodded. Exchanged a quick look with Parker. She could see the same frustration in his eyes. To keep the prince safe, they would have to return to the one place she was not.

CHAPTER 32

> They would be both troubled and ashamed of a bloody victory over their enemies; and think it would be as foolish a purchase as to buy the most valuable goods at too high a rate. And in no victory do they glory so much as in that which is gained by dexterity and good conduct without bloodshed.
> *Utopia by Thomas More (translated by H. Morley)*

If only the river weren't in spring tide.

Parker looked out onto the Strand and grimaced at the heavy foot traffic.

But with the tide low, they would not get past the bridge, and Jules and his men would only need to wait for them to come in to dock and pick them off, one by one.

The river was out as a way to escape.

It had taken time for Peter Jack and Harry to bring Will inside. By now, Jules could have circled back and be waiting right outside Durham House again, along with whichever of his accomplices had hit Will.

If his helper was Jan Heyman, the musician would have more

than spying charges to worry about. Parker would see to it personally.

He glanced across the room.

Susanna had Will half-raised on her lap, holding a cup of water to his lips and letting him take little sips now that he had awakened.

Henry Fitzroy sat beside them, watching them in fascination, his grip white-knuckled on his small longbow.

"We need to go." The mellow light of afternoon filtered through the windows, and Kilburne looked too pale in its golden glow. He needed a healer as quickly as possible. Harry had already sent one of his lads to fetch Maggie in Parker's cart—if it was still in one piece from this afternoon's roadblock to stop Wolsey.

It was ironic the Hospital of the Savoy was just a short walk away, the next large building down from Durham House on the river banks.

But Parker knew for a fact the master of the Savoy was a surveyor to Wolsey, and there was no circumstance under which he'd put anyone connected to himself under the hospital's care.

Anyway, Kilburne looked too bad to move, and Will would be better off remaining still, as well. There was no doctor he would trust over Maggie, in any event.

"Do you want to take the prince's cart?" one of the guards asked, and Parker turned to him, considering the offer.

"Would you consent to act as decoys?" He looked from Croke to the guards, and they all nodded.

"If you take the cart, with a sack under some blankets to look like a boy, and ride as fast as you can away west, towards Green-wich, that may confuse them. They will be familiar with the three of you as the prince's companions by now. It would make sense that you would be the ones to spirit him away."

Croke paled at the implication, but he nodded again. "I would agree that is a good plan."

"Wear a leather jerkin under your cloak." Parker placed a

hand on his shoulder. "If we get the cart ready, we can open the gates and you can ride out at a gallop. Take them by surprise. I think it will serve to draw them off."

"And draw them out." Harry was at the other window, but he dropped the curtain to speak. There was a hard look in his eyes. He was angry about Will, and perhaps about Kilburne, too. Parker knew he'd grown to respect the captain during his time with Susanna in the Tower.

"And draw them out," Parker agreed. "But we cannot engage them now. Not until Fitzroy is safely in the Tower. What I would say is we get some of the lads to stay behind, see where they go. I am almost certain they will follow the cart, at least at first."

"And then what?" Harry lifted the curtain again, looking out into the street.

"And then we hunt them down."

"I'll stay here with Will and Captain Kilburne." Susanna spoke from her seat on the floor. "Someone needs to let Maggie in, and I don't trust the servants. Not if there's a chance one or more are in Jules's pay."

Parker stared at her. "I wouldn't leave you here for that very reason." He glanced back at the window. "They may decide to check inside the house if they realize the cart is a diversion. You won't be staying."

"I'll stay." Peter Jack had been quiet, leaning against the wall, and Parker knew he was almost asleep on his feet. He hadn't slept in over a day and night, and it was taking its toll. He was not up to a wild ride through the streets of London.

He nodded. "That's sensible." He held his hand out to Susanna, and she took it reluctantly. As he pulled her to her feet, he drew her against him, touched his lips to her ear. "You are too precious to me. I cannot let you out my sight now."

She sighed in acquiescence, but her eyes lingered on Will. "At least Maggie should already be en route."

Croke cleared his throat. "We will be off."

"Don't forget that leather jerkin." Parker let Susanna go. "Good luck."

Croke walked over to Fitzroy and bowed. "Good luck to you, your lordship. Heed Master Parker well. I know he is a great friend of your father's and will take care of you."

Fitzroy bowed back. "I will, sir." His gaze rested on Will and Kilburne a moment, and Parker knew he had realized this was no game. Croke had done a good job with the boy. He was thoughtful enough to understand others had been harmed helping him.

Perhaps Fitzroy on the throne would be no bad thing.

Croke gave an encouraging smile. "We will see each other soon." He exchanged a last look with Parker and left the room, with the guards following behind him.

"As soon as they leave the front gate, we leave by the side alley." Parker waited for Harry to drop the curtain and step away from the window. "And then we ride as if the demons of hell are at our heels."

❀

HARRY WAS ONLY A SLIGHTLY BETTER RIDER THAN SHE, BUT Susanna was grateful he was at the reins as they struggled to keep pace with Parker, who had Fitzroy tucked before him and covered over with his cloak.

The streets of London always carried danger, but now it seemed to her every small movement was an archer lifting a bow, or an assassin unsheathing his knife.

Their best defense was to keep moving forward at the bone rattling pace Parker had set.

Ahead, on their right, the Hospital of the Savoy loomed, and there was a collection of the wounded and ill loitering out the front.

It was easy to see how Jules and his men had easily kept watch on Durham House. There were so many people standing or sitting on the side of the road, they would not have stood out.

A man stepped into Parker's way on the road ahead, and Harry drew his knife as they closed the distance. Parker danced the horse around the man, but he moved to block the way again, reaching up to grab the reins.

He was filthy. His legs were covered in something dried and black, caked to his leggings, and as they came level with Parker the stink of it enveloped her. It could have been nightsoil just as easily as mud.

The man was shouting something unintelligible, and at last Parker drew his sword, smooth, clean and efficient.

"Let us pass." He lifted the sword to show he was armed and as a warning, but the man did not notice or did not care.

He made another grab for the reins, and Susanna saw Parker's face harden. She guessed this was not one of Jules's men, but Parker had had enough, and he was not prepared to take more of a risk than he already had. Fitzroy had been partly revealed by the horse's panicked movements—Susanna could see his blond head emerging from Parker's cloak—and if any of Jules's men were watching, the secret was out.

Parker's sword came down, and the flat of the blade struck the man's upper arm as he lifted it to make another grab at the horse's mouth.

He howled as if his arm had been sliced open, and Parker followed it through with a smack to the man's ear.

With a shriek, he toppled over and crawled away, and Parker moved on, sword slashing out as he went.

The crowd parted, and as they followed close on Parker's heels, Susanna locked gazes for a moment with a woman pressed up against the wooden fence along one part of the hospital front.

Her eyes were tired, worn through to her soul. No one would commission a portrait of such a woman, such a subject, but Susanna knew she would paint it. The raw exhaustion, the lack of any emotional shield, was as riveting as it was disturbing.

She stared, trying to memorize every detail, and at last, unnerved, the woman turned away, pressing her face into the wood.

The horse jerked to the side a little, and Susanna clutched at Harry's waist to find her balance, looking back at the woman a final time.

A tight, cold hand of fear gripped her neck. The woman was staring down the road, the way they had come, her mouth open, and Susanna twisted in the saddle to look behind her.

A man was standing in the middle of the road, crossbow raised.

"Danger. Behind us." Susanna grabbed hold of the ends of her cloak and lifted her arms out, creating wings of black wool that lifted and billowed in the late afternoon breeze.

She hoped the fabric blocked Parker and Fitzroy from view.

Parker turned back and she brought her arms in for a moment so he could see, then raised them out again.

They had been moving as fast as they could, before, but now Parker showed the crowds no mercy. He let out a cry that sent a shiver down her spine—a war cry that had a place on an ancient battlefield, and forced his mount into a canter, sword swinging left and right.

Harry followed tight behind, and Susanna wondered what the people leaping out of their path thought of the mad warrior with a child tucked up against his chest, and the dark horse, a Pegasus with wool wings spread wide, following behind him.

She braced herself for Jules's bolt through her back. Braced herself for him to rid himself of her meddling, but then they thundered over Strand Bridge, bore right with the curve of the road, and suddenly, the Savoy Hospital was no longer behind them.

They only had the whole of London to ride through to reach safety.

CHAPTER 33

> For it has often fallen out that many of them, and even the prince himself, have been betrayed, by those in whom they have trusted most;
> *Utopia by Thomas More (translated by H. Morley)*

"This way." The words were hissed from a darkened alley, and Parker lifted his sword in response.

"Wait."

He recognized the hand as it shot up in defense. Or rather, the rag-covered mitt.

"Gladys Goodnight?"

"Aye. In need o' the back alleys, Parker? I know every one in the city."

Parker nudged his horse into the alley, and Fitzroy clung tighter to him. The dingy passage stank, ripe with the choking smells of the latrine and rotting food. He sensed Harry behind him, and heard Susanna's choking gasp as the smell enveloped her.

They moved in deeper, to where the alley twisted left, so they could not be seen from the street.

"This your fancy lady?" Gladys peered up at Susanna, looking like a tiny, wizened crone from a folk tale, with her lined face and startling, sharp blue eyes.

Parker nodded, although he would never have described Susanna as fancy. Beautiful, yes, but she held no airs about herself. He turned to her. "Gladys and I are old acquaintances from Belin's Gate. She knows the back ways to the Tower."

"What're you in such a hurry to get there for, anyhow?" Gladys skittered back and forth in place, a strange dance of nerves. The slightest movement taken amiss, and she would disappear.

"The boy." Parker said nothing more, but Gladys stepped closer for a look at Fitzroy in the shadows and then jerked back as if struck by a snake.

"Well. You've certainly come up to quite a level, Parker. Quite a level. To be holding the likes of 'im afore you on a horse." For once, Gladys was completely still as she looked at Fitzroy. "'Course, the thing to do is for you to ride on without him. Give 'em someone to follow. I'll take the lad and your lady through to the gates of the Tower itself."

She was right. He didn't like that she was right, but that didn't change the facts. He didn't want to leave Susanna alone. But if he stayed with her, he was endangering them all.

Jules would be looking for them, and who knew how many he'd paid for this job. If he had been working with some of the spies and informers de Praet had cultivated before he'd been thrown out of London, he could have called on quite a number to help in this. They were already double agents to their own countries, what did they care about the life of an English prince?

Even if Jules didn't know he had Fitzroy, he knew it was a possibility. And if Parker took the main street now, he could lead them a merry chase while Gladys slipped her way like the tiny, invisible mouse she was, through the back alleys and streets of London.

He turned to Susanna and found her watching him, her eyes grave.

"I don't want you to . . ."

He raised a hand to his lips. He'd caught sight of Gladys, and she had flattened herself against the wall, her full concentration on the way they'd come in.

At last, he heard it, too. The sound of a footstep in the alley-way, the careful tread of someone wanting to make as little noise as possible.

His decision had been made for him.

He exchanged a quick glance with Harry and Harry swung down from the saddle as Parker lifted Fitzroy, still clutching his bow and arrow tight, up and over. Put him before Susanna on Kilburne's dark mare.

Harry took off his cloak, rolled it up, and tossed it to Parker.

He grabbed it, held it to his body and covered his own cloak over it, like he was cradling a child. Drew his sword with only the faintest song of steel.

As he lifted the blade, Susanna extended her hand, clamped it around his sword arm.

Her eyes glittered in the dim light filtering in through the narrow passageway.

He lifted his arm closer to his face, and bent his head. Kissed her fingers. Then he kicked his stirrups, flicked his reins.

He felt her grip tighten for a moment before she let go.

With a shout, he shot from their hiding place and turned the corner, surprising a tall, blond man with a crossbow just a few steps from where they stood.

Jules.

He slashed out with the blade, but the horse was moving too fast to be accurate. He only managed to strike the crossbow itself.

He had the satisfaction of feeling the blade bite into the wood, and then he was out the passageway, on the Strand, and he turned the horse right, heading straight for Temple Bar.

He heard a cry behind him, and glanced over his shoulder,

cloak billowing, to see Jules exploding from the alley, raising his bow.

Parker turned back, low over his horse's neck, and rode.

GLADYS MOVED QUICKLY, FLINCHING AS PARKER SHOT PAST her, and seemed to melt into the shadow ahead.

Harry grabbed the reins and led Kilburne's mare after her, but Susanna sensed him hesitate, unsure of where she'd gone, when they reached a split in the alleyway.

They stopped and for a moment heard nothing but the slap of a loose shutter above in the rising breeze.

Fitzroy sat still as a rabbit before her, but she could sense him trembling, and she put her arms around him, and held the pommel.

"What you waiting for?" Gladys's hiss from the darkness to the left made them all jerk. Harry moved towards her.

"Couldn't see you," he muttered, and Susanna thought she heard the old woman laugh.

"No one sees Gladys unless she wants them to."

Her route plunged them into passageways so narrow the horse grew nervous, and Susanna's boots scraped the walls on both sides.

Fitzroy was silent, pushing back against her, his arrow notched loosely in his bow. She lifted one hand from the pommel and gripped his waist, but he pushed it away.

More than once the buildings almost touched each other above them, and the way became pitch black, the dank smells almost overwhelming.

No one spoke, and she felt trapped in some waking nightmare, lulled into a half-wake state by the gloom and confusing twists and turns. She had no idea where they were.

She was jerked from her daze by Harry swearing softly, and she peered ahead. Light flowed in from a curve in the way ahead, the heavy, thick light of falling dusk, and with a jolt she realized they could soon be journeying in the night.

The prospect of being in this place with no light at all put her on the edge of panic.

"Do you see her?" They had not come across anyone since they started after Gladys, but Susanna whispered the question.

She'd had the sense more than once that eyes watched them from hidden places, and she had the same sensation, now.

Harry shook his head, and seemed to make up his mind to take the right curve, toward the light. The relief at his choice brought tears to her eyes.

And then the way was barred.

A man stepped as if from nowhere into their path, and Susanna wondered how long he'd been there, watching from the shadows. It certainly explained Gladys's disappearance. She was so attuned to the dangers of the alleys, so accustomed to looking out for only herself, she had probably gone to ground without a thought.

The man said nothing, but his eyes were eloquent enough. They flicked over Kilburne's mount, over Harry and herself, and Fitzroy, and at last Susanna saw a length of pipe in his hand. It looked like it had been smashed off a longer piece with a hammer, the top end buckled and rough, with sharp, jagged edges.

Harry drew his knife, and for the first time, the man showed a chink in his calm.

Harry looked like he'd been handling the weapon all his life, and the blade caught the light even in this gloomy alley.

But it didn't have the reach of the pipe, and the man swung his weapon in an opening play.

The reins went slack as Harry dropped them, and Susanna took them in. There was no place to turn, but Kilburne's horse, already nervous, sensed troubled and edged back.

Harry widened his stance. There would be no circling, no feinting, here. There wasn't the room.

Susanna extended her arm a little and flicked, and the blade Parker had returned to her dropped, cool and comforting, into her palm.

Fitzroy looked at her hand, and then up to her, his eyes wide with astonishment to see her suddenly wielding a knife.

She adjusted her hold on the knife into a throwing grasp, and waited for a clear target as Harry and their attacker edged closer.

As if a bell had been rung, they rushed each other. The attacker's pipe swung in a wide arc and Harry ducked under it and came up right in his face, knife raised.

His pipe useless with Harry so close, the man slammed his forehead into Harry's, but Harry saw the move just a moment before, and jerked back his head.

He grunted as he took the lesser hit and stabbed out wildly, landing a cut on the attacker's upper left chest and then danced back.

The man roared as the knife slashed him and clutched at the wound. Enraged, he swung the pipe, backhanded, and Harry dived straight at him again, slamming against his legs.

They both fell, the pipe flying from the attacker's hand. It chimed like a bell as it struck the stone of the alley floor.

"You little *turd*." The man raised himself up on his elbow, and Susanna could see the bloodlust in his eyes. He wanted to tear Harry apart. He struggled to rise, his hand groping backward to find his pipe.

He had been dangerous before, but now he was the injured bear, the enraged boar with arrows in his back. He got his legs under him and at last slapped his hand over the end of the pipe. Came up fast and swinging.

Harry was still down, vulnerable beneath him, scrabbling back so he would have room to stand. But before the attacker could lunge forward, he stopped dead. Lifted a hand to the arrow at the base of his throat, and made a strange, choking sound.

His eyes lifted to the horse, to Fitzroy, who was shaking like it was mid-winter before her, his hand still back and up from where he'd released the arrow.

The man collapsed back down, limp and silent, but as he struck the ground he began to writhe, grunting and gagging, his hands scrambling at his throat.

"Make it stop." Fitzroy put his hands over his ears. "Make it stop." His cry jerked Harry into movement, and he scrambled to his feet and struck, slicing the knife across the attacker's throat, from ear to ear.

The man let out a gurgle. His hands at last went limp, and he stared at Harry, eyes wide with surprise, blood pouring from his wound.

Harry took a step back, and his hands were shaking as he wiped his blade on their attacker's breeches. He breathed deeply, watching the blood spread in a pool beneath him.

She could hear nothing but the drip of water from a nearby drain and Harry's deep, stuttering breaths. They echoed the shivers of the boy before her.

Harry seemed to shake himself out, suddenly, and turned to them.

She could see his face at last and it was pale as he grabbed their attacker under the arms and pulled him around the corner he'd leapt from.

When he stepped back into the alley, Gladys was just behind him, appearing like a dark goblin from the shadows.

He sensed her, and spun with a shout, knife raised, until he saw who it was.

She cringed back, a look of shock on her face at what she saw in his. "Sorry."

Susanna wondered if her apology was for startling him, or abandoning them to their attacker.

Harry said nothing. He came back to the horse, took the reins and lifted his eyes to hers.

She held his gaze, her heart thumping in her chest. "Thank you."

He nodded. "I saw it done, once." He cleared his throat. "Never thought I'd have cause . . ."

"You protected us all, Harry." She spoke softly.

He looked down, to where his hands grasped the reins. There were smears of blood on his fingertips and he rubbed them on his breeches.

Fitzroy straightened, his back ramrod stiff after the shaking. "My father will reward you, page. You truly saved us from death."

Harry lifted his eyes from his hands, and looked straight at Fitzroy. "You saved me from death, too. I need no reward." He turned back to face Gladys. "Lead the way."

She gave a nod, like the bob of a robin on a branch.

"And if you do not warn me, next time," he called after her, and Susanna saw her stop. "I cannot say what I will do."

CHAPTER 34

> I can have no other notion of all the other govern-
> ments that I see or know, than that they are a
> conspiracy of the rich, who, on pretence of
> managing the public, only pursue their private ends,
> and devise all the ways and arts they can find out;
> first, that they may, without danger, preserve all
> that they have so ill-acquired, and then, that they
> may engage the poor to toil and labour for them at
> as low rates as possible, and oppress them as much
> as they please;
>
> *Utopia by Thomas More (translated by H. Morley)*

Jules had somehow gained a horse. Stolen, Parker had no doubt, from some unfortunate traveller.

They'd danced an elegant chase, through the arch of Temple Bar and onto Fleet Street, dodging people, carts and animals.

The closer they got to Bridewell, the more Parker sensed Jules pushing to gain ground. He would assume they were headed to the king's residence, and knew he would lose them the moment they rode through the gate.

It was time to draw the Frenchman off north or west—as it was, they were running parallel to the alleys. It was too close to Susanna for comfort.

At the Fleet Conduit, Parker veered left and took Shoe Lane, out to Old Bourne Rd and the fields north of London.

He risked a quick glance back and saw Jules slow a little, drawing on his reins while he tried to understand why Parker would head for the open fields, rather than the safety of Bridewell.

But Parker was all he had—the only lead—and when Parker looked back again, he was coming at a gallop.

Shoe Lane ended in an orchard with an arched gate at the far corner, and Parker raced through it, the smell of ripe apples crushed under hooves tickling his nose. He came out onto Old Bourne, and took the way left.

The road rose and fell as it followed the canal running beside it, and without warning Parker took a rise and came down amongst a dense herd of cows.

They were packed tight, caught between the canal and the wall, and Parker's curses served only to distress them. They shuffled closer to each other than before.

He couldn't get through. Not before Jules was upon him.

Parker looked back, saw Jules cresting the rise, and turned his mount to face him, his sword drawn.

Jules pulled hard on the reins, taking in the scene, and they eyed each other while their horses blew, sides heaving from the pace.

"Why did you take the boy out here?" Jules eyes were on the bundle tucked beneath his cloak, and Parker looked down at it, too.

He's almost forgotten about it, but saw he'd held Harry's rolled cloak carefully the whole way, as if it really were a child.

The subterfuge would not last long, however.

He would milk it while he could.

"There are just as many enemies in Bridewell as on the

streets. I do not know who commissioned you to kill the boy. But I do know he will be at Bridewell. I could have brought the boy into the presence of the one who wished him dead." Behind him, cows lowed and bumped his horse's haunches, and he felt his mount's vicious backward kick, felt the muscles bunching beneath him in distress. There was an overwhelming stink of mud and cow dung in the air.

"No one would try anything there, under the nose of the king." Jules turned his head and spat on the ground.

"You tried in Fitzroy's own home."

"You know that's different." Jules's hand went to his belt and he grabbed hold of his crossbow, lifting it in a smooth move, his eye going to the sight.

Parker threw the bundled cloak, and in reflex, Jules swung the bow in line with the throw, shot the bolt. It made the sound of a spade biting into mud as it pinned the bundle to the ground.

Jules stared at the cloak, mud-soaked and loose on the path, lifting at the corners in the mild breeze, the bolt through the middle, and then up at Parker, eyes hard.

He reached back for another bolt, fury making his hand shake, but Parker had his knife ready. Threw.

Even though Jules flinched left, he was too late. The knife didn't go through his throat, as Parker intended, but buried itself just above his right collarbone.

His cry of pain echoed off the water in the canal, off the high wall on the other side, and his bolts dropped with a thud into the damp earth of the path.

Jules turned his horse, dancing it around to face the other way, urging it back down the path they had come. His face was white with pain, the knife still sticking from his shoulder.

Parker drew his sword and charged after him. He could not allow Jules too much distance, in case he somehow found out which way Susanna had gone.

There was a shout beside him, making his horse rear again,

and Parker caught sight of the open-mouthed astonishment of the cowherd before at last they surged forward.

They were coming back past Shoe Lane, and Parker's hope that Jules would ignore it, would continue along Old Bourne, keeping to the outskirts of London, died as he turned his mount through the arch.

Whatever happened, Parker could only follow now, and keep Jules in sight. As helpless to determine the route they travelled as Jules had been before.

GLADYS LOOKED STRAIGHT AHEAD AT THE CAUSEWAY TO THE Middle Tower, with its soaring height and arched entrance, and vibrated with fear.

"Our thanks, Mistress Goodnight, for your help." It felt wrong addressing her from atop Kilburne's horse, but Susanna was sure any sudden move to dismount would send Gladys skittering into the shadows.

"Our sincere thanks." It was Fitzroy's first words since the alley, and it was well done, humble and honest.

"Aye. You saved us." Harry turned to her and gave her a nod.

The woman dipped her head, her eyes darting, and Susanna withdrew a coin from her pouch. "For your trouble." She held it out, and Gladys took it so fast and light, one moment it lay on her palm, the next it was gone.

And then, in the blink of an eye, so was Gladys herself.

They all looked toward the Tower, white and soaring. The dusk sky seemed huge, endless, after so long in the dark, narrow passages of the back alleys.

The stink of the king's menagerie drifted across the causeway to her, musky and rank, and Susanna heard the low, throbbing growl of a lion, like a warning to stay away.

She was not surprised they were all unwilling to move forward. It felt wrong, completely wrong, to be returning to the one place she would like never to go again. And they would need to move soon. The curfew hour within the Tower was surely approaching.

"I hope Master Croke is safe." Fitzroy's voice was small, more like that of the child he was.

"I hope so, too." It was the most honest thing she could say. She thought of Parker, and was suddenly in need of a deep breath.

"State your business."

Susanna realized two guards had noticed them blocking the way to the causeway, and were watching them from the other end of it.

"Captain Kilburne sent us." It was the truth, and she could not think of anything less complicated than that. She nudged the horse with her knees, and it began walking forward. Harry exchanged a quick look with her and took hold of the bridle again.

They crossed without any hurry, as reluctantly as condemned prisoners.

The guards moved back, letting them step off the causeway, and in the last sliver of daylight, Susanna recognized one of them as Kilburne's second-in-command, Lewis, now demoted, it seemed, to gate duty.

Because of her.

He stepped closer, and looked up at her, his face hard. Fitzroy shrank closer to her within the cloak, sensing his hostility.

"I would speak urgently to the Constable." She looked down at Lewis, relishing the advantage of height. "Your captain sent me with a message for him."

Another two guards had joined Lewis and his companion, and Lewis looked sidelong at them, agitated. "How can we be sure of that?"

She caught his gaze, and she flinched at the anger in his eyes. This man would bring her down if he could. He blamed her for his fall.

"You can be sure that by letting me in, you will for once be serving the wishes of both your masters."

Lewis flinched at her direct mention of his betrayal of Kilburne, and the other guards shifted uneasily. "You go too far."

Harry, tired of waiting, tried their luck by simply walking forward, and Lewis blocked their way with his hand to his sword.

As Harry was forced to a halt, Susanna fingered the king's ring, still within her sleeve. She may need its power yet.

She would never have believed she would be fighting to get within the Tower. That instead of forcing her in, the guards were denying her access. The irony pressed down on her, like the shadows from the Tower wall.

"We are pursued by assassins," Susanna was loathe to say even this much, the words scratching her throat as she spoke them. "We need the safety of the Tower."

Lewis's eyes darted behind her, to the darkening road and buildings behind them. "Assassins?" At last he moved aside as if to let them pass.

"At long bloody last," Harry muttered as he started forward. "They could have shot us six times over, in the time you took—"

Lewis raised a hand and struck out at Harry's head, but Harry's arm came up to block. They stood poised against each other, Harry's forearm raised high, Lewis's mouth twisted in temper.

Susanna reached her hand into her sleeve, and began to work the King's ring loose.

THEY HAD COME TO A PARTING OF WAYS.

Parker could tell Jules was merely trying to stay ahead of him. He had no clear destination in mind. He did not want to lead Parker to his home, and he had no way of knowing where Susanna had taken Fitzroy.

Two carts had crashed together up ahead, just past St. Paul's

Church Yard, and the chaos and blockage to the traffic forced Jules to turn up a narrow side street, or turn back to face Parker.

Parker followed him, suddenly weary to his bones. The lives of Wolsey's two men weighed heavy on him again, as he faced what he might have to do up ahead.

He knew these streets well. Jules had trapped himself in a dead-end.

"Are you laughing to yourself, Englishman?" Jules had taken the alley all the way to the wall that ended it, and turned his horse to face Parker. He held his crossbow like a club. The place where Parker's knife had struck him was dark and crusted with blood through his clothes, and his lips were thin with pain.

"No." The stark truth of his answer stripped some of the bravado from Jules's face.

"You don't give up. Why don't you give up?" Jules did not seem to expect an answer, but Parker gave it to him, anyway.

"You threatened my betrothed. If you had not shot at her, had her imprisoned, hounded her, I would have left you alone."

"This is because of the woman?" Jules's mouth gaped. "The artist?"

Parker met his gaze and did not look away.

"*Encroyable. La femme.*" Jules closed his eyes. "I promise to leave her alone now."

"You seem to have moved on to other, more lucrative pursuits. Does the emperor not pay you enough?"

Jules gripped his saddle. "No. He hasn't paid us at all since de Praet was kicked out of England. When de Praet was here, he made sure we got our money, but these new ambassadors?" Jules spat on the ground. "They couldn't find their arse with both hands. And that de la Sauch, he looked at us as if we were something unpleasant under his boot. This private job was just what we needed to stay afloat."

"Why are you still working for the emperor, then?" Parker asked.

"We had a letter from de Praet, promising he would get de la

Sauch to pay us. And then your woman's brother arrived. He has too many loyalties, that one. Margaret of Austria, de Praet, his sister. He was supposed to meet us at the docks with details of the letter the emperor's aunt had given him, but we missed him, and then Jan Heyman wasn't in his rooms when Horenbout came calling on his way to his sister. By the time he'd seen her, he'd taken fright and given her the missive. We had no choice but to try to shut him down anyway we could."

"He took fright because you tried to kill her through the window of my study."

Jules stared at him. "He hadn't given it to her yet? Before I shot?"

So many things fell into place for Parker. "Shooting at her forced him to give it to her. He would have done what you asked, said nothing, betrayed Margaret in favor of the emperor, but once he thought you were double-crossing him, trying to kill him and his sister anyway, he did the only thing he could think of to save her. He gave her the missive so she could tell the queen. He thought once the damage was done you would no longer have a reason to see her dead."

"I wasn't shooting at her," Jules said. "I was shooting at him."

Parker let a smile twist his lips. "No. You were shooting at me."

Jules swore. "I wondered why Renard looked so guilty. He was supposed to tell me if anyone else came into the house after Horenbout. That's probably why I haven't seen the bastard in two days."

Parker titled his head to the side. "You haven't seen Renard for a few days because an assassin, sent by the French king, killed him."

Now Jules truly went white. "Jean? Jean knows we are in de Praet's pay? My king knows?"

Parker said nothing, and Jules lowered the crossbow to the saddle, his head bowed. "I saw Jean just a few days ago. He couldn't have known then that I was reporting to de Praet. I told him—" He lifted his head sharply.

"Yes, Jean was kind enough to pass on that someone was looking for an assassin to kill the king's son."

"This is how you knew? Jean . . ." He could not get the words out, forced himself to take a deep breath. "And how is it the assassin for the French Crown tells you these things?"

Parker said nothing.

"It does not matter. I'm finished in London. If you know my secrets, I'm sure the cardinal will know soon enough, too, and it won't be safe for me here any more. I will truly leave your woman alone, sir."

Parker narrowed his eyes. "Do you think that's the end of it? That I will let you go now? You tried to kill the king's son."

Jules's stolen horse moved restlessly beneath him, and he lifted the crossbow again. "No. I suppose you will want to take me."

The Frenchman readied himself to make a move, and Parker lifted the sword he had held ever since the chase began. It seemed to weigh more than it should.

Jules gave a cry and forced his horse into a canter, charging Parker down like they were taking a turn at the lists.

There would just be enough room for the two to come abreast, but Parker tried to block the way by angling his mount to the middle of the alley.

He braced himself for the impact, knowing as his arm came up and across he was only going to strike with the flat. If he could knock the Frenchman down, he could take him prisoner. Let the Tower deal with him.

He wanted no more blood on his hands in this matter.

As he swung the blade, he realized Jules was no longer sitting in the saddle, that in the short run from the end of the alley he had slipped his feet from the stirrups and was balancing in a crouch on the horse's back. A moment before his horse ran into

Parker's, he jumped, throwing his crossbow at Parker's face as he cleared his horse's head in a headlong dive.

The horses clashed, flicking their heads back, screaming in agitation, their hooves a thunder on the cobbles.

Parker held on to his saddle, twisting to look behind him.

Jules had landed badly, tumbling to a halt and then rising awkwardly, holding his leg with one hand, the other covering the place where Parker had stabbed him. He turned the corner at a limping run, and was gone.

Parker called softly to the horses, soothing them, stroking his mount's neck to calm it. His cheek stung where Jules's bow had clipped him.

And somehow, he could no longer find the energy to care that the Frenchman had managed to escape.

He turned his horse around, and headed straight for the Tower.

CHAPTER 35

> It is the fear of want that makes any of the whole race of animals either greedy or ravenous; but, besides fear, there is in man a pride that makes him fancy it a particular glory to excel others in pomp and excess;
>
> *Utopia by Thomas More (translated by H. Morley)*

"Mistress." The call from within the Tower grounds swung every head in that direction.

It was Eric. He was running towards them, where they stood by the Gate, but he slowed and then came to an uncertain halt just below the portcullis at the sight of the guards blocking their way.

His appearance created a subtle shift in the tension. Eric being Eric, he had befriended most of the guards.

"Who is that beneath your cloak then?" Lewis asked, stepping back from Harry in the sudden silence. "I thought it were him." He jerked his head towards Eric.

Susanna was loath to give him any information, but they needed the safety of the Tower. The king's ring lay heavy and loose on her middle finger, turned inwards until—if—she had need of it. "It is the king's son, Henry Fitzroy."

Lewis cocked his head. "What do you take me for, mistress? The king doesn't trust traitors with his only son."

She closed her eyes, sat taller in the saddle. "Fetch the Constable, if you please. I'll speak to him, and no other." Susanna tried to force down her agitation, but her voice trembled as she spoke. If they were turned away, or if she were taken within, and Harry and Fitzroy left outside—it was unthinkable.

"They would deny us the safety of my father's Tower?" Fitzroy looked at her in astonishment.

"It seems they are considering it." Harry stood back and looked down the causeway. "If we're forced away, who knows who will be waiting for us?"

The matter-of-fact talk between them made the guards more uncomfortable still. One of them called to a man amongst the small crowd of guards gathered to watch the spectacle, standing near Eric, just within the portcullis.

After a brief word, the man turned and disappeared into the darkness. Susanna was glad it was not Lewis who had sent him. Less chance of the cardinal being summoned, if he were still within.

Eric caught her eye and then turned as well, and disappeared after him.

The guards in the tight crowd muttered amongst themselves, and Susanna had the sense one, at least, was watching her. She looked up, and her heart stumbled in her chest.

Jean looked back at her from amongst the men, his face unreadable.

Had he been trapped within all day? The way he eyed the road beyond told her he had, and he was thinking of a way to use this as a means to escape.

She had wanted to warn Kilburne of the danger of his being here, but she had not, for her own sake, and for Parker's and everyone who depended on him. But by doing so, she may have risked Fitzroy's life.

Desperate, needing to think, she nudged the horse around, so it faced back the way they had come, as if she were staring into the growing darkness beyond, looking for signs of danger.

It put her back to Jean, put her body between Fitzroy and any weapon Jean may have to hand.

The movement startled the guards, and one lunged for the reins. Kilburne's mount flinched, nervous, hungry and ready for its stables.

A few of the guards stepped forward to assist.

"I see someone out there."

She was not sure if it were Jean who called out, but three men ran down the road a little way. Atop the dancing, panicked horse, Susanna saw one of them turn to look back, caught the flash of a smile from under a helmet.

They disappeared into the dark with the sound of running feet.

Now all Susanna wanted was to turn the horse round again, get herself between Fitzroy and Jean, standing somewhere in the darkness, with an easy escape.

Better yet, she would like the thick, pale walls of the Tower between them.

She could only hope Jean did not want the fuss that would come with a royal assassination. That he was content to take one of the largest diamonds in the world and run.

THREE GUARDS APPROACHED HIM, WEAPONS OUT, AS HE CAME through the Bulwark gate, and Parker threw back his robe to show his chain of office.

They stopped, and touched their hats, and then one of the guards continued past him.

"I'll check Petty Wales," he called.

The way he pronounced it, as it most likely was originally pronounced—Petit Wales—made Parker whip his head around to follow the man's progress out the Bulwark gate.

Jean.

The assassin didn't turn around and the night swallowed him from sight.

Parker knew, even if he raced to follow the Frenchman, he would be nowhere to be found. He had most likely been looking for a chance to escape the Tower all day, and he would not waste it.

He urged his mount forward, trailing Jules's mare behind him. He'd been unwilling to abandon the horse in the alleyway.

Ahead, he saw a tight knot of people at the Middle Tower gate. Guards on one side, and could that be—?

"Susanna!" He urged the horse faster.

"Parker." She fought Kilburne's horse around to face him, and her smile, her delight at the sight of him, made it difficult for him to breathe. Fitzroy sat before her, his face pale against the dark wool of her cloak.

When he reached her, even though her horse danced and shied, he hooked an arm around her and for a sweet moment felt the soft press of her body as she leaned against him, felt the warmth and life of her.

With an angry snort, Kilburne's horse wrenched them apart.

He caught a glimpse of Harry, standing to the side. Something in the way he stood, the set of his face, chilled Parker.

Their trip had not been easy.

"What is this? What is the delay?" Parker frowned down at the guards.

"They will not let us in." Fitzroy spoke, his words clear and accusing.

"It is near curfew. And the Constable has instructed me to tell you that your woman is no longer to be confined here, by order of the king." The guard's words oozed spite.

Susanna gasped, staring at the guard who had spoken. "You could have told me at the start, Lewis. You accused me of being a traitor, even though you knew already the king had dismissed the charges." She turned Kilburne's mount around again. "Let us be off. We will find no welcome or safety here."

Parker caught a glimpse of someone running across the drawbridge to them, and Eric darted into the light thrown by the torches.

He stopped when he saw Parker, and smiled almost as widely as Susanna had when she'd seen him. "Sir." The word left him like a relieved sigh.

"Did they fetch the Constable?" Harry asked.

Eric shook his head. "He is dining with the cardinal, and would not be disturbed."

"Wolsey is here?" Parker thought the cardinal would be long gone. But his presence changed things. He would not stay in the Tower with Wolsey lurking. The cardinal had too much power here.

"We're off?" Susanna asked, her face tense with the effort of holding back Kilburne's horse.

Parker gave a nod. "You and Eric take the extra horse," he said to Harry, jerking his head back at Jules's mount.

"Where will we go?" Fitzroy watched him with wide eyes, but Parker did not answer.

He would not give any hint of their direction to the guards standing around them. It was not a question of whether one of them may be in Wolsey's pay, only how many.

While he waited for Harry to swing up into the saddle and haul Eric up before him, he took Fitzroy from Susanna, leaning across to lift the boy up and tuck him under his cloak.

"Let's go." He wheeled about, and took the causeway at a canter, wanting them to have a good speed by the time they exited by the Bulwark gate, in case Jean or Jules or some other threat waited for them there.

Behind them, he could hear the pounding of feet, the shout

of voices, and he turned to look. Saw Wolsey and the Constable standing by the Middle Tower, fighting for breath, staring after them as they took the king's only son into the darkness.

CHAPTER 36

> The hardest point of all is, what to do with England; a treaty of peace is to be set on foot, and, if their alliance is not to be depended on, yet it is to be made as firm as possible, and they are to be called friends, but suspected as enemies
>
> *Utopia by Thomas More (translated by H. Morley)*

P arker held his arms out to Susanna, catching her as she dismounted. She slid down his chest, breathing in his scent of horse and leather, and came to rest in his arms. She did not want to move.

They stood in the courtyard at Bridewell Palace, though, and she moved back at last.

Harry and Eric had dismounted as well, and were grabbing the horses by their bridles and leading them to the stables.

Fitzroy stood, uncertain and lost in the massive space. "Where do we go now, sir?"

"Within. I need guards around us, until I can find your father." Parker stepped close to him, and knelt on one knee. "We will make sure you are safe, my lord."

The courtyard was almost completely empty at this late hour, but somewhere outside the palace walls Susanna could hear the thunder of hooves. Not just one or two horses, but a cavalcade.

Parker rose, sword drawn, and Harry and Eric came running out of the stables, followed by some of the stablehands.

She braced as the noise became a roar of iron-clad hooves on cobbles, and what looked like the king's hunt came bursting into the yard.

The king was in the lead, his face set white, his eyes dark pools of fear and fatigue.

"Your Majesty." Parker bowed in relief, and Susanna saw he had blocked Fitzroy completely with his body. The boy stood behind him, unnoticed.

"Parker. I went from my hunt to Greenwich for the night, and Master Croke was there. He told me—" Henry swallowed convulsively. "I have sent a guard to the Tower. Croke told me you were taking Fitzroy there."

"They wouldn't let us in there, Father." Fitzroy stepped from behind Parker. "But I am safe."

"Wouldn't let you in?" Henry leaped from his horse and scooped the boy in his arms. "You are well?"

"Aye. Master Parker and his lady and pages risked their lives for me today. Many times over."

Henry looked over the boy's head, and caught Susanna's eye. She hastily lowered her gaze.

"I would like to hear the story." He swung Fitzroy up in his arms and moved towards the doors. "Parker, bring your lady and your pages. I would know who threatens my son."

Parker sheathed his sword again, and held his arm to Susanna and she took it, glancing back to make sure Harry and Eric followed.

The rest of the king's party began to dismount, and the courtyard echoed with noise behind them. It was a relief to step into the quiet hall of the palace.

"My chambers, just us." Henry led the way, his servants scurrying ahead to light the sconces and open doors.

At last they were in Henry's private quarters, and he sank into a chair near the fire in his study, and drew Fitzroy onto his lap.

"What is this, Parker?" Henry shook his head. "This comes from nowhere."

Parker rubbed his chin and nodded in acknowledgement. "I was given the information this afternoon, and went straight to Durham House. Just in time, too. The attempt was made no more than a half hour after I arrived."

"Croke told me. He told me you acted with great courage and that one of the Tower guards was severely injured."

"Captain Kilburne. He was there to escort my lady to her appointment, to paint his lordship. He was struck by a bolt while blocking Master Fitzroy with his body."

"Croke also told me you carried my boy yourself, mistress, covering his body with your own as you ran." Henry was watching her, his eyes unreadable. Given their last conversation, the way he had deliberately hurt her, threatened her, she could not know what he was thinking now. She merely bowed her head and murmured assent.

"She held me on the horse, she drew a knife to protect us." Fitzroy's words were muffled, exhaustion seeping into his voice. "And Master Parker." The eyes he lifted to Parker were full of hero-worship. "He drew them off, using himself as bait, and then he came for us at the Tower, like a dark knight from a story."

"What is this about denying you entrance there?" Henry's voice shook a little, and Susanna realized it was not relief at having his boy, but rage.

"The cardinal had no proof of Susanna's treason by nightfall, and Susanna was no longer a prisoner in the Tower. They refused her entry and did not believe her when she said they were pursued by assassins and that she had Master Fitzroy with her." Parker crossed his arms over his chest.

"Did they not call for Wolsey? I am told he is still at the Tower."

"He was dining with the Constable and would not be disturbed." Eric spoke, daring and cheeky in the circumstances.

"Who was behind this, Parker?" Henry frowned at Eric as he spoke, and if trying to remember why he was there.

Susanna wondered how much Parker would say. How much would be dangerous to Lucas. "Some foreign spies, sir. Turned loose by their master and without funds. They were approached by someone at this court. Took the job for want of the money."

"Who at court?" Henry was very still.

Parker shook his head. "I do not know. And the spies are all dead, or disappeared now. I deemed Fitzroy's safety more important than running them down."

"Aye." Henry rubbed a hand through Fitzroy's hair. "You chose wisely." He set Fitzroy off his lap and stood. "You are all commended for your help. Parker, will you take Fitzroy to a bedchamber, and make sure he has an appropriate guard? Master Croke was only just behind me, and should be arriving soon."

Parker nodded, and stood back for Susanna to leave the room before him.

Henry shook his head. "I would speak with Mistress Horenbout alone."

Parker bowed and caught her eye. She shared a look with him, and he took Fitzroy by the hand, led him out followed by Eric and Harry.

Susanna waited, head bowed, until the door swung shut behind them.

"You have me at a disadvantage, mistress." The king sat again beside the fire. "I recall our last meeting was not amicable. And yet, I am now deeply in your debt."

She said nothing.

"What have you to say?"

"You owe me nothing for helping to save Fitzroy. As it is, I bought the information on the plans for his assassination with something of yours. And what I risked of my life for him, I did freely, for him alone. Not to create a debt of obligation from you." Her voice shook as she spoke. She did not know when she'd decided to tell Henry about the Mirror. But now was the time, if there ever was to be a time. Now, while the flush of happiness at his son's safety was strongest.

"It was you who discovered the plan to kill Fitzroy?"

"Aye." She drew out the letter Jean had given her and past it to him. "The French assassin who tried to steal the Mirror of Naples in March tracked me down to the Tower. Offered what he knew of the plan in exchange for the whereabouts of the Mirror."

"And you told him." Henry's voice was flat as he read the short missive.

"I thought you would gladly exchange the Mirror for information that could help to save your son, Your Majesty." She had never been so daring.

There was a startled silence. "You are right. Fitzroy is my male heir. He is beyond the price of diamonds."

"If it would make it easier for you to accept, the Frenchman told me he does not plan to return the Mirror to King Francis. He plans to have it cut down and sold, for his personal purse."

She watched Henry from the corner of her eye, saw him absently drum his fingers on the arm of his chair. "That does make it easier. I need not inform anyone of its disappearance. The French will not officially have it back. There is no loss of face."

She stood quietly, waiting for her dismissal, her hands curled into fists. She could feel the gem of the King's ring pressing into her palm.

Henry stood. "Take your leave, knowing I will not speak against your betrothal again. And there will be no more slurs against your loyalty. From Wolsey or anyone else."

She dipped in curtsy and made to go.

"One last thing."

She turned with her hand on the door.

"I bade the queen show me the likeness you made of my

daughter. Make sure you finish that painting of Fitzroy in time for his acceptance into the Order of the Garter. And make sure it is just as good."

She nodded. Opened the door.

"No."

She paused again.

"Make sure it is better."

CHAPTER 37

A prince ought to take more care of his people's happiness than of his own, as a shepherd is to take more care of his flock than of himself.

Utopia by Thomas More (translated by H. Morley)

"Norfolk." Parker closed the door of Fitzroy's private chambers and stepped into the passage, his body blocking the way. He should not be surprised that Norfolk had the nerve to come here. To see for himself whether his plan to kill Fitzroy had come to nothing.

"I hear of great escapades, Parker. Of rides through the streets of London, with the king's son beneath your cloak."

"And I hear of French spies accepting a job to kill the king's son from a nobleman of this court, and have someone who saw one of those spies visit a particular nobleman's house during the negotiations."

Norfolk drew back, his head jerking as if Parker had slapped him with his glove. "And what have you done with what you have heard?"

"I have only my informant's word on where the spy went. But

I will try to find proof of that nobleman's identity, and then, of course, I will take all I know to the king."

"Of course." Norfolk took a step back. "Of course you will." His lips formed a thin, bitter line. "You know, it would serve me well to have you killed Parker. You are nothing but a thorn in my side."

"I might say the same." Parker's gaze flicked over Norfolk's shoulder, saw the two guards who had helped him at Durham House coming down the corridor.

He accepted their salute, and felt a lift of tension. These two, at least, could be trusted. "No one comes in without Master Croke's approval. And you escort his lordship wherever he may go, within the palace or without."

They nodded their agreement and took up place, hard-eyed, before the door.

"You might take this advice," Parker said as he and Norfolk walked away. "If any accident should befall Fitzroy, I will go to the king with your name, whether I have conclusive proof, or not."

"He would not believe it." Norfolk barked out a laugh, but Parker could smell the stink of his fear, sharp and sour.

Parker stepped away from him, turned back to the king's rooms to find Susanna. "Perhaps he won't." He shrugged. "It's a chance I'll take to bring you down."

As he walked away, the spot between his shoulders twitched. If Norfolk could, his dagger would be buried there. To the hilt.

He only regretted there was almost no hope of connecting Norfolk to the assassination attempt. The word of a street boy against the Duke of Norfolk would never stand. And he was sure none of the spies had been foolish enough to remain in London. They were long gone now.

And once again, Norfolk weaseled himself free.

Susanna closed the door behind her and stared at it.

"King got your tongue?"

She choked back a scream and spun round. Saw Will Somers leaning against the passage wall. She lifted a hand to her heart and took a deep breath. "That was not kind."

"I am not kind. Or so they say." He lifted a shoulder.

"I say they are wrong." She slipped the ring from her finger, and held it out. "And I thank you. I did not need to use it, but there were many occasions on which it would have saved me, had fate not been on my side."

"Ah. Fate or your own cleverness, mistress? I think it would be hard to tell." He took it from her with a smile, and it disappeared into a pocket. No doubt later he would slip it back where he had found it, and no one would be the wiser. Except for her. He had risked a great deal for her.

"Why do you help me?"

"I would say that it is merely a whim, but the truth of it is—"

"Susanna?"

Parker was suddenly standing behind the King's Fool, almost invisible in his dark clothes in the gloom.

She held Somers' gaze. "The truth of it is?"

"Nothing. Nothing that cannot wait for another day." He turned to Parker and bowed. "My congratulations on a rescue of great daring, sir. You are flying high in the king's favor now."

"That could change in a moment, as you know." Parker watched Somers with a strange look in his eyes. "But it would take a lot for you to be out of favor with me, Fool. I am in your debt for the aid you leant us."

"I ask you but one thing, regarding this esteem in which you hold me, and the deed itself." Somers backed down the passageway.

"And what is that?"

"Do not tell anyone of it." The Fool laughed, a high, mocking sound. "It would quite ruin me."

CHAPTER 38

> Another proposes the gaining of the Emperor by
> money, which is omnipotent with him;
> *Utopia by Thomas More (translated by H. Morley)*

"Lucas?" Susanna slid down from Parker's horse, and looked from her brother, loading his bags into a cart at the front of the house, to Parker. Parker said nothing, urging his horse round to the stables, giving her a moment alone with him.

"Your boys told me you were safe, and pardoned." He placed another trunk in the back of the cart with care. His head was bound, neat and tight, and Susanna knew Maggie must have been round to dress his injury.

"Where are you going?" She looked from the bags to him to the lamp-holding carter, waiting patiently on the driving bench, and then stepped in close, put her arms around him. "I was so worried about you, about your head."

He moved back, disentangling himself from her embrace. "Your betrothed doesn't share your concern." He spoke without bitterness.

"Parker told me how you tried to save me. What you risked

by giving me that missive." She paused and then looked straight at him. "What made you go to work for Uncle Louis?"

She would never understand that. Why would he risk everything for Louis de Praet?

"He made it sound like an adventure. A lucrative adventure." Lucas looked away, at the cart horse, blowing its impatience. "Then Margaret gave me that letter and I made the mistake of not just sending word to Uncle Louis, but Heyman, as well.

"Uncle Louis asked me to keep up correspondence with him, and as we had been friends, it was easy to do. No one on either side looked twice at the letters he sent, but they were written in pre-arranged code, and I passed his information on the English court along.

"If I had not sent that letter to Heyman before I left, telling him what Margaret wanted me to do, thinking myself so useful, I would never have caused this trouble. I didn't know the lengths Heyman would go to to keep that letter out of Queen Katherine's hands." He rubbed his forehead.

"It's all right. By chance, this trouble uncovered another plot, to kill the king's son, Henry Fitzroy. It saved his life."

Lucas looked up at that. "Then I am glad some good came of it." He lifted a satchel. "I am going home, Susanna. I am sure you will see us all back here, Father and Mother and I, but later this year. I need to cut my ties with Uncle Louis, and I need to help Father pack up his *atelier*. If he truly wishes to come here, there is much to do before he can leave."

She nodded. "I might not wait for your return to marry."

He accepted that with a nod. "Do not expect Mother to be happy with that. But I understand. Your betrothed is a better protector than Father or I have ever been." Lucas leaned forward and kissed her on both cheeks.

"Going?" Parker was suddenly beside her. She had wondered what was taking him so long but now she wondered how long he had been listening.

"You will be pleased to know the answer is yes." Lucas bowed formally. "My apologies, sir. I have not been the best of guests."

"No." Parker shifted, as if relenting. "I spoke with de Praet's spies. They were acting of their own accord, not under his orders. Your life should not be in danger."

"My thanks for that," Lucas said. "Did you ever find Heyman?"

Parker shook his head. "He is under suspicion of conspiring to kill the king's son, so if I were you, I would not associate with him any more. And I am convinced he is the one who struck you on the head."

Lucas gave a slow nod. "I would like to think not, but I will be wary of him. He may have fled back to Ghent." He put out an arm and hugged Susanna awkwardly. "Farewell." Then, with a look that was pure Lucas, he swung himself up next to the driver. "Don't get too comfortable in my job."

As she stood looking after him, disappearing down the lane with his back to her, she realized her hands were tight-clenched fists.

THE KNOCK WAS CAUTIOUS. RESPECTFUL.

Parker glanced at Susanna and she looked towards the door in dismay.

They had gone to Maggie's house before going to bed last night, checking on Kilburne and Will, and it had been well after the bells of St. Michael's had rung matins before they had gone to sleep.

Will was already sitting up, complaining about being bed-bound, whereas Kilburne was still pale and weak. But he would recover, Maggie had told them.

They had slept late, and neither felt inclined to do much more than sit and contemplate their good fortune. Parker knew Susanna wanted to get back to painting Fitzroy's portrait, but he wanted just half an hour longer of peace in her company.

The knock came again.

Parker pulled himself out of his chair and went through to the hall. He swung open the door, not sure who he expected. It certainly wasn't Jehan de la Sauch.

He stepped back to allow the diplomat in.

"Master Parker." De la Sauch extended his leg and made a bow. "I have come to enquire after Mistress Horenbout. Since your visit I have thought of little else but her imprisonment and could stand it no longer. I need to know if she fares well."

"She was pardoned last night. But come in and see for yourself." Parker showed him into the study, where Susanna stood next to her chair.

"Mistress Horenbout?" De la Sauch bowed deeply. "Your father painted my family—"

"I remember the picture. He caught your likeness well, sir. I recall him working on the piece." Susanna curtsied. "Parker told me you made efforts on my behalf to have Uncle Louis declare my innocence to King Henry. I thank you."

"Any letters from de Praet have not even been received yet, so any help I gave was useless, but I am pleased beyond words to see you have managed to untangle this knot on your own."

"It is my good fortune to be in good standing with the king."

De la Sauch looked away at that, as if embarrassed. Parker gestured to a chair. "Can we offer you refreshment?"

"No, no. I will not stop long. I wished only to know if Mistress Horenbout was still a prisoner. I shall write again to de Praet. Let him know the change in circumstance."

"You can tell him that Heyman has fled, and so has Jules, the Frenchman he turned. Renard, the other Frenchman, is dead by the hand of the French Crown, and the emperor's lack of pay to those in his service caused some of them to take on the job of attempting to murder the king's son." Parker did not hide the coldness in his voice, and de la Sauch took a step back.

"You know far more of my business than I do, sir. More than I truly wish to know." He fingered the gold buttons of his doublet. "But there is one thing I might tell you, in exchange for the information you have given me."

Parker waited.

"I have the emperor's envoy staying at my house. He is freshly arrived from Spain, and carries correspondence for your king."

Parker stood straighter, and saw Susanna was leaning forward a little, her hand on the back of her chair.

"He passed through the court of Margaret of Austria on his way, and she ordered him to suppress one missive, which the emperor had wished him to convey to King Henry."

"What missive is that?" Susanna gripped the top of the chair.

"One in which the emperor tells the king he is desperate for money, and if Henry will not relinquish Princess Mary's dowry to him now, and send her to be married and live in his court, he will have no choice but to renege on the betrothal and marry Isabella of Portugal."

"That is precisely what de Praet's men were trying to prevent me telling the king," Susanna whispered.

"No doubt the emperor wished to convey the information himself, through an official missive." De la Sauch shrugged. "But whatever the reason, Margaret has managed to get her way. She took the missive away from the envoy, so he cannot give it to King Henry, in any event. She wants more time, so between her and Katherine, they can persuade Charles that he must still marry his English princess."

"Do you think they will succeed?" Parker watched de la Sauch carefully.

The Lowlander shook his head. "There is no money in the emperor's coffers, and Isabella of Portugal comes with a million pounds. Henry would be mad to relinquish Mary's dowry so soon before she can marry Charles, and Charles knows it. He will take the bride who is of age to marry him, and comes with cold, hard cash over the child who comes only with promises. A child who could die before she is old enough to marry him, anyway."

"I think you are right." Parker knew he was. No matter how much time Margaret had bought with her scheming, she would not sway her nephew from the only course a cash-strapped leader could take.

De la Sauch drew himself up, his arms stiff and formal at his sides. "I must be away. I have taken enough of your time. But I would like to have you to dinner at my residence, both of you. I miss talking of art and home, some days, as I'm sure you do, too." He bowed to Susanna.

"I would like that." Susanna smiled at him and then stepped forward, and kissed him on both cheeks.

Parker showed him out and watched him walk down the path to the lane, and thought de la Sauch's walk was a touch too light to be that of a man weighed down by a job he did not want.

He also thought of what Jules had said in the alley at the end. How he'd approached de la Sauch for funds, and been denied, although de la Sauch had denied any knowledge of the turned French spies.

If Charles's ambassador wanted Henry to know that the emperor was not trying to hide his motives, that it was Henry's own wife and the emperor's aunt whose hand was at play, preventing information getting through, he had picked the perfect courtier to confess his secrets to.

The taste of being used lay on Parker's tongue. Bitter and cold, unpleasant as a slug.

When he returned to the room, Susanna was staring out the window, as grim and implacable as the carving on a ship's prow. "Princess Mary will be cast aside."

"I think that is a good possibility."

"It isn't fair."

Parker shook his head. "No. But I am willing to give the Queen as much time as she can to change Charles's mind. Even if it seems an impossibility."

Susanna nodded. "Yes. Of course we will."

Parker looked back at the door. "De la Sauch hopes we will tell Henry that Margaret is trying to suppress the information about him considering marriage to Isabella."

Susanna frowned. "Why would we?"

"Because we are loyal to the king."

Susanna stepped toward him, slipped her arms around his waist and brought him close. "Every involvement I have with Henry's court makes my loyalties clearer."

"And where do they lie?" He let his lips brush the top of her head.

"Only to you." She lifted her face to his. "Only, my love, to you."

DANGEROUS SANCTUARY: A FREE SHORT STORY

DANGEROUS SANCTUARY is a short story set between IN A TREACHEROUS COURT, the first novel featuring Susanna Horenbout and John Parker, and KEEPER OF THE KING'S SECRETS, the second novel also featuring Susanna and Parker. It is available only in ebook form, and is exclusive to members of Michelle Diener's New Release Notification list. Go online here to sign up and receive your copy: https://BookHip.com/PZWBDNA

Members of the list get emails about new releases and occasionally about free books and giveaways. You can unsubscribe at any time.

Readers who are already subscribed will be sent an email from Michelle with a link to Dangerous Sanctuary.

About Dangerous Sanctuary:

Artist Susanna Horenbout is commissioned by Henry VIII to paint a picture of the ceremony in St. Paul's Cathedral to commemorate the capture of the French king, Francis I, in battle, and to give thanks for the death, in the same battle, of Richard de la Pole, the last serious rival to the throne of England.

While Susanna is working on a sketch, just before the ceremony is about to start, she witnesses a strange meeting between two men, and soon realizes she might be the only one who can stop an attack on the king without causing a blood bath.

With her betrothed, Parker, caught up in the out-of-control crowds on the streets as the king makes his way to the cathedral, Susanna finds herself weighing the balance between social order and a man's life.

AUTHOR'S NOTE

This is a work of fiction, but as in my previous two novels in which Susanna Horenbout and John Parker appear, I have tried to incorporate as much real history as I can into my plot.

Henry VIII's illegitimate son, Henry Fitzroy, whom he called 'his worldly jewel', was accepted into the Order of the Garter on June 7th, 1525, and shortly thereafter was given numerous titles and positions. Henry was clearly displaying him, and showing his nobles and the rest of England where Fitzroy stood in the pecking order.

At the ceremony of the Order of the Garter, Fitzroy was placed at Henry's right hand. A rather clear signal. And this did not go down well in all quarters.

The queen was watching the ceremony from the gallery above. One can only image what she thought, although, to her credit, she never bore Fitzroy himself any ill-will. She kept it all for Wolsey, who she considered the architect of her husband's plans.

As for Jan Heyman, I based the idea of a musician spy on a real musician in Henry's court who was a double agent, Pierre Alamire. Alamire (not his real surname, which was most likely

Imhoff, or something similar, but rather made up of the musical pitch A and then the solfege musical notes la, mi and re) was supposedly spying for Henry VIII and Wolsey on Richard de la Pole, posing as an instrumentalist, composer and dealer in manuscripts and crossing between England and the Continent between 1515 and 1518, bringing back information for his English masters. But it turned out he was in fact de la Pole's agent, and wisely did not return to England once the secret was out.

Double agents, it seems, were a common problem in the courts of Renaissance Europe. I had a real stroke of luck while doing my research on the emperor's spies and ambassadors in London for this book. Louis de Praet had been arrested and tossed out of England by Wolsey in complete breach of the diplomatic rules just months before the action in this novel takes place. The cardinal wanted to be rid of the meddling ambassador, even if he had to resort to breaking the rules of diplomacy to do it, because he knew de Praet was sending the Emperor Charles missives which urged the emperor not to trust either Henry VIII or Wolsey.

It was perfect for my purposes.

An ambassador banished too fast to have any real replacement put in place, and what is more, he had at one time been mayor of Ghent, the town where Susanna and Lucas Horenbout were from. What a wonderful coincidence for me.

Most of the places mentioned in this book are real. Or were real, some are no longer in existence, like the Lieutenant's Lodgings in the Tower of London. Durham House was the place where Henry put Fitzroy, Croke was his tutor, and the administrator of the Hospital of the Savoy really was Wolsey's surveyor, and thus not a place Parker would have wanted to go.

I drew heavily from Brewer's Letters and Papers, Foreign and Domestic, Henry VIII, Volume 4: 1524-1530, Alison Weir's Henry VIII: A King and His Court, and various online sources for this book. My thanks to Sword Forum International's posting of the Belgium Longsword rules of play and the Association for Renaissance Martial Arts' website for their fascinating articles on the art of longsword fencing. All and any errors are my own.

Michelle Diener

ABOUT THE AUTHOR

Michelle Diener is an award winning author of historical fiction, science fiction and fantasy.

Michelle was born in London and currently lives in Australia with her husband and children.

You can contact Michelle through her website or sign up to receive notification when she has a new book out on her New Release Notification page.

Connect with Michelle
www.michellediener.com

ACKNOWLEDGMENTS

My thanks to 100Covers for the amazing cover design, and to Edie & Liz——critique partners extraordinaire. To beta readers Jules, Bridget & Jo, you rock!